MY CHEATING HEART

MY CHEATING HEART

Contemporary short stories by women from Wales

Edited by
KITTY SEWELL

HONNO MODERN FICTION

Published by Honno
'Ailsa Craig', Heol y Cawl, Dinas Powys
South Glamorgan, Wales, CF6 4AH

Copyright © The Authors, 2005
Copyright © This collection, Honno 2005

British Library Cataloguing in Publication Data

My Cheating Heart

ISBN 1 870206 73 8

Published with the financial support of the Welsh Books Council

Cover design: Gomer
Cover image: Getty Images
Printed in Wales by Gomer

CONTENTS

Foreword

My Cheating Heart is a collection of stories about infidelity and betrayal, by women, and almost exclusively from a woman's point of view.

I was asked to edit this anthology, partly because of being a writer myself, but mainly because of my background in psychotherapy. Does the study and practice of counselling and psychotherapy make me an expert in this field? Certainly not. In my opinion there can be no such expertise. Infidelity certainly formed part of the large range of human experiences that I listened to over my thirteen years as a practicing therapist, but it never ceased to surprise me how differently people experience adultery, on both sides of the fence, those cheating, and those being cheated on.

Infidelity touches our deepest and most primitive emotions. Every culture has its own taboos regarding infidelity, but the structure of human society is based on the unity of the nuclear family. The notion of fidelity permeates society in a broader context too, the sense of loyalty that unites us, such as patriotism, the betrayal of which carries the worst possible stigma and the severest possible punishment.

But let me not mislead you. This anthology is also about fun. Life is such a serious business and many of these stories will help us have a cackle at ourselves. Jenny Sullivan's hilarious *Erik* tells of middle-aged lust and the lengths to which a woman will go to titillate a gorgeous gardener. C. P. Davies' *Laetitia Jones' Fancy Man* is a poignant and witty reminder of village tittle-tattle getting out of hand. Kay Byrne's *Love The One You're With* and Vashti Zarach's *The Romantic Trollop* entertain us with valiant efforts at promiscuity and show how love conquers all in the end.

Some of the stories treat us to a touch of the surreal, like the quirky and memorable *The Dancing King* by Maria Donovan. A mysterious dancing partner sweeps a young woman off her feet but her ethereal lover soon tires of her and she is left perceiving the sounds of music and laughter as her dancing king seduces yet another woman. In contrast, the sinister *Speaking in Tongues* by Marion Preece warns that infidelity and betrayal can have dire consequences, as its ventriloquist antihero ends up savaged by his own alter-ego.

But these stories also take us far out and away into more complex realms of infidelity. The subject of Oedipal obsession in Elizabeth Morgan's *Florentine Spring* made me shudder with unease, as the lone woman on holiday gets sequestred by a man whose sexual relationship with his mother, real or imagined, threatens to unhinge him. The heroine in Frances-Anne King's haunting story, *Mrs. Morgan's Boulders*, left me feeling the impotence of women in the not so distant past. In Joy Tucker's *The Mari and Me*, we suffer a child's perception of an eccentric Welsh tradition involving the head of a horse, which, connected with the breakdown of her parents' marriage, becomes warped and menacing.

Sheer illicit pleasure is the subject of Deborah Davies' *Wood*, a story that shines in its elegance and simplicity. The ending of a love affair is austerely and skilfully evoked in Jo Verity's *There Must Have Been Some Good Times,* and Candice Morgan's *Girl Standing at a Window* eloquently tells of the gradual deterioration of a woman artist's complicated relationship with her lesbian lover.

As some of the authors indicate in their stories, infidelity can have positive aspects, heightening confidence and self-esteem Ruth Joseph's *The Dog's Blanket* tells the story of a wife and mother who is continually rebuffed by her husband, and whose sexual dissatisfaction and frustrated fantasies makes her the willing victim of seduction. If infidelity escapes detection, this renewal of sexual interest can be re-introduced into the marriage or *core relationship* with surprising results. The fantasy of an affair can have the same effect, such as in Karen Buckley's *In Love with John Travolta*. Or conversely, as in Elizabeth Morgan's *Indian Summer*, rejection or a misunderstood gesture of romantic interest can have a devastating effect on a woman's self-worth.

Food and sex are often connected in the female conciousness. In Barbara Michael's *The Ultimate Betrayal* the heroine struggles to integrate her identity as Matriarch, widow and torch-bearer, with her new-found love for a younger man.

Recent research seems to indicate that women regard infidelity increasingly with less condemnation, and are having as many extra-relationship affairs as men. This goes hand-in-hand with women regarding sexual exploration and satisfaction as their personal right.

Studies have shown that there is an 'infidelity gene', a predisposition in some women to cheat on their partners. Well, what can I say? Let that not give us free rein, because regardless of what genetic baggage we may be made to drag through life, both men and women experience infidelity and betrayal mainly as destructive. Jealousy is no doubt the overriding negative emotion, as in Holly Cross's story *Green,* in which a woman's life is corroded by bitterness and resentment as she is forced to be a bystander to her ex-lover and his new partner's pregnancy.

What can never be denied is the tremendous impact that these experiences will have on both the betrayer and the betrayed (I'm referring to situations involving secrecy and concealment, since both presently and historically, infidelity has at times and in places also formed a fairly normal and acceptable part of society, *so long as the nuclear family remains intact*). It seems that infidelity is a catalyst, a make-or-break, for most relationships. Cecilia Morreau's *The Business Trip* warns of the consequences of serial infidelity, as an ageing husband tries to boost his flagging ego with affair after affair, and just as he realises that he doesn't want or need any lovers but his wife, he finds his fate already sealed.

An affair can certainly be a catalyst for a period of growth and exploration, sexual and emotional, in a relationship. It invariably changes a relationship, most often in a permanent way. Certainly, with the new emphasis on openness, the advent of relationship counselling, and the myriad of books, articles on self-exploration and studies on the nature of male-female interaction, issues like infidelity are much more difficult to hide.

Whereas a Victorian wife might be well aware of her husband's infidelities but for reasons of shame, discretion, timidity or even tacit approval, she might not even mention her knowledge to her husband, these days such a scenario is most unlikely. Communication is the buzzword for the new generation, and we are encouraged to *bare it all*, and *have it out*.

There is no telling how much the authors of these stories have touched on personal experience -- I should not like to ask -- but invariably writers rely on what they see, hear feel and live. I was struck by the vivid and heartfelt candour of some of these tales.

Lastly, a thank you to all who have contributed to the Anthology, including the staff at Honno who have been extremely patient and supportive of this time-honoured project.

Kitty Sewell

Laetitia Jones' Fancy Man

C P DAVIES

Laetitia Jones' hair was much darker than was reasonable for a woman of her age, and possessed a youthful gloss in good light. It was cut in a neat bob that the local ladies described as 'continental'. They did not mean this kindly. In her sleek dark suits, it was true that Laetitia Jones would have looked very much at home on the Paris Metro, but in Brynmawr she was atypical in a way that made gentlemen interested and ladies jealous.

Her elegance might have been understandable had her father been rich or her husband successful, but they were not. It could have been tolerated had she been jolly or dim-witted, but she was neither. She was a knowledgeable and highly efficient librarian, and attended Chapel with a regularity that was unsettling. Worse than that, though, was her inexplicable detachment. She had an obvious disdain for the endless conversations that flowed like torrents down Brynmawr's main street. It was inevitable, therefore, that she became the subject of many of them, though she was a poor source of material. Laetitia Jones' life was as regular and correct as anyone's ever could be, though it had to be said that no one knew what she did on her half-day on a Tuesday.

The ladies of Brynmawr never missed a chance to improve their local knowledge, however, and on one wet Wednesday afternoon, deep within Brynmawr's Lending Library, Nerys Morgan's attentiveness behind the large print books was rewarded by overhearing an interesting, if strange, remark.

At around five o'clock, a time when weariness and insufficient snacking can often take a librarian off her guard, a gangly youth approached the desk with a large volume under his arm.

'Can I take this out for two months?' he inquired, pushing his luck.

Laetitia Jones peered at him over her half-moon glasses. 'The loan period is one month. You can renew after that provided no one has reserved it.' She turned the book over as she reached for the date stamp. '*Reptiles for the Home*,' she read. 'Hmm. I have a reptile at home.'

'Yeh? I've got three iguanas and a pair of geckos. What have you got?'

'None of those,' she said, smiling, as she handed him the book. 'You'll need to renew on 24th March.'

Nerys Morgan told Marian Hughes, who promptly informed Hannah-Jane Pugh, that Laetitia Jones kept some very strange animals inside her modest home. Within hours, the information had seeped through the streets of Brynmawr, and was certainly common knowledge by Sunday. It was no surprise, therefore, that the Minister's wife would sidle up to Mrs Jones after morning service.

'I hear that you have taken up a new hobby,' she said, a smirk creasing her powdered face. 'I'm told you have taken to keeping interesting pets.'

'Pets?' retorted Laetitia, stony-faced. 'I disapprove of pets of any sort. You have been misinformed, Mrs Evans.'

Queries placed with Laetitia Jones' next-door neighbour, Mrs Edwina Thomas, confirmed that no pets had ever been seen in either the front or back garden, and Mrs Thomas had to be actively dissuaded from calling the Environmental

Health Department after a reference to snakes.

However, Nerys Morgan insisted that she had heard the word 'reptiles' with her very own ears, so what on earth had Laetitia been talking about? It took the brains of Agnes Bowen, piano-teacher, aided by an old Biology text-book, to fathom out that the late-waking, slow-moving, heat-seeking creature to which Laetitia had been referring could only be her husband.

Matrimonial discord is a fine fuel for the engines of speculation. The ladies of Brynmawr talked of nothing else for days, but by Wednesday week their enthusiasm was wavering in the face of the evidence, or, more precisely, the lack of it. Laetitia Jones may have been tiring of her husband, but she didn't seem to be doing anything about it. Unless, of course, she was doing it on Tuesday afternoons. The truth had to be known – there would have to be some half-day trailing.

Since the only trustworthy lady in the locality who had the use of a vehicle was Dilys Davies, widow, she was an essential member of the surveillance team. Unfortunately, however, Mrs. Davies had arthritis in her left wrist, and moreover had mislaid her bifocals at a Bring and Buy. So Marian Hughes, who was a big girl, was appointed gear-changer and Hannah-Jane Pugh, who had had an eye test the previous month, was nominated road-watcher. Nerys Morgan would sit next to her in the back looking out for signs of infidelity.

With great excitement, the ladies assembled at Dilys' house the following Tuesday, and equipped with Tupperware boxes full of sandwiches, and Marian's giant Thermos, they squeezed themselves into Dilys' Mini-Minor. Given that three different people were collectively trying to drive the car, progress towards the library was a little hesitant, but they did arrive before it closed, and managed to park. In fact,

Hannah-Jane piloted them into a rather devious position alongside a Volvo estate where they had a good view of the library, but could not easily be seen themselves.

Loath to miss an opportunity for refreshment, the ladies were soon partaking of tea and sandwiches, and consequently the car windows soon steamed up to the point of opacity. They might have missed Laetitia's exit altogether, had the Town Hall clock not chimed one o'clock and reminded them of their priorities. Marian wound her window down furiously, and Dilys rubbed the windscreen with a lace-edged hankie, just in time to catch sight of the librarian reverse her car into the lane.

Driving was not a talent that the ladies had thought to add to Laetitia Jones' lengthy list, and so were somewhat taken aback at the speed with which she turned out of the lane into the main road. In fact, within five minutes they had quite lost sight of her, and the mission might have ended there had not Marian Hughes suggested that their quarry might have gone home for lunch. They were much relieved to see her little grey Renault parked up next to her house, and took up watch again five houses up the road behind a Transit Van.

They didn't have long to wait, for at 1:45 precisely, Laetitia Jones re-joined her car, and reversed smoothly into the road. For one dreadful moment they thought she was going to turn her car towards them and drive right past. She would surely catch sight of them and their sandwiches, and even if she didn't, their pursuit would be scuppered since there was no way Dilys Davies could do a three-point turn in under ten minutes. Fortunately, however, Laetitia Jones turned her car away from them, and the chase was on again.

The Renault got to the main road, and turned right into the A267 heading for Penymynydd. This was a relatively wide, straight road, and, egged on by her companions, Dilys Davies put her foot down, bringing the Mini-Minor to an alarming fifty miles an hour. It was just as well – had they been travelling any slower they would have missed the Renault's left turn down the B road leading to Bryngwyntog. They followed as quickly as Dilys' poor old car could manage and saw the Renault coming to a halt outside Soar Chapel.

Dilys edged her car into the lay-by on the other side of the road and turned off the engine. She looked at Marian uncertainly. Marian turned to Nerys hoping for encouragement. Nerys peered at the gravestones. Hannah-Jane, however, with the benefit of her 20-20 vision, could see what was going on.

'That's a hearse parked up by the Chapel door!' she declared. 'Laetitia Jones is going to a funeral!'

They could hardly hang around waiting for her to come out; they might be there ages, and anyway, they would surely be recognised. With heavy hearts they retreated back to Brynmawr, planning the next phase of their espionage as they went.

For the next two Tuesdays in a row, the watching women headed off in pursuit of Laetitia Jones, and on each occasion they were perplexed to find her at a funeral. Thorough research into the backgrounds of the variously deceased revealed no obvious relationship between them and their town librarian. Did she just like funerals? On the following Tuesday, they didn't bother with the car because they knew that Edmund Phillips, grocer, was to be commended to his Maker at their own Chapel in Brynmawr that afternoon, and so the four ladies took up suitably concealed positions behind the bus shelter. It was a cold day and the funeral started half-an-hour later, so there was much rubbing of hands and cursing. But they were not disappointed, for Laetitia turned up at the rear of the entourage, decked out in a calf-length black coat and matching pill-box hat.

Marian's house was the nearest to the Chapel, so once their

observations were complete, the four numb ladies trouped over there to warm themselves with tea, jam doughnuts and apricot brandy. In Brynmawr this particular combination of delicacies was well-known to have therapeutic properties, and to be a potent enhancer of cerebral function in ladies of a certain age, such as Dilys Davies.

'You know what I think,' she announced, half way through her second brandy, 'I think that either Laetitia Jones is a female vampire, or she's got the hots for an undertaker.'

Her three companions stared at her in stunned admiration.

'But that's it!' exclaimed Nerys when the shock had worn off. 'She thinks her husband is a reptile, and spends her Tuesday afternoons ogling an undertaker!'

'But which one?' asked Marian, topping up the glasses.

'Most of them are half-dead themselves,' remarked Hannah-Jane, 'there can't be many fanciable ones.'

Indeed there weren't, as a quick look in the Yellow Pages testified. There were only five funeral directors in a ten mile radius of Brynmawr, and the only one with a hint of good looks was Peregrine Cadwaladr, who just happened to be single. Moreover, research carried out the following day – ironically, at the town library – revealed that he had directed the proceedings at each of the four Tuesday funerals at which Laetitia Jones had lately paid her respects. Bingo! Her passions had been revealed, and morbid ones, at that!

The ladies made quite sure that they did not keep this juicy information to themselves, and the story of Laetitia Jones and her fancy man circled the town like an unambitious whirlwind for weeks on end. Intermittent Tuesday afternoon forays confirmed Laetitia's ongoing funereal tendency, and also Mr. Cadwaladr's constant attendance. The fact that he was the only undertaker in the district who ever undertook funerals on a Tuesday afternoon (it being half-day) was also noted, but not broadcast.

None of the formidable foursome had ever contemplated interference in any of the many matters of local interest over which they had media control. In general, they were content to observe and report. But in the case of Laetitia Jones they felt differently. She was so much more attractive and clever than they were, and so irritatingly aware of it. She carried her superiority before her like a new handbag. That such a woman could get away with weekly adultery was insufferable – why, the hussy had even got the Grim Reaper himself to assist in her clandestine plans! How could such a creature sit so serenely in her Sunday pew?

All the same, no action would have been contemplated had it not been for the incident with the chocolate. Nerys Morgan began her account of the experience by explaining that if you suffer from borderline hypoglycaemia you have to be prepared, indeed, you should be pre-emptive. And that was what she had been, she maintained, when Laetitia Jones had found her scoffing a Mars Bar between 'Pets' and 'Alternative Medicine'.

'Do you think she would listen to reason?' Nerys inquired of her companions as they tucked into her cherry genoa. 'Do you think Her Majesty the Librarian wanted to know about hypoglycaemia?'

'She probably knew all there is to know about it already,' commented Marian, oblivious to Nerys' scowl. 'She always won first prize in our Sunday School tests.'

'But what did she *do*?' asked Hannah-Jane impatiently.

'She said I was breaking a by-law, and asked me to leave,' continued Nerys. 'I told her that I wouldn't until I'd renewed my book. So d'you know what Madam Perfect did next? In earshot of Mrs Evans from Chapel and Miss Lewis, the schoolteacher, she announced loudly: "your book on re-cycling old clothes is overdue. So before you leave with your illicit food you'll have a fine to pay.'"

'What a *dreadful* thing to say to you, *and* in front of everyone!' sympathised Marian.

'That woman made me feel like a worm,' continued Nerys bitterly. 'And I mustn't let her get away with it, though I don't know what I can do.' She frowned in unproductive contemplation.

'I do!' declared Dilys, once she'd dispensed with the last of her cake. 'She wouldn't look half so proud of herself if you caught her and that undertaker of hers together "in fragrant delicacy", or whatever it is they say. You should confront her with her own sin!'

Once again the ladies turned to her in awe, wondering whether she had secretly discovered a new and yet more potent dessert.

'Dilys, you are absolutely right!' retorted Nerys with glee. 'We'll sort her out! We will fight in the chapels, and on the burial grounds! We will fight in the fields and in the streets! We will never surrender!'

Thus it was that on the following Tuesday the ladies once again squeezed themselves into Dilys Davies' Mini-Minor and followed Laetitia Jones' grey Renault to Ebeneezer, a small chapel on the outskirts of Penymynydd.

In addition to the Renault, the only car parked up on the grass verge was an ageing black saloon, the sort of car an undertaker might own. The hearse was positioned, as usual, alongside the chapel doors. The ladies were itching to get on with their mission, but they could hardly let rage interfere with respectability. So they sat in the car and waited until four weary-looking men in black returned to the hearse, and set off. This was the cue for the sandwiches to be put away, coats to be buttoned up, and battle to commence.

The graveyard at Ebeneezer was large, and rose steeply upwards behind the Chapel, and the new grave was on its far right-hand side on the edge of the diminishing 'unused' green belt. Two grave-diggers armed with shovels were progressing slowly towards it, whilst the officiating minister was heading, with much greater speed, in the opposite direction. Laetitia, sporting a double-breasted black jacket and jaunty black beret, promenaded a few yards behind, accompanied, as expected, by her 'beau'.

'This is it, girls!' hissed Nerys as they peered around the side of the vestry. 'You don't have to come if you don't want to. This is between me and her.'

'We're right behind you!' whispered Marian, who was hardly going to miss the chance to listen in on this most newsworthy of events.

Nerys advanced up the path as quickly and quietly as she could, though the 'lovers' were too deep in conversation to notice her, and nothing much could be heard in the strong wind.

Laetitia jumped visibly when Nerys Morgan suddenly appeared in front of her, with three further puffing ladies scurrying behind.

'I suppose you thought you could get away with it!' declared Nerys breathlessly, pushing an errant scarf from her face.

'What on earth...?' cried the librarian.

'We know what you've been up to!' Nerys proclaimed.

'What are you talking about, Mrs Morgan?' demanded Laetitia.

'You an' him. You've been meeting in secret every Tuesday afternoon. We know all about it, and we think your husband should know about it, too!'

'How dare you!' retorted Laetitia.

Peregrine Cadwaladr stepped up to face their assailant. 'You should be ashamed of such an outrageous accusation!'

'Do you deny it, then?' asked Marian sidling up to

Nerys.

'Of course!' declared Laetitia.

'But – but what's the point of going to all these funerals then?' asked a bewildered Nerys.

Mr Cadwaladr raised an eyebrow at her. 'Did you notice how many mourners came here today?' he asked.

'Well, no...that is to say, we didn't see anyone except you two, but then...'

'That is because there weren't any others.'

Hannah-Jane edged forward, followed by Dilys, who had finally caught up. 'But what has *that* got to do with *her*?' inquired the latter, pointing at Laetitia.

'Mr Emanuel Price, late of this parish,' continued Peregrine Cadwaladr sonorously, 'had no living relations except a nephew in Australia. He was a quiet man with few friends, and spent his last years in a residential home. Though he had managed to make provision for his funeral, he had not paid anyone to attend it.'

'So, do you mean...?' Hannah-Jane began, crestfallen.

'I mean that the late Mr. Price, and many others, would be grateful to know that at least one person paid them the respect that was their due as they embarked on their last journey.'

Nerys Morgan pursed her lips in irritation. 'So there is nothing between you two, then?'

'Of course not!' retorted Laetitia. 'Do you really think that I...'

But she broke off her reprimand as her eyes met those of Peregrine Cadwaladr, whose face, as all the ladies noted, was contorted in abject devotion.

In the circumstances, the ladies had no choice but to beat a retreat, and the four of them maintained a dejected silence as they levered themselves back into Dilys' car. All was not quite lost, though, for it took them such a long time to adjust themselves and the Mini-minor's gear-box that the other cars started off before them. They were thus able to observe that Laetitia's Renault did not make the expected divergence from Mr Cadwaladr's saloon upon reaching the main road. Indeed, Laetitia followed him into Penymynydd, thus casting doubt on the validity of her denial, and ensuring that she could not possibly return to Brynmawr in time to make her husband's tea.

Years after that windy afternoon, Nerys Morgan was still recounting the events at the Ebeneezer funeral to anyone who would listen, and proudly taking credit for the comeuppance of Laetitia Jones. It could not be denied that she left her job, and the Chapel, and indeed, the town. It was also true that she became divorced from her husband (forever after referred to as 'The Croc' behind his back), and the residents of Brynmawr were fond of commenting that Laetitia Jones had swapped a reptile for a vampire bat.

None of the ladies ever pointed out, though, that these apparent blows were actually improvements. Laetitia Jones became Deputy Chief Librarian at Penymynydd District Library, and in time, she also became Laetitia Cadwaladr. She moved into her new spouse's large but dilapidated house, and was driven around – especially on Tuesday afternoons – in his large, though dilapidated, black saloon. And though she had indeed lost her reptile, the companion she gained was most definitely warm-blooded and particularly active at night!

In Love with John Travolta

KAREN BUCKLEY

Mark had only been away a week when I fell in love with John Travolta. It happened that Saturday night. I was lying on the settee, sipping Martini and thinking how good it was not to have to watch *Babylon 5*, when that film *Michael* came on the telly. Afterwards, it wasn't Mark's hands I imagined up inside my nightie. It was Michael's, creeping over my breasts, his fingers on my nipples, that dimple in his chin buried in my pubic hair. And it was a lot better.

The next morning I woke up and stretched my legs across the bed, enjoying the coolness on Mark's side. Then I lay there for awhile, trying to work out why I'd fallen in love. I should have been up doing my marking. The film hadn't been that good, really. William Hurt as a cynical hack, sent to investigate this guy in the Mid-West who's supposed to be an angel, and bring him back to Chicago. Of course Michael can't go by plane. He can't get his wings into the seat, so Hurt and another hack, and Andie MacDowell, who's pretending to be an angel expert, have to drive him east. On the way, Hurt and the rest get in touch with themselves, and by the time Michael dies, on a sidewalk in Chicago, they know he really is an angel.

Michael didn't do much for me at the start. He waddles downstairs with his belly flopped over the top of his boxers and a cigarette hanging from his bottom lip, and starts groping around in the fridge. His wings don't even look that special. They're grey and limp. All l could think about was how much weight John Travolta had put on. Even those blue eyes look piggy because his face is fat. I've never really gone for fat men. One belly between two is enough in bed. I'd rather feel the bones of a man, like I can with Mark.

I remembered John Travolta had been chubby in *Primary Colors*. Mark had rented it for us a few weeks before. A compromise between *How To Make an American Quilt*, which I wanted to watch and *Star Trek Insurrection*, which he wanted to see for the third time. Anyway, there was Travolta as President Stanton sneaking out to Dunkin' Donuts at three in the morning, grey and portly in his tracksuit. But there was a sparkle about him. He made you feel like Stanton's a nice bloke really, because he has time to chat to the guy behind the counter, and even if he has got his friend's daughter pregnant, he can't help himself.

I was still trying to work out why I'd fallen in love as I was opening a tin of beans for my lunch, but I just kept seeing Michael in his denim dungarees, hunched over the kitchen table in that shack. If there's one thing I can't stand it's men in dungarees. The way their buttocks hang. And he's so scruffy. Not that I mind scruffy, that much. I did have a thing for Bob Geldof once. Even Mark was a bit scruffy, when I first met him. He'd just got back from a dig in Italy, all tanned limbs and black curls. Now it's shirts and ties and regular haircuts. It was touch and go with Michael, though. The way he wolfs his breakfast, dribbling stuff down his chin, and that big old gabardine he puts on over his wings. But that's at the beginning of the film. After that he's just scruffy enough. Apparently he smells of cookies. All the women notice it. I thought maybe that had something to do with the way I felt. Not just the cookie smell, which I wouldn't mind, but the way women fall for him. Every waitress in every seedy diner just about drops his dinner in his lap, and he ends up dancing with her to something on the juke box, because of course this is John Travolta. Then he dances her back to his room for sweet, cookie-smelling, uncomplicated sex.

I spent most of that Sunday thinking about Michael. I was supposed to be preparing a handout on *The Color Purple* for my A level group, but I spent more time staring at the computer screen, reliving the film. Then I got it. It's that scene where he comes out of his motel room in Iowa. He walks over a rich brown field into this beautiful orange sunrise, raises his arms and looks at the sky. Then he sits on a tree stump and cries because his time is nearly up, and he doesn't want to leave all this behind. You can tell he doesn't have long left because the camera keeps zooming in on the feathers floating from the tips of his wings. And I realised I wanted to be a waitress, lying in his bed, picking feathers out of my hair.

When the phone rang, I knew I should have been thinking about Mark. The first thing he said was, 'Are you missing me yet?'

'Oh, you know how it is. Piles of marking. How about you?'

'You know I'm lost without you, Sal. Have you met somebody else already?'

'Oh, only John Travolta,' I sighed.

'Lucky you. What's he doing over there?'

'Shagging me soon, I hope.'

Mark laughed and I remembered how much I liked his voice on the phone. He was in New Hampshire, staying with his brother. We were having a trial separation. We'd agreed on a month. Except for which videos to rent and what to watch on telly, we agreed on most things really. That was part of the trouble.

It was that lunch time a couple of months earlier that had

made me think of the split. Things were hectic at school, and I should have used the time to mark Year 10 comprehensions, but I'd decided we ought to meet up now and again, escape a little. I dashed across town to get to O'Leary's for half past twelve, then sat on my own, trying to ignore the couple at the next table who were giving me sympathetic looks. After ten minutes I thought I'd head for his office. I was bound to bump into him on the way. But I didn't. He was still behind his desk, phone clamped to his ear, reeling off figures. He beckoned to me with his eyes to sit down, as if I was working for him, and I hated him.

Back in O'Leary's we ordered lunch, talked about work, glared at the clock on the wall and then at the lad behind the counter who was pouring coffee in slow motion.

'This is hopeless,' I said.

'It is a bit, isn't it?' Mark smiled, reaching across to take my hand. His fingers were always warmer than mine. 'We'll have to go out for a meal one night instead.'

'Yes, but how many late meetings are you going to have this week? And I've got a Parents' Evening on Thursday.'

'I know. Sal,' he sighed, glancing at his watch. 'I'm going to take some leave soon. God knows I've earned it. We could go to the States. Phil's always asking.'

'But I can't go until the summer and that's still a long way off.' I pulled my hand away. 'Mark, I'm tired of going on like this.'

'Like what?' he asked, fiddling with the popper on his Filofax.

'Just drifting along, too wrapped up in work to even talk. Where are we going?'

'Oh. Sal, what do you mean? We're just busy, that's all. Is it about a baby again? We can have one any time, you know.'

'It's not a baby I need. Look, why don't you take your

leave and go and see Phil.'

'On my own?'

'Yes. It'll give us time to think.'

'What about?'

'You know, about what we want.'

'Oh, Sal.' He was already making for the counter to pay the bill, talking to me over his shoulder. 'I know what I want.'

I followed him, grabbed his arm and whispered into his collar, 'Well, maybe I don't.'

The Monday morning after *Michael* I was in the staffroom trying to think up some new essay questions on *The Rainbow* when Jenny came in and sat beside me.

'Nice weekend, Sal?' She smiled the way she did when she was talking to some pupil struggling with calculus, her head tipped to one side.

'Fine, thanks. You?'

'Oh, you know, washing, ironing, kids fighting over the Nintendo, marking till midnight. The usual. Heard from Mark?' she quizzed, shuffling a pile of papers on her knee.

'Yes. He's okay. It's really hot over there, and his brother's taken time off to show him around. I think the break's doing him good.'

'You must be missing him though, Sal.' She straightened the pile and slid it into a plastic wallet.

'Jenny,' I gulped. 'I've fallen for somebody else.'

I didn't mean to tell her. It just came out. The way it does when you're in love. The way it had when I met Mark. Jenny used to listen all the time then. She was sipping her coffee but she didn't take her eyes off me. I could see where her eyeliner had smudged.

'Who is it, Sal?'

'It's John Travolta, and I don't know what to do.'

I thought she'd laugh or choke on her coffee, but she just smiled this grown up sort of smile, patted my arm, and said, 'Enjoy it while it lasts.'

And that's what I did. Not that I had a choice. You know what it's like when you're in love. You can't stop thinking about someone and somehow you keep bumping into them. Suddenly John Travolta was everywhere. When I called at the Spar for some milk on the way home there was *Pulp Fiction* right at eye level in the video rental section and I had to take it out, even though it was due back the next day and I had forty essays to mark.

I didn't put the kettle on when I got in. I didn't feel like coffee and digestives anymore. I closed the blind to keep the sun off the screen, flopped onto the settee and fast forwarded over the trailers. This time John Travolta is Vincent Vega, a thug in a dark suit with slick hair. His skin looks pitted and greasy. The dimple in his chin is like a little hollow in a pudding. I did wonder how I could love a gangster who shoots a boy in the head and has to shower to get rid of the blobs of blood and brain. But Vincent doesn't mean it. The gun just goes off when he turns round for a chat, and maybe, like he says, Jules has hit a bump in the road. Anyway, none of it matters because Vincent has been to Amsterdam and he knows that a Quarterpounder with cheese is a Royale with cheese in France. And he's the one who's trusted to look after his boss's wife, and dances with her in that slow, drugged dance, but never touches her. And – Oh God, the bit where he takes her home after he's stabbed the adrenaline into her heart. She's staggering and her face is grey, but he just watches her go and blows her this gentle kiss over the palm of his hand.

It was that night that the dreams started. I'm watching him dance, pointing his fingers and drawing his arms up and back over his shoulders. He's pointing at me and when our eyes meet, that spaced-out look turns into the Travolta smile. Then he blows me a kiss over his hand. I can feel his breath wafting along his fingers and stroking my lips, and it smells of cookies.

A couple of days later I was sitting in the staffroom with a heap of exercise books, trying to make sure I put red ink on every page, when Jenny handed me a coffee. She lifted the books on to the floor, and sat down.

'When have these to be done for?' she asked, picking a book from the pile, and scowling at the streaks of Tippex on the cover.

'First period,' I groaned, knowing my chances were even slimmer now.

'Oh come on, Sal. Give yourself a break. Tell them you've handed their books to the Head of Year because they're so awful.'

I put the lid back on my pen.

'What's wrong?' she grinned. 'Is it John?'

'Jenny,' I whispered, 'I think he loves me.'

She didn't say anything. She just bent over her enormous leather bag, raked around in the papers, marker pens and J-cloths, and pulled out a video.

'*Grease*?' I laughed.

'Yes. Nicola had it for her birthday. I thought you might like to borrow it. Keep you company while Mark's away.'

I looked at the box. John Travolta. Tanned face and smooth neck, sculpted hair, blue, blue eyes, top lip like a bow, and the neat little dimple in his chin. But Olivia Newton John is gripping his shoulders as though she owns him. Red fingernails digging into his black T-shirt.

That night I'd lit the candles and was singing along to 'Summer Lovin'' when I had to press pause and answer the phone. I felt irritated, leaving Danny Zuko frozen on the screen while I chatted to Mark about work and the weather, and he told me about the Baseball Hall of Fame.

'Is it still on with the other bloke?' he asked, just as the pause gave out and the screen started to fizz. 'Yes,' I said. 'I'm with him now.'

'Oh, I'll leave you to it. Do you think he'll mind if you ring me next time?'

We were laughing, but things felt serious now. I put the phone down, went into the kitchen, took the bottle of Bergerac out of the wine rack, and blew the dust off. We'd been keeping it for a special occasion. I was twisting the corkscrew when Mark's photo on the pinboard caught my eye. He's in a white T-shirt and faded jeans and he's crouching, one arm stretched round his dog's neck, his fingers caught up in the long black hair. He's smiling, but I remembered how he cried when Paddy died. The only time I'd seen him cry. I noticed the veins in the back of his hand and I wanted to kiss them, but I pressed my palm over his face and poured myself a glass of wine.

I thought Danny Zuko might help to wean me. During that weird 'Beauty School Drop-Out' bit, I tried to remember how I'd felt when I saw *Grease* for the first time. It was at the cinema with my friend Cheryl. We'd managed to get in to see *Saturday Night Fever* and she'd giggled and elbowed me every time Tony Manero moved. She was just as bad during *Grease*. Even now I could see what she meant. Danny has a perfect body and he's cute when he sings 'Stranded at the Drive In', but there's something missing. He's young and he's frightened of women. And all those thirty-something actors pretending to be High School kids. Then there's the ending. Sandy is sweet in her yellow cardigan, singing 'Hopelessly Devoted to You'. Then she comes out in leathers and stilettos. thrusting at Danny in 'You're the One That I Want'. I couldn't help thinking she'd got it wrong.

Jenny was doing her hair in the toilets when I handed the video back.

'How was he?' She grinned at my reflection in the mirror and I recognised the look from the Monday mornings when I used to tell her about my weekends in bed with Mark.

'Oh, I don't know, Jenny. Maybe I'm getting old. It wasn't so good.'

'Sorry, Sal.'

'It's okay. It's probably for the best,' I said. 'Mark will be home soon, and I can't sort things out with him if I'm thinking about some star I'll never meet, can I?'

I suppose not,' she sighed.

What I couldn't tell Jenny was that *Grease* hadn't stopped the dreams. Some nights it was Michael tickling my thighs with his wings, some nights Vincent, smiling at me through streaks of blood. Once it was Stanton, offering me a huge donut with chocolate sprinkles. But now I knew it wasn't just Michael or Vincent or Stanton. It really was John Travolta. In my dreams we knew each other. Sometimes at work I forgot about the films and I looked at the clock, worked out the time difference, and wondered what John was doing while I was talking to Year 7 about the apostrophe.

The Monday before Mark came home. Jenny came into my form room and caught me with the biography. I was reading about the obscurity years of *Look Who's Talking*. I'd found the book in Smith's that Saturday. Fate again. I'd spent most of the weekend with it, poring over the photos. Young John Travolta with his arms round his parents. John Travolta in a white dinner jacket at Cannes, flanked by Stallone and Tarantino. John Travolta in a black suit, bending to kiss his wife.

'I thought you'd given him up,' Jenny said, snatching the book from me and frowning at the sultry close-up on the cover.

'I'm trying, Jenny,' I explained. 'I thought this might help.'

'How do you work that out?' she laughed.

'Well, I don't really know anything about him, and I thought if I did I might be able to get rid of the mystique.'

'Found anything yet?' she asked.

'He's done some terrible films.'

'And isn't he one of those Scientologists, like Tom Cruise?'

'Well. yes. but face it, Jenny. If you'd twisted your ankle and John Travolta came up and said, "Hey, I'm into Dianetics. Let me give you a contact assist," would you mind?'

'There must be something.' Her smile subsided as she noticed a couple of spotty faces peering in at the window, and shooed them away. 'What about all those fans? There must be millions of them.'

'Yes. He gets thousands of letters every day.'

'So? Doesn't it put you off?'

'I'm not one of them.' I smiled. 'It's different with me.'

'Oh, you're a hopeless case, Sally Taylor.' She was shaking her head. 'By the way. When's the cuckold back from the States?'

'Friday night.'

'Well, good luck.'

After registration my A Level group came in. I scribbled a question on the board about symbolism in *The Rainbow* and told them they had fifty minutes to complete it. One girl groaned about the lack of warning, but I explained it was practice for the exams, and settled down behind the wall of papers on my desk to carry on with the biography. I knew Jenny was right. It didn't matter what the book said. The thing about the fans didn't bother me at all. I was more worried I'd find out John Travolta was impotent. But of course he isn't. He lost his virginity at thirteen, nursed his first lover until she died of cancer, and then there's Kelly Preston. He says he married her because she'd sit for hours and just talk to him, and I didn't mind because I knew that's how it would be with me.

By the time the bell went, I was sure he was meant for me. John Travolta, eating chocolate ice cream during interviews, flying his plane, holding his baby, crying when his mother died. He even bought Andie MacDowell a tea-set when they were filming *Michael* to make her feel at home on location.

My classes had a lot of tests that week. I knew I'd regret it when I had to mark them at the weekend, but if I couldn't break it off with John Travolta, I thought the least I could do for Mark was to finish the book and put it away before he came home.

I read the last chapter in bed on the Thursday night. I was finding out about the flop of *Mad City*, the way Hoffman took ages to prepare for a scene and John Travolta just did it. A real professional. Then I was dreaming. It's Michael again. He's standing in that Iowan field, his wings suddenly white in the sun. There's a little wiry terrier, limp in his arms, and he's crying. Big, generous tears running down over that dimple in his chin. I'm in the dream, watching, trying to make sense of it. I'm telling myself this is the bit where a juggernaut has just flattened the dog that's been pestering Hurt and the other hack. They've tried to abandon it. But when they see Michael holding the corpse, they beg him to bring it back to life, and this begging is meant to show their faith has been restored.

After that something a bit more original happens. I'm standing beside Michael, breathing his cookie smell, stroking the little dog's head, curling my fingers round its neck, feeling for a pulse. Its fur is still warm. But when I look up again it isn't Michael. It's Mark. And he's looking at me. The little dog's nose starts twitching and sniffing the air.

Mark is smiling, but there are tears in his eyes.

That Friday night I thought I'd better make a start on the test papers that were piling up on the coffee table. I'd only done three when I heard the taxi pulling up outside. I listened as Mark turned his key in the lock and heaved his suitcase into the hall. Then I put my marking down. He came into the living room. He was wearing a linen jacket he must have bought in the States. It was creased and the pockets were saggy. The pale grey suited him.

'Hi, Sal.' He smiled, glancing at the heaps of paper. 'You've been busy.'

'Not really. Want some coffee?'

I got up and he followed me into the kitchen. I took the kettle to the sink and held it under the tap. He came up behind me, wrapped his arms round my waist, and kissed the top of my head.

'What's it to be then, Sal? A white suit and dancing lessons, or shall I just take the case and go?'

I turned the tap off and put the kettle down. I could smell his smell. It wasn't cookies, but I liked it.'

'A baby?' he asked, stroking my cheek.

'No,' I smiled. 'What about a dog?'

The Ultimate Betrayal

BARBARA MICHAELS

Her main concern was not the sexual infidelity. The issue at stake went far deeper. It would be a denial of all that she believed. The structure of her entire life would undergo a dramatic change.

The ritual Friday night dinner was an important part of this structure. Brought up in the Jewish faith, Stella had always viewed Friday night – the start of the Sabbath – as the apex of the week. Tonight was no exception, but this was no normal Friday. Once she had made her announcement, there could be no turning back.

Stella did not belong to the Orthodox Jewish faith, with its strict laws and taboos. She was a member of the more modern and liberal-minded Reform synagogue. Nevertheless, as for most of her friends in the prosperous North London suburb, the big brick-built synagogue was the core of her religious and social life. The traditional Friday night meal was an essential ingredient.

As the children grew up and married it had been important to her to continue the pattern. Now, as she placed on the white lace tablecloth the silver candlesticks, which had belonged to her mother, Stella's preparations were overshadowed by the knowledge that this could be the last Friday night dinner she would make for her family.

'Am I crazy to jeopardize the closeness of our family, to

throw away everything that I know?' she asked herself for the thousandth time.

Rhys had told her, laughing, that they had been unable to help themselves. It was the pheromones. He had a habit of imparting odd bits of scientific data, always with a self-derogatory smile. Stella was inclined to take such information more seriously. From the distance of maturity (at fifty-six she was ten years older than Rhys) she thought that it was more likely due to too much testosterone. That had been in the beginning. When she could have stopped.

She had struggled with a feeling that she was somehow being unfaithful to Daniel, even though she knew it was ridiculous. Daniel had been dead for almost five years. Yet a sneaking sense of disloyalty lurked at the back of her mind. There could, however, be no doubt whatsoever that she was being untrue to the tenets on which her life was based. In the eyes of the Beth Din – the official body governing Jewish Orthodox faith - she would be regarded as an outcast.

Was it really worth the humiliation of being ostracised?

As she put the bottle of kosher wine and the plaited *cholla* loaf on the olive wood breadboard beside the candles, she told herself to stop dithering and concentrate on what she was doing.

Pushing her problems to the back of her mind, she began to fold the white linen napkins into the shape of a swan. It was a trick her mother had taught her, learnt from her own mother – Stella's *Bubba*. The old lady had been an Orthodox observer of the Jewish faith all her life.

She wouldn't have understood – how could she?

The weather was too warm for hot food. No chicken soup tonight. Instead, she had made borscht: chilled beetroot soup. It was a family favourite – her grandmother's recipe, handed down first to her mother, who had passed it on to Stella. She had poached a salmon, already decorated with cucumber and keeping cool in the fridge. Smoked salmon and rollmop herrings completed the Sabbath feast, along with crisp green salad, coleslaw and new potatoes.

There was ice cream for dessert, and fresh strawberries. The children would be pleased. Stella had made an apple strudel – Martin's favourite. It was a very Jewish trait, this obsession with food and everybody's likes and dislikes. Stella chided herself for it, while admitting that it also gave her pleasure. She wondered if tonight's announcement would bring it all to an end.

Suddenly, it was impossible to concentrate. Her mind whirled with a mix of excitement and apprehension. God, she felt more like a teenager than a grandmother. She must get a grip on herself. But, as she placed a vase of sweet peas in the centre of the table, her hand shook so much that she knocked against one of the thin glass wine goblets, rocking it on the slender stem.

Unexpectedly, her heart gave a lurch. The glasses had been a wedding present from her aunt – her mother's youngest, and favourite sister. Stella tried – and failed – to imagine what Aunt Deborah, who had married a Rabbi, and was now living in the United States, would say when she heard her news. The family jungle drums – in the shape of transatlantic phone calls and e-mails – would work overtime.

Involuntarily, Stella glanced towards the big oak carver at the head of the table. It had been Daniel's place. Their son Martin sat there now, had done so since the terrible Friday night five years ago when Daniel had been in hospital, awaiting major surgery. The family – her daughter Lisa, Martin and his wife Rachel, with their two children – were all there as Stella had lit the Sabbath candles. Their thoughts with Daniel, they had tried to eat as they willed the operation to succeed. In vain – he had died three days later.

It had been many months before Stella was able to enjoy

a Friday night. Despite having her family around her, it emphasised the fact that she was on her own. Slowly, the sharp edges of her anguish had smoothed. She had managed to rebuild her life, once more taking pleasure in her work as a language teacher, going to a film or a concert with a girl friend.

But she hated the feeling of coming home alone to an empty house. Weekends were the worst. On Saturday afternoons she would invent any number of trivial errands to delay returning home. Bank holidays drew the weekend out still further. That was why her eye had been caught by the advertisement in the Sunday paper:

'Enjoy the Bank Holiday weekend at a country hotel in Wales.'

'Why not?' she had thought to herself. With some trepidation at the thought of staying at a hotel on her own, she had booked the weekend away.

That was when she had met Rhys. She had first noticed him when she was sitting in a corner of the bar, having plucked up the courage to order herself a glass of white wine. He stood out from the rest of the hotel guests. For one thing, he was younger than most of them. And, while the other men were the type to be wearing sports jackets and shirts with collar and tie, he wore a black open-neck shirt with beige chinos.

Her wine was only half finished when the waiter came over to say that her table was ready. As she was carrying her drink in to dinner the glass had tipped.

'You're going to spill that.'

Rhys, walking in to the restaurant behind her, had stepped forward to take the glass from her hand. As he did so, his touch had sent a shiver through her entire body. Unexpected as it was, the frisson of desire had been unmistakable. It had been an immediate coup *de foudre* for both of them.

It was completely different from the way she had felt
about Daniel. Marital sex had become less and less thrilling
over the years. Affectionate, yes – passionate, no. Yet after
his death she had desperately missed the physical closeness
of his body next to hers in the night. Rhys was quite unlike
Daniel in looks. He was tall, with a spiky shock of dark hair,
while Daniel had been stocky, his mid-brown hair already
thinning.

She had been open to love when Rhys came into her
life. But she had not allowed for the strength of the – well,
lust was the only way to describe it – that came over her.
Nor had she dreamed that it would have such far-reaching
repercussions. It was a last fling, that was all. (Although she
ought to have known herself better – a casual relationship
negated all the principles by which she lived). But if anyone
had said to her that she would contemplate leaving all that
she held most dear to begin a new life in a remote corner of
North Wales – let alone with a man ten years younger than
herself, who was not even Jewish – she would have declared
them crazy.

She glanced at the clock on the wall. It was getting late.

'If I'm going to bath, I'd better hurry. They'll be here in
half an hour.'

Prone to running late, a quick shower was usually all Stella
had time for on Friday evening. Tonight, that would not do.
Yesterday, after work, she had been to the hairdresser and
had blonde highlights put in her hair. She needed the moral
support of feeling and looking good.

Upstairs, in the bathroom, she turned on the tap over the
bath and poured in an extravagant quantity of her favourite
bath essence. As she relaxed in the warm water, the tension she
had felt all week eased. She felt sensuous – voluptuous, even
– and young. The thought of Rhys made her feel thrillingly
adolescent. She allowed herself a minute of anticipation then,

knowing she didn't have time for such indulgence, she got out of the bath. Quickly she dried herself, smoothed on body lotion, finished with a sprinkling of perfumed talc under her breasts and between her legs.

Any minute now there will be a ring on the doorbell.

In her bedroom she plonked herself down on the stool before the dressing table to put on her make up. Peering at herself in the mirror, she pushed her dark hair back from her face and saw that she was faintly flushed – from the bath, or from excitement, or both. She'd better not put on too much blusher. She was vain enough to know that her clear grey eyes fringed with lashes that curled naturally were her best feature.

Swiftly, she emphasised them with a touch of eyeliner, a coat of brown mascara.

She slipped her favourite summer dress – the print, purple on white, made her eyes look almost violet – over her head, was just putting her feet into high-heeled sandals in a lilac colour which complemented the dress perfectly when the bell rang. She ran down the stairs to open the door, smiling a welcome.

'Hello – you're nice and early.'

She greeted her son and her daughter-in-law, then bent to hug Sharon, who was four, and Nigel, six. Considering himself too old to be cuddled, he immediately wriggled free.

'Lisa's not here yet,' she told the others.

'She's not coming,' Rachel announced. 'I popped into her office at lunch time and she told me she had a pounding headache and was going home to bed. She said she was sorry and sent her love.'

A feeling of guilty relief. Of them all, Lisa would find her mother's news the hardest to accept. She had been so close to her father – he had always referred to her as 'baby' even after she had qualified as a solicitor and bought her own flat. They had adored each other.

Belatedly maternal, Stella hoped her ailing daughter would soon feel better. But it would be easier to break the news to the others first. And Rachel was not a blood relation.

Perhaps I can count on her as an ally.

She loved them all so much.

But I have my own life to lead, whether or not they approve.

With the family gathered around the table she lit the candles, shielding her eyes against the brightness as she murmured the blessing to mark the beginning of the Sabbath. Martin, wearing on his head the dark blue silk *yarmulke* that had belonged to Daniel, pronounced the Hebrew blessings over bread and wine, then sprinkled the *cholla* loaf with salt. As they did every week, they all wished one another 'Shabbat Shalom' – a peaceful Sabbath – before sitting down.

It was not until the borscht had been served and pronounced 'Delicious,' that Stella decided it was time to tell them her news. She was absurdly pleased that they had enjoyed the chilled soup, wanting everything to be perfect – an affirmation of her love for them.

'You know that weekend I went to Wales on my own?' she began. 'I was carrying a glass of wine into dinner when it tilted. I would have spilled it, but this man behind me…'

She had their attention all right. Martin and Rachel were looking at her expectantly. Then, to Stella's annoyance, there was an interruption. Nigel knocked over the silver cup of Kiddush wine, which was still half full. A dark red stain flooded over the delicate Brussels lace of Stella's best tablecloth. Anticipating being told off, Nigel immediately began to wail.

'Don't worry, darling, it will wash out.'

Sighing inwardly, she fetched a cloth and wiped up the spillage. Eventually, conversation resumed, but the family had forgotten that she had something to tell them. As was normal on Friday nights, talk centred on what the children had done at school that week.

They never think I have anything important to say. Well, this time they are wrong.

She offered second helpings of dessert half-heartedly. As they all pronounced themselves 'Too full to eat another thing,' the observant Rachel remarked: 'You don't sound very enthusiastic. That's not like you.'

'I'm just a bit tired. It's the heat.'

'You don't look tired. That mauve colour suits you – a new dress, isn't it?'

Small Sharon chipped in: 'You smell nice, too, Grandma.'

'Yes – you're wearing a different perfume from your usual one,' said Rachel. 'It's quite exotic. You've worn the same one for years. What made you change?'

'Oh – Lucy at work bought it for my birthday,' Stella improvised, embarrassed. Rhys had bought the extravagant present for her.

Hoping to divert Rachel's attention, she gathered up the dirty plates and took them into the kitchen. Rachel followed her out, saying as the swing door shut behind them: 'What's going on? You're not like you tonight, but you look great. Weren't you going to tell us something?'

Stella remembered that here was a possible ally.

'Yes, I do have something to tell you, but not now when the children are tired and you want to get home. I'll pop in at teatime on Sunday, if that's all right. And, Rachel – I'll be bringing someone with me.'

Her mystified daughter-in-law nodded her assent. In the adjacent dining room, the children started to bicker.

It was still only 9.30 when Stella closed the front door behind her family, breathing a sigh of relief. Swiftly, she cleared away the debris of the meal. She carried the candles, still flickering gently in their silver candlesticks, into the sitting room. The pointed flames – emblem of the tranquillity of the Sabbath – glowed golden, as they did every Friday night, and had done for as long as she could remember. It was not correct to blow them out.

Daniel had always worried about their safety. He had been such a cautious man. She thrust away from her the treacherous thought that at times she had felt stifled by his care, restless and dissatisfied by a relationship that was more like father and daughter than husband and wife.

Determinedly, she turned her mind to the present. Suddenly, her mood changed. Feeling buoyant and upbeat she went to fill the ice bucket, took it into the sitting room. She placed it, with two champagne flutes alongside, on a small side table. The Veuve Cliquot would stay in the fridge until it was required.

The still evening air was suddenly filled with a raucous noise. It was the sound for which Stella had been waiting. Seconds later, the motorbike screeched into view past her window. It braked to a halt. The rider swung one long leg off the bike and turned to look towards the house.

Her heart beating fast, she moved swiftly to the front door and opened it. Leaving the door swinging wide, she ran down the path. Suddenly, she couldn't wait another moment. Who cared what the neighbours would think? She was through the gate – and straight into the arms of the tall young man in black leathers.

'Hey there, babe! Hold it a moment!'

Rhys drew back to remove his crash helmet, before bending his head to kiss her.

With the salty, road-dusted taste of his kiss on her lips,

Stella abandoned herself to the sense of completeness that she always felt with Rhys – coupled with a sense of physical well-being. In a moment of clarity, she recognised the frisson of sexuality that ran through her as the missing factor in her previous life. From now onwards, her home would be with him.

Together, they went into the house. While Stella locked the front door behind them, Rhys threw his leathers off in the hall. His hand on the small of her back, he steered her into the sitting room. As he did so, something fell out of one of the pockets.

He picked it up with a smile, reached for her and swung her around.

'Know what this is? A pair of tickets for that rock concert I told you about – on Friday. I tell you, I was lucky to get them – rare as hen's teeth, they are.'

He added carelessly: 'For once, you'll have to miss Friday night dinner.'

Stella opened her mouth to protest that she couldn't possibly go to the concert – not on a Friday night. Instead: 'Why not?'

She smiled at him, stretching up to curl her arm around his neck. Stepping outside the boundaries drawn by creed and culture was going to be hard. Her children might not – would not – approve. But she had to take that risk.

Rhys drew her closer to him, reaching for the buttons on her dress. A sudden breeze came through the open window. The bright flames of the candles flickered in their silver holders. For a few seconds, they guttered disapprovingly, before another gust extinguished them completely.

There Must Have Been Some Good Times

JO VERITY

The first flakes fall, like a shake of washing powder.

'It's snowing,' Chloë shouts at the bathroom door.

'What?' Alex's razor stops buzzing.

'It's snowing.'

'Much?'

The particles swirl into the umbra of the street light outside the bedroom window, then rush into the darkness.

'No. Not much.' She lets the curtain drop back and returns to the dressing table, leaning close to inspect her make-up.

'You look sexy.' He comes up behind her and runs his fingertips down her spine, pushing his hand inside the plunge of her dress.

She arches her back and pulls away. 'We'll be late.'

'You can't be late for a party.' He tries again to sneak his hand round towards her breast. 'Come on, Chloë.' He licks her ear, watching himself in the mirror.

'No.' She clamps her arms against her sides. 'I've got to tidy this mess.' She gestures towards the clothes strewn across the bed and littering the floor.

'If I wanted nagging I'd get married. What's the matter anyway? Something's the matter.'

'I don't know.' She keeps her face turned away from him. 'I just feel edgy.'

He shrugs and goes to check the weather.

Gathering up an armful of clothes she walks out onto the landing and tosses the bundle towards the laundry basket that stands in the alcove next to the bathroom. A black sock snags on the woven cane and hangs there like a fruit bat.

'It's getting thicker.' It is the first time she has spoken since they left the house.

'It'll be fine. The gritters have been out. We can't let Dave and Rachel down, can we?'

They drive on in silence. As they turn onto the bypass, Alex pushes a CD into the player and turns up the volume. The flakes, larger than pennies now, flash past in the headlights, hypnotic against the darkness. The heater warms the windscreen and the wipers push the slush to left or right. Now and again they squeak on the glass. When Chloë lowers the window the wind is so fierce that her eyes stream and she pulls the coat collar up around her face, shutting her eyes.

'For Christ sake.' Alex reaches across for the button and the window slides up.

He parks the car and she sits, seatbelt still fastened.

'When it freezes it'll be impossible to get out of here,' she observes.

'We'll have to stay then won't we?'

'You'd like that.'

He swivels in his seat and holds her face between his gloved hands, preventing her from turning away. 'Look. I don't know what's got into you tonight. All I want is to spend a few hours with friends. Have a chat. Bit of a laugh. It's Christmas, Chloë. That's what people do.'

'*Your* friends.' She pushes his hands away.

'Yours too if you'd give them a chance. Come on. I'm not sitting here all night.'

Stilettos are no match for the slush and her feet are numb by the time they reach the front door. Lights shine in every window of the party house. The front door is on the latch and Alex pushes it open, allowing warmth and music to spill out into the garden along with a hail of greetings.

'Here he is. The man himself.'

'Hi, Alex. Coats upstairs. Booze in the kitchen.'

And with that he pushes the car-keys into her hand and melts into the crush, abandoning her in the hall. She catches a glimpse of herself in a mirror at the bottom of the stairs, pale and frowning, and she forces a smile but there is no one to appreciate it.

Upstairs she locates a room with coats heaped on the bed and adds hers to the pile. It looks like a hotel room. Anodyne prints above the bed. Pot-pourri on the sill. Pastel colours and everything matching. She searches for proof that life exists here but there is nothing. No photographs on the wall, dressing gown on the back of the door or book on the bedside table.

The thudding beat of the music and laughter of strangers keep her upstairs.

A man comes in and tosses a duffle-coat and red scarf onto the bed. He spots her in the shadows and points his finger. 'You look as though you're hiding.' Older than Alex, forty maybe, hair sequinned with snowflakes, he seems not at all surprised to find her there.

'I am, sort of.'

'Well, I promise I won't tell them where you are.' And with a grin he is gone.

The adjacent room proves to be the bathroom and Chloë inspects the shampoos and aromatherapy oils on the shelf. She moves on to the cough mixtures and antiseptic creams in the medicine cabinet. Predictable, right down to the never-floated toy boat on the edge of the bath.

The next door along is shut and she leans close, listening before turning the knob and slipping inside. The bedside lamps are on and she detects signs of habitation – a wine-glass on the dressing table, a towelling bathrobe flung across the bed, a pile of coins on the chest of drawers.

She crosses the room and pulls the curtains an inch or two apart. It has stopped snowing and stars stipple the clear sky. It must be freezing hard. There is a small armchair near the window and she shoves it against the radiator, sits down and draws her feet beneath her.

For a while now she has been reading Alex's email, although she isn't at all proud of herself. His 'inbox' contains the usual laddish communications. Cars, drinking, football, smutty jokes. A few weeks ago there had been mail from 'Stella'. It read as a harmless note from an acquaintance who had lost touch, mentioning friends and places in the time before Alex met Chloë. It finished by suggesting that they 'get together to talk over old times'. At first Stella mailed Alex every few days but recently the pace quickened and, from her words, it was apparent that he had been responding.

It was his practice to clear his mailbox regularly but he kept the most recent communications, obviously confident that Chloë would never stoop to spying. The tone of the messages has become more familiar. Flirtatious. Suggestive. Intimate. Last night's confirmed that she would be at the party.

Chloë has been upstairs for half an hour but he hasn't come to find her. The music pounds and the front door slams as more people arrive. Her feet tingle and she unwinds herself from the chair, flexing her ankles and rubbing her insteps. Leaning against the radiator she inspects the street below. The snowfall has chamfered the corners of roofs and garden walls. Cars line the kerbside like monster marshmallows around the edge of a Christmas cake. And all along the suburban street, fairy lights garland front porches and snow-laden trees, casting rainbows on the pale lawns.

Someone leaves the house and crosses the road, high-stepping over the frozen car tracks. Once or twice he slips and holds his arms out to regain balance. The street light on the pavement opposite reveals the red-scarfed man. He stands beside a car, shifting from one foot to the other whilst he fiddles at the lock.

'It's frozen,' she explains to herself.

He goes to the passenger door, wading through the snowdrift that merges road with pavement. He fares no better on this side, gives up and re-negotiates the precarious route back to the house. If she leans her forehead against the double-glazing and peers straight down, she can see him stamping his feet before coming back inside.

The man and woman writhing on the floor don't notice her as she rifles through the pile of coats. She finds her own but it takes a while longer to root out the duffle-coat and scarf.

On the landing, a man, can of lager in one hand and cigarillo in the other, squeezes past her. He rubs his groin against her hip. 'You're not going, are you, darling?' His words slur. 'Don't be like that,' he adds as she shoves him away.

From the stairs she can see down into the kitchen. Alex is sitting on the worktop next to the sink, his knees apart. Facing him, standing between his legs, with her back to Chloë, is a dark-haired woman. His arms are around her waist, pulling her close to him and causing her short red dress to ride up. She stares, waiting for him to sense her presence and look up but he doesn't take his eyes off the woman's face.

'You've come out of hiding.' The owner of the duffle-coat stands at the foot of the stairs, grinning up at her.

Without acknowledging his comment, Chloë points at the woman in the kitchen. 'D'you know her? The girl in the red dress?'

'No. I don't think so.'

'Her name's Stella. Stella the star.'

'I had an aunt called Stella. She played the oboe.'

She looks at his lips as though trying to interpret a difficult language. His thick hair, barely touched with grey, lends him a boyishness but there is slack skin at his neck. Nearer fifty than forty. 'Can we leave?' she asks.

'I'm not absolutely sure I know what we're talking about.'

'I think you do. Come on.'

Without arguing he follows her and his coat. Stepping outside, the sub-zero air is a slap in the face after the fug in the house and within seconds she is shivering.

'Here, you've got next to nothing on' He loops his scarf around her neck and drapes her coat over her shoulders. She hangs on to his arm, steadying herself as they edge down the glassy road. When they get as far as Alex's car she dips into her bag and pulls out the keys, heavy and cold. Holding them away from her to catch the light, flicking them this way and that, she identifies the right one.

'You must be very important to be the keeper of so many keys,' he mocks gently.

She glares at him. 'They're my boyfriend's keys and he's not at all important. He's a fool to keep them all on one key ring. Lose one and you lose the lot. And they're so heavy.' She is sitting behind the wheel now gesturing for him to get in. 'I don't want to talk about him. Just get in the car.'

The car starts on the third turn. She guns the accelerator and it slithers at the kerbside, rear wheels spinning, bedding down in the frozen slush. She tries again but they stay where they are.

'You were a little heavy on the accelerator,' he comments.

She begins to cry, leaning forward against the steering wheel. 'I don't need a bloody driving lesson,' she spits out.

'In that case you shouldn't proposition a driving instructor.'

She twists round to face him, wiping her nose with the back of her hand. 'You're not, are you?'

'Would that be so dreadful?'

'But you seem too...'

'What? Cultivated? Middle class? Don't you fancy me now you think I'm a driving instructor?'

'Who said I fancy you?'

'I'm teasing. Here.' He passes her a folded handkerchief.

She wipes her nose and dabs at her eyes, smearing mascara across the white cotton before handing it back to him. 'I'm freezing. I can't feel my feet.'

He, too, has twisted in his seat so that they are facing each other. 'Give them here.' He puts his hands under her knees and draws her legs around, pulling off her wet shoes and cradling her feet in his lap. She leans her cheek against the headrest and watches him as, working slowly and with great concentration, he massages her feet back to life.

Eyes closed, she smiles and sighs. 'That's wonderful.'

'Aren't you glad you propositioned a reflexologist?'

'I don't care what you are. Or who you are. Just keep doing it.'

He keeps doing it and she tells about Stella and the emails. He lets her talk, nodding, massaging and occasionally muttering, 'I see,' or 'go on,' until he knows everything about her two years with Alex. 'But there must have been some good times,' he says when she stops.

'There must have been, mustn't there?'

He raises her feet, one at a time, and brushes his lips against her toes. 'There. Warm as toast. Now what d'you want to do?'

Several party-goers burst out of the house, rowdy and singing Christmas carols. They pelt each other with snowballs, staggering and falling in the snow, their clothes soon sodden. 'They're crazy. I saw a thing on the news about the drunks that freeze to death every night in Moscow during the winter.' She leans across and kisses his cheek. 'I need to go home.'

They walk down to the main road and wait in the bus shelter for the taxi to pick her up. 'Are you sure you don't want to come?' she asks.

'Of course I want to come but I don't think you really want me to.'

'Maybe you're right.'

'What do you expect if you proposition a mind reader.'

She loops her arm through his. 'Thanks for everything. I don't usually behave like a tart. I shouldn't have dragged you into my mess.'

He shakes his head. 'Extenuating circumstances. Any idea what you're going to do?'

'Well, I know it really is over this time. I'll probably go to my sister's for Christmas, then take it from there.'

The taxi arrives, crunching to a stop in the grit-spattered slush.

As she climbs in to the back seat, she pulls the scarf from her neck but he raises his hand, palm towards her. 'No. Keep it.'

'What about you?'

'The kids always give me scarves and gloves for Christmas, so I'll be OK.'

'Oh.' She smiles brightly.

She pulls an old sweater over her dress and, moving swiftly from room to room, she stuffs his possessions into black bin bags. When one is full, she tears another from the slippery roll and carries on, pausing only to listen as the answering machine takes his calls. 'Chloë? Darling? Pick up. Shit.' By two-thirty she has compressed Alex into eleven refuse bags.

The icy wind takes her breath and makes it visible as she carts him out of the front door. The night is silent but for the hiss of swirling flakes, striking the plastic bags.

The Mari and Me

JOY TUCKER

I still dream about the Mari. And they are dreams I would
not wish on anyone. They begin sweetly enough, with bright
lights, coloured streamers, singing voices. I am surrounded
by laughing faces – some from the present, some from the
past – and some are of those mysterious people – the film
extras of our imaginations – given a brief existence for our
own subconscious reasons.

And there we all are – happy, eager, waiting for the chime
of the clock, a New Year, and the arrival of the Mari Lwyd. I
love that part of the dream, when for a brief, flaring moment,
I am a child again, Eve before the apple. It is the moment to
wake up. But in the dream, of course, I never do.

The tempo changes. Lights dim. Voices fade. There are
no chimes – only thick, silent darkness. Then the banging
on the door begins – loud, hollow, urgent – followed by
chanting voices, raucous laughter. Surely someone will open
the door. But no-one does. Hidden hands push me forward.
No, it can't be. No one would make a child open the door
– not on New Year's Eve. Not to the Mari Lwyd.

I try to scream as I wait for my dreamscape to fill with
the stuff of nightmares. It will all be there in the Mari Lwyd
– the pale fleshless bone of a horse's head – the dark gaping
eye-sockets and loose, clacking jaw – the white, clownish yet
shroud-like, cloth hiding the man inside, his protruding legs

and feet seeming suddenly, surprisingly, comically human.

The noise from the door is louder than ever - the hands are pushing me, closer and closer. The door rears up before me – old and black and wooden, with a brass handle almost too big for my fist to grasp. The heavy door swings open to a dark, empty, twisting street, white with frost. There are no revellers. And there is no Mari Lwyd.

As I turn to go back inside I suddenly see a man's figure, with a spade over his shoulder, walking slowly towards the corner where the houses stop and the mountain begins. And when I waken, I realise the man was my father.

I know more about the Mari Lwyd now than I did as a child. I know that the custom is an old, bawdy and rumbustious, wassailing tradition once found in some parts of Wales, with likenesses in Poland, Romania, Nigeria. It was already a fading tradition in the days of my childhood some fifty years ago. But there was a certain thrill in the event, something that brought a shiver of pagan recklessness to a normally respectable community. And in our village, deep in the hills of south-west Wales, we were proud of our Mari Lwyd, and the group of loyal revellers – streamer-wavers, bell-ringers, beer-drinkers every one – who brightened so many Eves of so many New Years.

My father was one of their most loyal supporters. There was money in it – and you couldn't blame him for being glad about that. He was the landlord of the local inn, and if the Mari Lwyd and its followers filled the bars in his brief festive season – bringing a bit more life to the long winter of the village – it was a good thing for us all. So my mother would have it. 'Long live the Mari!' she said.

She didn't take part in the reciting and the romping – not at first anyway. She would stay in the background, keeping busy filling glasses, but she always had a smile in her bright, dark eyes for the revellers, and a special pat for the Mari's rump when he came close. For she knew that under the traditional trappings the incongruous human legs probably belonged to my father. And if not, they would be those of Uncle Trefor, who was, at that time, the main organiser of our village's Mari Lwyd.

'Why do you and Uncle Trefor do it Da?' I remember my brother Gethin asking.

'It's quite an honour, you know,' was the reply, 'and it brings the customers in.'

'But what's it all for?' Gethin persisted.

My mother laughed, her eyes twinkling as brightly as the tankards she was polishing.

'It's a bit of fun, Gethin – we all need a bit of fun from time to time. And we can't let Trefor down.'

'No, that would never do,' my father's tone was sharp. 'And once you've seen the Mari Lwyd, don't forget, you two will be off upstairs, smart as can be. It's no place for children.'

When he left the room, my mother said, 'His mother – your Gran – she didn't approve. I can hear her now. "All these goings-on," she would say, "It's overly licentious."'

Before I could ask what that meant, Gethin had more to say. He was in the top class at primary school then and often had more to say.

'Mr Morris-Roberts says the Mari Lwyd has 'degenerated' in this village. They don't do enough of the 'poetic contest' – only two or three verses on times – and Mr. Morris-Roberts says there should be at least fifteen, before the door opens.'

'Oh, does he now?' said my mother.

'Yes – and here they use a wooden head for the Mari. It should be a real horse's head, Mr Morris-Roberts says, with all the blood taken out and the eyes, and the skull scraped clean, and treated with lime and buried for...'

'Stop it Gethin! You'll be upsetting your little sister. That new teacher will have your Da and Trefor to deal with if he keeps on.'

My mother had had enough of Mr Morris-Roberts – for the moment.

But he was a persuasive man – as persuasive as Uncle Trefor. For before long, he had talked the village round to his way of thinking. Plans were made for the coming January, with appropriate costumes being prepared for the whole group and informal classes held in the back room of the inn so that there would be a proper 'poetic contest'. The wooden head would have to do for the time being, but Mr Morris-Roberts and Uncle Trefor were already talking about the future, vying with each other over their ideas for the following year.

'I don't hold with all this poetry nonsense,' my father grumbled to Uncle Trefor.

'It'll be all right on the night, man,' Trefor said. 'You can't back out now!'

'It's just a bit of fun,' my mother reminded them. 'And fair play, you have to admit that Mr Morris-Roberts is making his mark in the village.'

'So it would seem,' said Trefor.

New Year's Eve was to be the first public display of the new 'regenerated' ceremony. As my excitement mounted, even Christmas seemed to lose a little of its glitter. My temperature soared – and it wasn't all excitement. There would be no sighting of the Mari for me – I had flu and had to stay in bed. Pleading was no use and all I could do was to leave the bedroom door ajar and hope that I would stay awake till after midnight – as if anyone could have slept through the shouting and the singing, running footsteps, giggling, doors slamming – as the old inn echoed and shook to a rowdy rhythm that my Gran would not have liked at all.

I remember wondering as I fell asleep if 'overly licentious' was the name of the special late-night licence Da had to apply for.

I woke in the dark to a clash of raised voices, and there was no merriment in them. A staccato knocking on wood, the deep rumble of men's voices and a woman's scream brought me out of bed.

I crept towards the top of the stairs, near my parents' bedroom. The voices grew louder and suddenly the door of their room burst open to a flurry of bodies. I had a quick glimpse of my mother, wrapped in a shawl and cowering against a mirror – and then, there was my nightmare Mari Lwyd, looming huge and white with staring black holes for eyes, loping down the stair, its jaw unhinged, and my father chasing the apparition, lashing out at its silly wooden head with a stick.

'You must have been dreaming,' my father said next morning. 'You're still feverish. Your mother said you're to stay in bed another day.'

He turned at my door, trying to smile. 'She's gone to visit your Auntie Lily for a few days – Lily's got that bad back of hers again.' He left quickly before I had time to say that Auntie Lily lived in England, far away, and when was Mam coming back?

'Don't be such a baby,' Gethin said when he came in and found me crying. 'You're always having bad dreams and Mam will be back soon – Da said just a few days.'

I forgot to ask him about the poetic contest, and if he had heard the shouting.

A few days passed, and several more – and they were all grey days. There was no news of Auntie Lily's bad back. My father didn't say much but there were tears in his eyes when he found me after school one day, sitting inside the wardrobe where one of my mother's dresses still hung, breathing in her scent from the soft material.

Da closed the inn for a while, when he had a bout of my flu, which seemed to be raging round the village, faster than the gossip about Mam. He said Uncle Trefor had it too – which was why he hadn't been over for some time. But Gethin told me he had seen Uncle Trevor up at the school, talking to Mr Morris-Roberts.

'What were they talking about?' I asked.

'How should I know?' he replied. 'Shouting they were.'

'Do you think it was about the Mari?' I asked.

'Who cares?' said Gethin.

I cared. I worried. I knew I hadn't been dreaming. I might never know the details of that night. All I did know was that the Mari had lunged clumsily and carelessly across our lives and my mother had gone.

Then the fear came. It crystallised on a sleepless night when I heard my father go out very late and decided to follow him. He was carrying a spade. Round the corner, past the last house, and on up the hillside he trudged, dragging his feet as if it was the last place he wanted to be.

I followed, afraid to keep too close in case he would turn and see me, afraid to fall too far behind, as the sprinkled lights of the village faded farther away and the darkness closed around me.

He reached a clearing, where the branches of a mountain ash tree were etched black against a slatey sky. And there I saw him dig into the ground and heard a grating sound as the spade hit something hard, and hit again, and again, and again, until something splintered. When he stopped and sat on the cold earth with his head in his hands, as if weeping, I turned and ran. Rushing back towards the lights, my heart thudding, my head burning, I refused to think about what I had seen, afraid to accept the fear that my mother might never now come home.

But just occasionally, life is better than our dreams. A rainy day can turn hot and sunny, a dead tree unaccountably sprouts buds, blossom, even berries. And so one day, my mother did come home. There were no explanations. But my father smiled again, and only Gethin ever knew that for a bleak, blank time – so painful that even now I do not dare to know whether it was for weeks or months – I had thought that our father was a murderer.

It was Gethin who came with me to the hillside when we were all happy again. The sun shone in that unspeakable clearing and there were bright red berries scattered on the ground as together we searched in the earth and found the splinters of lime-bleached bone – all that remained of the next year's Mari Lwyd.

The Romantic Trollop

VASHTI ZARACH

I used to be a right trollop when I was younger. Well, I couldn't really help it, living in Mynydd. Mynyddgwyllt is an old slate quarrying village, out in the mountains in the middle of nowhere, and there isn't a lot to do apart from drink and have sex. A lot of the kids aren't entirely sure who their fathers are. My mum said my dad could have been either the school bus driver, one of the barmen at her local pub, or Huw, the randy red-haired guitarist who'd fathered at least a dozen of the village children. However, she knew it was Huw when I was born with flaming red hair. I never met Huw. He ran away to Cardiff to avoid responsibility for the dozen children.

I guess this is why I've always been attracted to musicians, what with my real dad being a guitarist. Mind you, half the men in Mynydd are musicians; there's not a lot else to do in the village except sit around strumming guitars and dreaming of stardom. Plus it gives them an excuse not to find a proper job. 'But I'm a musician!' they cry indignantly when the mothers of their children ask if they ever plan to find a job. I do love them though; men with jobs are so boring compared with singers and drummers and fiddlers. It's a shame I always have to buy the beer when we go out though.

Anyway, my trollop days ended when I found my true love. I was so glad to have found true love, because as much as I loved flirting with men over the pool table, vying with other local girls to see who could wear the shortest skirt, and waking up in the morning wondering which gorgeous, useless musician was asleep beside me; I'd always been a bit of a romantic. I'd always dreamt of finding my soulmate, and being passionately in love for the rest of our lives. Gomez and Morticia were my ideal couple; they're always so madly in love.

Finn wasn't from the village. He comes from Galway. He came over to North Wales to play a gig with his band, got very drunk, and woke up at an all-night house party in Mynydd. I met him the next day, as he was staggering into The Drunken Druid, my favourite pub, with a fiddle case tucked under his arm. He was absolutely gorgeous, with long dark dreadlocks, deep brown eyes, a genuine Irish accent, and oodles of Irish charm. Not to mention the fiddle. I rushed straight home to put on my very shortest skirt, before dashing back to The Drunken Druid to play pool. Needless to say, I had to take a lot of very difficult shots, which entailed bending quite far over the table. Before long, Finn offered to help me. Several pints of Guinness and glasses of Baileys later, he was back at mine.

It wasn't just a shallow attraction. I didn't just want him for his long dreadlocks, his Irish accent and his wild fiddle playing. And he wasn't just temporarily blinded by my fiery red tresses, my fabulous boots, and my job at the off-licence. We really loved each other. We shared lots of interests, such as drinking heavily, playing pool, dancing to wild music and having lots of sex.

He was named Finn after a mythical Irish hero, and he knew quite a lot about mythology. He explained to me that my namesake, Blodeuwedd, was a bit of a tart. I said he was wrong, that my mother had told me Blodeuwedd was a beautiful woman made from flowers. But Finn explained that

a wizard had created Blodeuwedd from flowers to be a bride
for a husband she didn't love, and she'd run away with her
lover Gronw Pebr, before killing her poor husband. It was all
in the Mabinogion. I reassured Finn that I was nothing like
the mythical Blodeuwedd; for a start I wasn't made out of
flowers, and secondly I had no intention of cheating on him
and then killing him.

We were very happy together. I was no longer interested
in shallow, meaningless flirtations in the village pubs. Finn
was my ideal man. However, there was just one drawback
to my charming, handsome lover. Most of the other girls
in the village fancied him too. I had never really suffered
much from paranoia or jealousy. I hadn't cared that much
for any previous boyfriends or one night stands. But this was
different. I was becoming insanely jealous. Occasionally,
Finn played gigs in the village pubs whilst I was working
late in the off-licence. I would find myself locking up early,
and sneaking into the pub to see whether some cheeky bint
was chatting up my man.

I had lots of competition. All the local women adored
him. The hairdressers and beauty salon was suddenly
booked up with former trollops getting facials and new
hair styles in vain attempts to recapture their youthful good
looks. Schoolgirls started hanging out outside our house in
skimpy outfits, with the magic resilience to cold which only
sixteen year olds possessed. Several of the younger women
developed imaginary close friendships with me, and took
to calling round to visit me; accidentally dropping in when
I was out at work. I would arrive home to find a couple of
flirtatious minxes draped over the sofa begging Finn to play
the fiddle.

Finn remained solid in his avowals of love, and refused
to listen to my fears. He claimed he only liked feisty red-
headed women with fabulous boots, who worked in off-

licences, and no one was going to change his mind. I was almost comforted. And then his distant cousin Maeve came to stay.

Maeve was a brown eyed, auburn haired Irish beauty; barely out of her teens. She had run away from home a few years previously, to live on the road with New Age travellers. She played tin whistle, and sang like an angel. She wore wispy, ragged dresses which were always falling off her slender brown shoulders, and fabulous big black New Rock boots. And she drove a green truck crammed with beer and whisky.

Every time I turned round, there she was; laughing and fighting with Finn, singing to his fiddle, floating barefoot around my house in transparent dresses. Finn drank his way through the whisky, and went out busking with Maeve.

'Isn't she terrific?' he'd ask me. 'You don't mind if she stays a few more weeks, do you, only there's something wrong with her truck?'

Finally, a few days before our first year anniversary; I came home early from the off-licence and overheard them plotting to go away together. As I crept past the living room window, I saw them huddled up on the sofa with some tickets. I sneaked quietly into the house, and listened through the living room door.

They were discussing a romantic weekend in Amsterdam, and Maeve was giggling. I threw open the door in fury, just as Finn shouted, 'I've never loved anyone so much,' and threw his arms around Maeve.

It felt as though I'd been physically kicked in the stomach. They sprang apart looking guilty, and I ran out to walk by the river and cry. After I'd stopped feeling hurt, I got angry. My inner trollop stirred. My wild woman cried out for vengeance.

I stormed back into the house, refusing to speak to Finn

and Maeve; and put on my scarlet thigh boots and my red pvc mini skirt. I applied lashings of crimson lipstick, shook out my long red hair, and stalked off out to The Drunken Druid.

As luck would have it, some teenage DJs were playing dub and reggae in the main bar of the Druid. The cutest one had blond dreadlocks and a muscular physique. I knew him slightly; he taught martial arts in the community centre on the high street, and often came to the off licence to buy Jamaican Rum. I danced around in front of the decks for a bit, until he came over and started chatting. He asked me where Finn was – even the men liked Finn – and I explained that I wanted to cheat on Finn. The cute teenage DJ liked Finn, but he clearly liked my red thigh boots more, so we left the other teenagers with the decks, and slunk away for a night of passion. Luckily he had the keys to the community centre, as apparently he still lived with his mum.

I awoke early the next afternoon in the community centre. We hadn't really had a night of passion, more like five minutes of passion; but nonetheless, revenge had been exacted. Leaving my teenage lover snoring on the floor, I popped home to change my outfit.

The house was quiet, and Maeve's truck had gone. I presumed Finn had gone with it. There was a note addressed to me on the kitchen table. Scorning it, I changed into my best biker chick outfit; and headed back out to The Dragon's Claw, a wild raucous biker pub at the edge of the village.

Although it was early afternoon, several bikers were already propping up the bar. My old friend Llyr, a fierce looking, sweet tempered, dark-haired biker from the next village was chatting up the barmaids; but he turned around as soon as I walked in. I strode across the Dragon's Claw in my leather mini and red biker boots, and sat down next to Llyr.

'Mine's a tequila, Llyr.'

Llyr had always flirted with me when I was a schoolgirl, but at that time I'd had a musicians-only policy. I had allowed him to take me for rides on his bike and buy me lots of tequila.

'Still only sleeping with musicians?' asked Llyr, buying me a double tequila.

'DJs and bikers are in this week,' I replied.

'I thought you had some Irish boyfriend these days? I heard you were love's young dream.'

'He's being unfaithful to me, Llyr.'

Llyr, as an old friend, was shocked and sympathetic; and as an old admirer, was delighted, and promptly offered to help me repay my unfaithful boyfriend in kind.

After a wild couple of evenings racing up and down the valleys on the back of Llyr's bike, and having slightly uncomfortable sex on the back of the bike; Llyr dropped me off back in Mynydd, as dusk was falling. Despite repaying Finn's infidelity with wild trollop behaviour, I was feeling quite flat. I was missing Finn. Unfaithful, revenge sex just wasn't as nice as romantic, loving sex. What was wrong? Was I losing my touch? Had my inner trollop turned into a Stepford Wife?

I turned towards home, but my spirits were low. I decided to have one final attempt at rekindling my inner trollop, and paying Finn back. I nipped into The Sheep's Head, and picked up a hunky farmer. We were strolling back to my house, brazenly snogging in the street; when an angry Finn hurtled out of The Drunken Druid.

'You unfaithful tart!' he shouted across the high street; much to the interest of a group of schoolchildren loitering outside Spar. 'I should never have trusted a woman named Blodeuwedd!'

'Well I should never have trusted a sweet-talking Irish

fiddle player!' I shouted back, as the farmer made a run for it.

'What do you mean, you should never have trusted me?' demanded Finn, as half the pub dashed outside to watch the action. 'You're the cheap trollop sleeping your way around the town!'

'Only because you slept with that auburn-haired bint!'

'I never slept with Maeve!'

'You did! You were running away to Amsterdam with her!'

The onlookers looked expectantly at Finn. To be fair, no-one was taking sides. They just enjoyed a good raucous argument of an evening.

Finn sighed. All the wise-cracking, fiddle-playing Irish charm seeped out of his being, and he slumped wearily against the pub wall.

'I was planning a trip to Amsterdam with *you*, Blodeuwedd. For our anniversary. Because I love you so much. Maeve and I were worried you'd overheard the plan. It was meant to be a surprise.'

Everyone held their breath. Some of the women sighed deeply, wishing their lovers had planned romantic weekends in Amsterdam for them, instead of getting them pregnant and then running off with the next door neighbour.

I stared at Finn in horror.

'You didn't cheat on me with Maeve? But I thought...'

Finn looked at me grimly.

'So that's why you've been sleeping with DJs and bikers is it? Oh yes, I know all about what you've been up to. Gossip travels quickly in small Welsh villages, Blodeuwedd.'

'I was only unfaithful because you were,' I said miserably.

'Ah!' said Finn, 'But there's the flaw in your plan! I wasn't actually unfaithful. Your supposed love rival, Maeve, actually left this morning to track down an old boyfriend in Ireland, and I was supposed to be catching a flight to Amsterdam with you tonight.'

The audience looked disapprovingly at me. This was all wrong. I was supposed to be the brave, modern woman taking revenge on my faithless lover, not the trashy guilty party.

'I'm so sorry, Finn, I got it wrong,' I admitted, tears filling my eyes. Now we'd never be Gomez and Morticia. I'd have to give up my one true love, and return to being a village trollop for good.

Finn sighed, and turned away from me. There was a hopeful ripple of interest from the watching women.

'I forgive you,' he said, swinging round suddenly. 'I'll take you back. After all, with a name like Blodeuwedd, you were doomed to cheating on your boyfriend sometime. However,' he added sternly, as I broke into smiles, 'You'll have to allow me to get my revenge for your infidelities. Let me see, how many people did you sleep with exactly?'

'Has he gone yet?' asked the farmer, who was quite drunk, veering suddenly back into view.

'I'm not a trollop anymore!' I shouted, as I was knocked to the ground by hordes of amorous women shouting: 'Be unfaithful with me, Finn!'

And that was how I settled down to a life of fidelity.

Girl Standing at a Window

CANDICE MORGAN

Sandra stared at the ceiling. She slipped her hand behind her head and swept her hair to the front. She took a few strands and curled them around her thumb and forefinger. Then, bored with the ceiling, she looked at the alarm clock. 10.47am. Saturday had become one of those nothing days. Every other week, Toni got up early and went to work and Sandra – not to make the day appear so long – resorted to spending the mornings in bed.

The duvet had been untouched on Toni's side. There was no dent in her pillow either. Sandra had spent the night alone. The arguments were becoming more frequent; a week didn't go by now when they didn't argue over some silly thing. Last night it was because Sandra hadn't ironed Toni's black turn-ups. Earlier in the week they had argued because Sandra got home late after teaching and was too tired to cook.

'You're not the only one who works,' Sandra told her.

'Yeah and you can pick and choose the hours you work. I'm stuck in that place from half-eight in the morning till half-five in the sodding evening. Anyway, you're never here,' Toni said.

Sandra stood in the middle of the room loaded with a bag in one hand and her folio carrying case in the other. She was staring at Toni who had her face stuck in the newspaper. Sandra could have counted to ten, twenty, thirty, a hundred...

a thousand... still Toni wasn't going to budge, showing no signs of getting up off her fat arse. She would sit there all night if she had to and do bugger all, except moan about the shit day she'd had.

Sandra stood there for a few moments, then in the end she lost patience. She went upstairs to put her folio carrying case in her studio. There was no time for brooding by the window. Sandra knew that if she locked herself in her studio, Toni would remain downstairs. After eight years of living together, there were no apologies any more.

Sandra went to the bathroom to scrub the charcoal from under her fingernails. As she leaned over the bath to reach for the nail brush, she caught a glimpse of herself in the black tiles. She pulled a face. The word that came to mind was haggard. She looked even worse in the cabinet mirror. Resembling a panda was one thing, but the silver streaks... If the grey kept growing at this rate, and if she continued to pluck them, it wouldn't be long before she would go bald.

As she left the bathroom and made her way to the stairs, Sandra thought about what she could do for food. Perhaps they could order a pizza or get a Chinese.

'I'm not driving. Too tired,' said Toni, after Sandra suggested the idea.

'But I've just got in.'

Toni rolled a cigarette and lit up. 'I don't fancy a pizza.'

'I really don't feel like cooking. It's been a long day, Toni hon', please try and understand.'

Silence.

'I'll drive,' Sandra coaxed.

Toni blew smoke in Sandra's direction. Sandra waved it away and went into the kitchen to look in the freezer. They didn't always argue like this. But recently, nothing that Sandra did was good enough. Toni didn't like violence as a rule, but there was one time when she pushed Sandra against the sink in the kitchen. They hadn't been together that long and Sandra – who also hated violence – suddenly turned on Toni after she had been pushed. She gave Toni a swift kick. *Up the arse.*

They vowed never to use violence again.

Toni was a shouter; Sandra threw things. She would throw anything, cushions, cups, photos at walls and doors after Toni had walked out. But they always made up before going to bed.

Sandra ended up cooking. She also washed the dishes and emptied Toni's ashtray. Everything was fine again until Toni asked Sandra to iron her trousers. Sandra put her foot down. If Toni wanted her trousers ironed for work Saturday morning, she was going to have to press them herself. Toni hit the roof.

'You won't do anything for me,' she said, dragging out the ironing board from under the stairs. 'You don't have to get up early tomorrow.'

'It's eleven o'clock at night, Toni. Why didn't you ask earlier?'

Sandra bit her lip. For a moment, she wondered whether it would have been better if she had said nothing and ironed the trousers to spare herself the grief. Toni threw her trousers onto the ironing board. A quick once over was Toni's way of ironing. It wasn't Sandra's.

'Damn it!' Toni shouted after she had finished. She had given herself tramlines down each leg. 'I can't wear these to work.' Toni's voice softened. 'You always do them better.'

Sandra stood in the doorway. She could've taken the trousers and ironed them properly, but she left them where Toni had dumped them on the floor. Toni went and sat in front of the TV and lit up a cigarette. The iron was still on the board and plugged into the socket. Sandra lifted the iron off the board and took the plug out of the socket. She placed the iron on the draining board to cool, then she folded the board and put it back underneath the stairs.

Toni ignored her.

She always ignored Sandra after one of their fights, preferring to sit in front of the TV. But it was only in recent months that she would stay downstairs and smoke well into the early hours. Sandra sat down at the other end of the settee. She looked at Toni, whose face disappeared into clouds of smoke. What could she say? What was there to say?

Sandra was asking that same question as she lay in bed the morning after. 10.59 a.m. Any minute now she would hear the beep for eleven o'clock. The sun peeped through a crack in the curtains. She could get up. Then again, what did she have to get up for? If Toni had spent half the night downstairs, God knows what mess she had made. Crisp packets, an overflowing ashtray, Toni's trousers in a heap on the kitchen floor... There was also Toni coming home from work to look forward to.

What was there to say?

Sandra rolled over, pulling the duvet over her shoulder. She could take a shower, leave the mess and go into town or, she could have a quick wash, clean up the mess and do some work in her studio. Depending on the traffic, Sandra could expect Toni home any time after three. That was if she decided to come home. Occasionally she didn't return for a day or two. 'I stayed with mum,' was one of her frequent lines. But at any other time, when things were OK, Toni didn't have patience for her mum.

The room slipped into darkness as the strip of light on the carpet disappeared. Perhaps it wasn't such a good day for going out after all, Sandra decided. She didn't want to make things worse between Toni and herself. Going out would only make things worse. She closed her eyes and yawned.

Another five minutes and then she would get up.

Sandra must have opened every window downstairs to get rid of the smell of tobacco. She emptied Toni's ashtray, picked up the trousers off the floor and put them in the washing machine. There was no trail of crisp packets, only biscuit crumbs and a half-empty mug of cold tea on the table.

It was after one when Sandra could finally think about doing some preparation work in her studio. When they bought the house, Sandra insisted that the square front bedroom would be her studio. There were two big windows, which not only allowed plenty of light, but also gave an excellent view of the street. Day or night, she could sit by the window with her sketchbook on her lap and observe others going about their business.

The woman opposite was a nurse and judging by the colour of her uniform, she was probably a staff nurse. And then there was 'Mr Tinky' from number thirty-four who loved nothing better than to tinker about with his car.

At night, Sandra would sit in the dark in her favourite window seat and watch the tom-cats prowl the silent street in search of a willing queen. Sometimes they would lie in wait, tucked in the dark under parked cars ready to ambush. As for humans, the weekends were the most lively. Number 46 had regular Saturday night parties that lasted until three, four o'clock Sunday morning. It was a 'shared house'. The landlord came once a month, parked his small blue van outside and then went into the house for ten minutes or so. Sandra could tell that he was a painter and decorator from the paint on his overalls. Dom, they called him. Sandra heard one of the young tenants call him that one day when she was working on a picture.

Hey, Dom, has Claire had the baby yet?

She loved her studio. She could keep all her art books and

equipment in one place. That was the advantage of living in a house instead of a pokey flat. One space for everything. The studio was *her* room which meant that when she wanted time to *herself*, she could shut the door and not be disturbed by Toni. Unless, Sandra gave Toni a reason to disturb her.

Immediately she opened the door, Sandra was greeted by the smell of oil paint and turpentine. There were a few canvases still drying out, propped against the opposite wall near the windows. Sandra pushed them open to let the air circulate.

People were Sandra's favourite subjects. Clothed and unclothed. There were a few old portraits of Toni hanging on the wall which Sandra had painted when Toni was her college life model. Her favourite was the one in which Toni posed nude, reclining lengthways in front of a large mirror. Sandra's eyes roved from the pouting mouth to the small breasts with the erect brick-red nipples. In the background, there was the mirror in which she had painted her own reflection. Then they had only just become lovers.

Toni had joined her art class as an inexperienced life model who just needed extra cash. She was also a mature student, returning to education after failing her school exams. At first, Sandra tried to ignore her feelings. It was easier to keep busy and avoid temptation altogether. But there was something about Toni. So willing to help, to listen. She was interested in Sandra, the real person. Sandra's past didn't matter. Toni was open, uncomplicated; Sandra was the opposite.

Sandra shook her head and turned her attention elsewhere.

There were a few self-portraits, some she had done in her teens, and then there were recent charcoal sketches of nude models from her class, along with her caricature studies of her neighbours, drawings of landscapes and buildings which she had taken into her class to show the students. The shelves were cluttered with books on artists: numerous books on Salvador Dali, Max Ernst, Munch, George Grosz.

By this time, Sandra had forgotten her dream and all that she had on her mind was doing some work before Toni got home. She wouldn't do any painting today. She wasn't in the mood, still feeling the after-effects of last night's argument and all the other arguments that had passed during the week.

Sandra looked up at the reclining Toni. Were the lips really pouting because Sandra had asked Toni to do that, or was Toni pouting because she couldn't have her own way? Was that desire in those piercing blue eyes, or just the look of smugness? Sandra approached the picture and touched the face. Gently. It felt rough, as if it had been carved and not painted. It also looked ugly standing so close. She could see where she had used the knife to cut lines into the paint. She couldn't do any work with her staring like that. The painting either had to be covered or taken down.

It was half-past three before Toni pulled up in her car. Sandra was sitting in her window seat, sketching when she heard the distinctive sound of Toni's engine roaring up the street.

She had spent over an hour soaking-up the sun, enjoying the quiet while she worked on the detail of Pepper, next-door's smoky-black cat as he dozed peacefully on their garden wall. Pepper was a sun-worshipper. Sandra often watched him from her studio window, following the sunlight round the garden. Today he was quite content with the wall, sprawled on his side with his back to Sandra. That was until the noise of Toni's car frightened him. Then he leapt off the wall, out of Sandra's sight. The picture wasn't finished, but Sandra had something else to hold her attention now.

She put her sketchbook and pencils to one side, watching Toni's small head appear as she got out of the driver's side.

As usual, she had a cigarette in her mouth and she was carrying a paper. Sandra wondered if she would look up at the window. There was a time when Toni used to look up at Sandra's studio and smile.

The first few years of their relationship were hardly idyllic. After not doing very well at college, Toni didn't want to know education. She wandered in and out of dead-end jobs. It was Sandra's money that kept them. Yet, they pulled together. It was when times were difficult that their relationship was really strong. Then, as Sandra's career progressed, Toni changed. Subtle changes in her mood, the way she looked at Sandra, how they made love. They didn't even go out and socialize as a couple any more.

Sandra showed no surprise when Toni kept her face directed at the pavement as she opened the gate. Then she heard Toni place her key in the door. Sandra froze. This was the moment she had been dreading from the minute she'd dragged herself out of bed. Was she going to go downstairs? Was she going to be the one to make the first move, say something like, 'Fancy going to see a movie tonight?' Perhaps it would help to bring Toni round.

After spending a couple of minutes deciding on her plan of action, Sandra, hearing Toni in the kitchen, left her window seat in the sun and made her way slowly towards the door. The painting of the reclining Toni had been left untouched. Sandra had chosen to work with her back to it instead. *Out of sight out of mind.* However it was only a temporary solution to her problem. Again, her eyes caught Toni's, and again that look served as a reminder of what she had to face downstairs.

As Sandra walked into the kitchen, Toni was leaning against the draining board, drinking a glass of water. Sandra was just about to come out with her rehearsed line when Toni said, 'I've already eaten so there's no need to worry about cooking a meal.'

As Sandra stood there and thought about what Toni had just said, she realised that it wasn't what Toni had said, but how it was said that cut into her.

'Actually, I thought we could go see a movie tonight,' Sandra said.

Toni didn't respond. There was something in her look. Sandra speechless, watched Toni as she turned her back and placed the empty glass in the sink.

Sandra was waiting, yet she didn't really know what she was waiting for. And then Toni spoke again. So matter-of-fact. The same coldness of tone. Sandra didn't hear every word – perhaps the first sentence or two; then out of the corner of her eye she could see the blue-bottle caught in the net curtain, buzzing.

The Dog's Blanket

RUTH JOSEPH

I thought I'd been enjoying my life at home with a husband and two children. Time had moved on and the children could look after themselves if they had a day off school, so it was my moment to break free and return to the job market. I wanted a job with variety, I could type but wanted to escape that life so, I'd started working for a small paper and sold advertising space.

I've tried to think why it happened. Matthew and I were happy with each other – we never rowed. Well, not major rows. There was the odd niggle if he forgot the wine on the way for our dinner party, or arrived home two hours late, because he had to keep some of his boys in and didn't think of ringing. But there was nothing major. Sex was still good though less frequent. He was a considerate lover and I never felt rejected. But maybe after fifteen years of pushing the same buttons and pulling adequate stops, there wasn't that spontaneous got-to-do it now feeling. Sex had to fit in with timetables, when the kids weren't in the house. A routine, maybe, like going to Sainsburys early on Monday to miss the rush, or filling up with petrol before the weekend.

I did try to speak to him about it. I tried to offer tentative discussions because we never did, not in detail like we talked over the new shed or the summer holidays. I suggested we took the old blanket and a picnic, took a trip up the

Abergavenny Canal as we had in the old days when … we'd moor the day-boat after a while and walked hand in hand in the forest.

I kissed his ear. 'It's years love, since you laid me down on the blanket with just the sound of birds about us. Remember the rush to navigate a tangle of clothes – all those buttons and zips. Then free at last. You made love to me amongst the blue bells and the mushroomy smell of the earth. It didn't matter that branches were digging into me through the blanket or that the ground underfoot was damp. Remember our bodies sighing, and we'd moan with the passion of it… it was exciting…it was unpredictable…and it was you and me.'

Matthew turned to me in disgust, as if those people hadn't been us but some others that he'd read about in his paper and then tsk tsked under his breath. Matthew was very conscious of his position as vice head, wanting and hoping to be head in five years. That spontaneity and passion had been washed away in a flood of school reports, marking, and a mound of sardine paste and cheese and pickle sandwiches.

'It's too risky,' he spat.

'But we're married. So what if there was a headline in the *Western Mail* or the *Penarth Times*, that Matthew Thomas and his wife were caught *in flagrante*, in the woods near Abergavenny?'

But he snapped his face, formed his mouth into a letterbox, and gave me a look as if I was a sixth-former caught smoking in the toilets. I only suggested it once.

Another time just before Christmas, after a day's shopping, I felt a closeness helped by a couple of glasses of red. I whispered to him that I might dress up as a tart and sit in a hotel bar, and that he could pick me up and take me back to his room. But there was that face again. So I gathered up my fantasies, popped them in the loft of my mind…well, tried to, and made do with long walks in the park looking at others and pretending not to see.

But then it happened. It was waiting in the wings of my life. The office decided that they would do a regular feature on antiques that would appeal to their AB readership and it was up to me to try and rustle up the advertising. I'd scanned *Yellow Pages* and planned my campaign but many of the antique shops were closed and those dealers I'd managed to see were either suspicious, thinking I was from the police or trading standards, or just gruff and uninterested. So when, on my last visit of the day, I pushed through the stacked frames and dusty chairs and tables, waiting to be attended to, I was surprised when a tall guy, late forties with a crinkled face, smiled at me and asked how he could help.

'I'm from the *Penarth Mirror*,' I said, offering my card and unnerved by his bright, blue-eyed stare. He understood that it was advertising and, yes, he might be interested and, give him a few minutes to get the waxes off his hands, and we'd go for a coffee to discuss details. His name was Rob. I looked in his eyes and something was triggered in me in a lonely space. Those emotions that I'd so tidily wrapped up were forcing their way out. I tried to convince myself that I was just excited, that after a grey wet day when the predominant answer had been 'no', someone was interested in doing some business. And if he was attractive, it made my job easier. But my frustration had been simmering for years.

He wasn't the first guy I'd fancied: there had been the odd taut bum, or glancing look. But, in the past when I returned home, I'd see Matthew sitting at a pile of books or hear him playing with the children and that small intimacy, that sweet connection, would suppress what I persuaded myself was lust. I stood at the back of the shop listening to running water and ignoring the querulous voice of my maiden aunt who sat on my shoulder and stabbed my conscience. Rob, even in worn beige chinos and an old blue sweater, looked so tempting. We walked to a small coffee shop and sat in the corner and I tried to concentrate on my business patter and admired the single orange gerberas arranged to offset the turquoise décor.

'It's very pleasant in here,' I murmured.

'Yes,' he said, crinkling his eyes and his mouth in a teasing smile. I laid out my papers to show him the rates for full, half page etc.

'Yes,' he said, his eyes fixed on my face and totally ignoring my spiel, 'Whatever it costs, I'll do it. But you must sort out the layout. I don't want any pimply adolescent coming round to finish the thing. And if I give you a series of quarter pages, then you must come with the copy each time.'

I nodded, heart pounding, thinking that there would be at least five more occasions when I would see him and I had to steady myself before I could climb into my car with a modicum of decorum. Damn it! I was kidding myself that it was work. My thoughts were no better than all these men 'playing away' that I'd ridiculed in the past. It was dark by the time I got home. But there was nothing to blame myself for…a little flirtation with my eyes, maybe.

Matthew was angry. He said he was worried and that I always rang when I would be late. He wanted to get on with a report but the children had cornered him. They had heard about this giant Schnauser puppy for sale. We had promised them a dog on Alex's fourteenth birthday and that was in three weeks time. I'd been thinking more of a Westie or even a rescue greyhound. But the two boys, and even Matthew, ruled me out.

'They're women's dogs,' they chorused.

'But it still has to be manageable,' I argued. But my voice

was lost. Here was the chance to get this oversized animal and the winter holidays would be a good time for them to get to know each other.

'And Mum. You promised. You said that if we got up every day before school and walked it, then popped in lunchtime...'

I saw a very large animated noose in front of me that would ultimately be my responsibility. I was angry. I looked at Mathew's expression and was dismayed to see a light of triumph. Perhaps he'd even like it if I had to give up work.

The next day, after a trek to Petsmart for a collar and lead and worming tablets, and a toy and basket, the puppy arrived. It already seemed the size of a large dog – a tangle of pepper and salt fur and bright blue eyes that glinted with devilment.

'It needs something nice and soft to put into the basket,' shouted Mickie.

Matthew had caught the children's enthusiasm. 'There must be an old rug or something in the airing cupboard for him – something snugly,' He rushed upstairs to root in the depths of the airing cupboard. After dragging out an old electric blanket that was too good to throw away, and a pile of grey towels bought by mistake in the sales, he found our rug. Yes, our rug, safely put away for sentiment – for me to get out now and then and remember sweet times.

'But you can't,' I cried. 'Not that rug.'

'Matthew looked at me as if I had been discovered playing on the slot-machines, in town, when I should have been in an exam.

'Not that rug,' I whispered, 'You must remember,' trying to pull it out of his hands.

'Now that is absurd,' he reprimanded, 'You're being menopausal,' and his eyes screwed with disgust as he opened out its shabby width. 'It's a rug for goodness sake, worn and full of holes. Look!'

I was insulted and upset. I tried to reason with myself. Don't be pathetic, he's right. It's a rug. It's a tatty tartan thing – well past its life. But I felt betrayed. He was able to discard our rug – and give our past – to a puppy who happily spent the next hour shredding the damn thing. So in the end, we had to use the grey towels in his bed. The whole incident was ridiculous and maybe it was just hormones – but then all the more reason to be sympathetic. Nevertheless that incident had crushed my reticence.

I'd arranged to meet Rob as soon as the layout was sorted. 'He's a special client,' I muttered in the office, 'Went for a series of six half pages straight away.' I tried to look casual pretending it was business, but when I picked up the phone to make the appointment to see Rob, my heart was thudding in my chest.

'Great,' Rob said. 'Let's do it over dinner.'

Why not? With any other client it would mean nothing, I would not have worried. I agreed to go to the shop and we would go on from there at seven.

Matthew was working late and the children had swimming club and chips after with a friend. It was all too easy. I took time dressing, putting on my new black trouser-suit and a bright top underneath. Why did I bother to put on my best underwear?

Rob had taken trouble with his appearance. The battered chinos were replaced by a smart pair of dark cords and a bright shirt. The thick mass of hair looked as if it had been washed and he smelt of expensive aftershave. He was waiting at the door of the shop when I arrived and produced a bunch of gerberas.

'You liked these in the coffee shop.'

'But it's not a date,' I whispered.

He guided me carefully to a small bistro at the end of the road. An invisible wire hummed between us. I was afraid to talk. He had reserved a table and we sat opposite each other. My briefcase containing his artwork seemed a redundant prop in the play we were acting out. We both knew that it would happen. We ate very little – a few mouthfuls of pasta and some red wine. Then in a husky voice he said 'Come home, with me…please?'

And in that second and the perfectly delicious moments that followed, I felt no guilt. I buried the querulous voice of my maiden aunt, that had sat on my shoulder prodding my conscience, beneath the shreds of a tatty tartan rug.

Green

HOLLY CROSS

I knew before he did, I'd never met her, never heard her name because I didn't want to. All I knew was she and Jonathan worked together and blah blah blah. The usual office fling, and then he left me. I always thought we were permanent, fixed – the thick and the thin – but it ended up just being thin. Being with John was so comfortable that when he left I felt I couldn't sit down on anything without hurting myself. It surprised me how easy it was for him to go. I was exposed without warning, with raw skin all over.

She was just another two o'clock appointment. 'What can I do for you today?' I glanced at her file. 'Leda?' She took her coat off and placed it over the chair as if she didn't want to dirty her clothes on the clinic's furniture.

'I think I'm pregnant.' The third time I'd heard it that day. So often it was teenagers, in with their friends, scared of being two days late and cocky with the thrill of telling an adult about their sex. She was memorable though; a very fine-looking thirty-something Miss, with rich clothes and a nice way of speaking. She is what men might call a catch: sexy, winsome, weak. I went through the usual questions: what contraception, if any, date of last period, did she want a test. I could feel her anticipation, her restrained excitement, like she was about to receive an award for personal achievement; willing herself up the duff.

She mentioned 'a passionate encounter', sweeping aside the idea of contraception as if lovers need not set up such barriers. 'We'll face the consequences.' I felt like a bit-part actor with a one-liner in her drama. So, the forgettable messenger, I suggested we should run the test just to make certain. I handed her the cardboard cup and she slipped discreetly into the Ladies.

I think of her, squatting, uncomfortable, poised over the toilet with her nice trousers off, hoping to quickly squeeze something out, trying to relax and not succeeding. Hormones racing in her body, her womb on red alert at the implantation of an alien thing, and me waiting for her to emerge with her warm cupful ready for testing and her eager ears ready for my words of authority. Yes or no, positive or negative.

It's absurd that every test which shows a woman to be pregnant is 'positive'. It's not a yes/no question, and I've seen so many women sigh with relief when I declare they have yet to take responsibility for the continuation of the human race. 'Thank you, thank you,' as if I decide. Leda was pregnant though, and I had to tell her.

'Oh he'll be delighted! I'm so relieved to know. I'm having a baby! Thank you, nurse.'

I resisted the joke that it wasn't me who'd knocked her up. I was reserved, sensible; she must remember the risks in the first few weeks, she must make an appointment with the doctor, and silently I wondered why 'he' wasn't with her. I wanted to suggest she be sensitive when telling him, he might not feel the same after all. I wanted to plant a seed too, of doubt; it was as if I knew whom she was going back to.

She would prove herself like bread dough swelling soft and even in a warm room with the effort of the yeast inside. Jonathan just had to provide some sugar and he did that well enough.

We'd decided that a clean break was best once he left; the

'clean break' meaning he didn't want to feel guilty any more and I didn't want to get any angrier. So seeing him again was like waking up from a coma; suddenly existing again after hours and days and weeks of void. I went swimming after work, and I wasn't even thinking about him until he swam into my line of vision just as I was coming up for air after a long peaceful glide under water. I swallowed two mouthfuls before getting my feet on the ground, then took my goggles off; aware of the hot red line on my face where they'd suckered onto me. My ripples shuddered as I submerged myself up to the eyes so I could see what he was doing.

He was always a bad swimmer, comical, every child's nightmare as he heaved past, washing wavelets of stinging water into their eyes at the shallow end. His elbows dipped in and out and his face came up gasping with streams gushing over it in a drama of drowning that was actually his front crawl. He was there with her; she was floating her legs up at the side, in a nice swimming cap with straggles of dark hair sticking to her neck. His hands on her, smiling, laughing, underwater doing something to make her shriek, coming up grinning and splashing off for another weaving length of the pool.

Jonathan with her. Enjoying something a little bit more involved than a mere 'passionate encounter' with the smug bitch from the clinic. Despite it all; despite the nausea that assailed me at the image of him with someone else, in spite of trust and love being left abandoned, I admitted to wanting him back. It was bad enough just knowing he was somewhere without me, but now I was getting this twisted look at the details. I'd rather he had died.

Did he know yet? Was the celebrated baby his even? I felt myself gravitating towards her as if the pool's filter had broken open and we were all getting sucked in. I fought against the pull. What did I think I was going to do? She looked up quickly and took off into a graceful breaststroke. My stomach lurched. I had to get out and away before I swished over and tried to strangle her with my goggles. Or was it him I wanted to strangle? No, if I had to get close to him I would – I would – I would cry.

In the slithering escape of the changing room, I immediately had a crippling attack of pain in my abdomen and blood raced darkly towards the tiles. The pressure of the water keeps the blood inside you – that's what I tell the girls when I do the school talks – so you can go swimming but be ready for the flow when you get out. I felt sick, doubled over on the sticky plastic bench not 20 feet away from Mrs Fecundity and New Dad. I would have gone straight home if I'd known, if I'd been able to predict any of this. My body was rejecting the rich lining it had been getting ready, as if it wanted to return an unwanted gift – faulty, flawed or useless. Eventually someone noticed the diluted blood washing away in the gutters and found me.

'Thank goodness, I half-expected to find a horrible accident.'

'I'm fine, honestly, just waiting for the pain to go away, you know how it is. It'll go, I'll be fine. Please, I don't need any help.'

'Come on, love, you can't be on your own in this state.'

'I'm fine. It's nothing.' I started to cry, my hands over my eyes, not sure if it was blood or warm swimming pool water dripping off me. I let the woman wipe my legs with my towel then wrap me in her own, although I couldn't look at her as she did it.

'Hey, hey, don't cry. It must be the moon. I know exactly how you feel.' She knew; my blood didn't embarrass her. We had that much in common already. I sat, dazed, with her arm over my shoulders in a comfy support, and looked down at myself. Yet again the sign of the amateur. How could I stand up and direct all those pregnant and hopeful women when I was nothing but a dilettante with all the equipment but none of the experience?

Once I was dressed and upright we introduced ourselves properly – names hadn't been important before – then Rita and I walked home together; she lives on the other side of the park. I liked her straight away, she was uncomplicated and practical, but it was too much to explain my wounded woman performance – something reminiscent of shame stopped me.

Weeks went by. I met up with Rita and told her the whole story. We had a bit of a laugh over it, she talked excitedly about coincidence and fate, but at work I was alone too often, and found a quiet afternoon in which to pick out Leda's file. I rang her doctor, then the hospital, surprised at the ease of my lies.

'She's my client. Can you update me on her progress please?'

I justified my findings – that was easy too – because Leda had not taken Jonathan, or any other partner, with her to antenatal appointments. If he didn't know, then things weren't running smoothly, and the baby may not even be his. I could protect him from the almighty bit of news that was about to strike him down. I'd foreseen what was going to happen. This was Rita's coincidence and fate.

I wrote a letter to him, an innocent one, chatting, flirty, but kept it burning in my drawer for a while. I took to writing to him regularly, never sending, just stashing them and imagining his responses. It was safer to hope than to act. Gradually I expanded to fill in the gaps, became engorged on pretended conversations, nurturing my wisdom privately, furtively. I pencilled myself back into his life, so when he arrived at my door with the threat of a storm blowing in the trees behind him, I thought I was prepared.

'What are you doing here?'

'Nice way to greet an old friend, Eve. How are you?'

Anger came up unexpectedly at his casual manner: didn't he know how I was, hadn't I been telling him? 'Old friend? I'll bet you haven't even whispered my name for months. What do you want?'

'Can I come in?'

'No. Talk to me here.'

'Oh, come on Eve, don't be like this. I just need a few minutes, inside. Please, I didn't have to come.'

I remembered how bruised I felt when he left, how he could press his thumb on that crushed bit of me, but with him right there I could feel his shape, feel what it was like to make love to him, so very smooth and warm with that surge of white blindness when I felt like someone else.

'Go on, then.' I stood aside. 'What is it, John?'

I was willing myself to tell him what Leda was up to, ruin him, break him up like hard toffee then help him get over it. The ideas I'd been breeding, feeding and storing carefully in a mental nursery of possibilities were on the verge of ripening. He asked me how my mother was, of all things. Mum had always liked him until he disgraced himself. It was strange, sitting with him in my kitchen with awkward small talk popping in my ears, and I was cold with the prospect of his impending pain, or mine, if I opened up.

'Leda and I are having a baby, Eve, in September, so I – I wanted to tell you that we're moving away.'

The scenery around us went blurry and I turned brittle, like a pane of glass. He was steaming me up with his breath. 'Why did you want to tell me?' I was totally flat.

'Because I'll probably never see you again – my last chance to do right by you, I suppose.'

Shattered. 'Oh, bloody hell! If you've come here to make yourself feel better you can leave now.'

'Look, I meant to come as...as a kind of gesture, to let you know in case you wondered where I was, or heard it from someone else or...'

'Well, you needn't have bothered. I already knew about the baby.'

'You knew? What? How did you know?'

'I'm a sexual health nurse, Jonathan. Remember that much? Leda was tested at my clinic.'

'By you?'

'Yeah. In fact, I knew before you did.' I forced a superior smile but he didn't see it.

'Well, I'm glad you've taken it so nobly. Strange how things work out, isn't it?'

He wasn't crushed; or ruined, or angry, and he took on that serene look I see in the glad fathers who can't stop placing their big unknowing hands on the round bellies of their pregnant partners. I'd accidentally made it easier for him to go.

'Well, goodbye, Eve. Wish me luck.'

It had stopped raining by the time he left, and I watched him tiptoe round the puddles on the path. He got into a car I didn't recognise, a family-sized car with a pregnant woman inside it. Leda looked straight at me, curious and amused, no sign of recognition. That was that then, dead again. I closed the door.

How could I have got it so wrong?' I'd stuffed myself full of evidence and imaginings about his regret, his love, and it was as useless to me as all that forced food is to the paté goose. Miscarriage of hope.

Time rotated past me for uncounted days and the park started leaning over the fence, buds busting with a mad March energy. I couldn't escape the green; the wrinkled delicacy of new leaves unfolding like an eyelid opening to take in the world, tough spears of daffodils pushing the earth aside, and that unripe perfume. I wanted to hibernate from the grass-growing, bird-mating spring. Vernal was my swearword.

I took to closing the curtains in the afternoon, to shut out the pressing dappled light that filtered greenly into the living room. I couldn't do anything. Just sit. Sit and think of him with her.

They've actually moved to the Dordogne. All that lushness; fleshy new valleys cupping the deep belly of the river with its brown fish and round stones. Breathe it all in, Jonathan, with your new woman standing out in her Indian reds and oranges, her protuberant stomach disgusting with wriggling life. I see them, half way to the sky; elated with some sick kind of love, looking down to the canopies of fierce pines frothed with growth. I bet they're not thinking about me.

There was a sensation of barrenness in me; a phantom of pregnancy and the ache of frustrated ideas. I stopped cleaning, and neglected to water the plants until I felt like a rotten insect inside an old chrysalis. I was still working, still helping women with that monthly mess of life and death that strikes those who haven't conceived, advising them how to avoid or organise new life, and feeling emptier and emptier.

Rita invited me out to a Spring fair one weekend. I sneered, having blown off the begrudged offers from other friends, but she insisted.

'You cannot decompose in your dark house all year. It's sad and boring. Come out just once and see if you can remember how good things are. I'll help you. Just a couple of hours; come on.'

'All right, but I won't have fun.'

I sulked openly but feeling sorry for myself was getting

difficult, and the new smell of daffodils in the Town Hall made me feel cleaner than I had done in ages. I wished I'd worn a dress to show off my legs, but I didn't let on.

'I prescribe ice cream and a new Easter cactus to heal your wounds.'

'Is that all I need? If only I'd realised sooner.'

'Stop being so jealous and sour Right now.'

I was sweetened gently by Rita's administrations of scorn and sympathy. She bought me the cactus from a stall out on the grass.

'The flowers are ready to pop, look. By the time they're out you'll be feeling a right plum for ever having wasted your time on him.'

'Hope so.'

'These flowers'll be so fancy – tarts craving attention – you should open the windows to let the bees in.'

'Rita! What's that supposed to mean?'

'I mean you. I'm serious. You're getting unhealthy.'

There was an old guy on the bandstand, playing a whistle, his lips pressing the mouthpiece with kisses of clear notes, and we listened until a watercolour moon drew a thin curve behind him. We kept glimpsing it in the gaps between the houses on the walk home; skinny but waxing.

Rita made tea whilst I looked for something to put the plant pot on. In the drawer I found the letters I'd written to Jonathan but not sent. It was like standing back and reading something I'd written years ago, so sly and aberrant. I folded one and stood the fleshy cactus on it, in the window. I'll water the plant and the words will seep away.

Down

KAREN BUCKLEY

When the others have left, Sanford kicks off his sandals and stretches out on my bed. I sit on the edge. There is nowhere else to sit in my room in the Residence Chapou. It is tiny. Just a wardrobe, a desk, a small hand basin behind a partition, and the narrow bed tucked underneath a wall shelf.

'This feels good,' he says, clasping his hands behind his neck and grinning up at me, but I am looking at the shelf above his head, at the little sachet of sugar that Tim gave to me before I left for France. Across the tear-off strip at the top he has written, *I'm sweet on you.*

'You have a beautiful smile,' Sanford says.

Through the wall I can hear the girl in the next room emptying her sink, then a light switch clicking off, and, below my open window, the deep, quick-fire French of a group of North Africans coming back from the TV room. Sanford is staring at me the way he has all evening, his blue eyes singling me out across the table in the Restaurant Maroc, ignoring the others. If he does not stay here tonight he will have to walk back into Toulouse and find a room in a hostel, and anyway, I know he has come back for me.

We met a couple of months ago in the Lavomatique. He was emptying crumpled carrier bags into one of the huge washing machines, fumbling in the pocket of his jeans for change. When I offered him a handful of coins, he smiled at me and started to talk. He said he was from South Carolina, a musician, doing Europe. His next stop would be Arles, and then Montpellier, where a friend had found him a job as a piano tuner. I told him I was in Toulouse for the year, part of a group of students from Britain. He said it was good to hear an English voice at last and asked if he could meet the others.

That night at the Boum he danced with each of us in turn and slept on someone else's floor, but the next morning he appeared at my door, rucksack on his back, and asked if I would walk with him to the station. We took the canal path to keep to the shade and, as we walked, he told me about his journey from Paris. We crossed the Place du Capitol, and were passing a music shop when he stopped talking, lowered his rucksack onto the pavement and stared in through the window. Then he hoisted his bag up again and pushed open the smoky glass doors. I followed him inside, and he turned to ask me if I could speak to the assistant. He wanted to know if they would let him play the piano in the window. He said he just had to. It had been so long.

I rested my elbows on the top of the Steinway and watched him playing Debussy, his fingers quick on the keys, his head swaying, black curls brushing his cheeks. Then he looked up, his eyes lit and then sad, as though he had composed the piece for me.

We said goodbye in the station foyer, and two weeks later, his letter arrived from Montpellier: *I have found a beautiful apartment here. I can lie in bed and listen to the Mediterranean. I look out at the crystal blue clarity of the ocean and think of you.*

That was when I knew I was part of his game.

'Don't you find it hot in here?' he says, rubbing his forehead with the back of his hand. 'Do you mind if I take something off?'

I watch as he unbuttons his shirt, sits up and throws it to the floor. On his back again, he unbuckles his belt, unzips his jeans, arches his back and wriggles out of them. Then he lies back down. He is wearing cotton briefs that must have once been white. I can feel his toes on my spine, tickling through my dress, gliding up between my shoulder blades, down to my coccyx, and I lean back against his foot. It is the first time we have touched.

'Lie down with me,' he says.

I feel tired now, from the meal and the Kir and the walk back from the city. I pull off my sandals and he shuffles up to the wall to make room for me. I lie on my side, head propped on one hand, and look at him, taking in his long black lashes and the strange, shallow forehead, the hairline coming down to a point – a widow's peak.

'Tell me about Charleston,' I say, and I close my eyes, breathing in his smell. His voice is a soft drawl. I hear, 'Blue skies, magnolias, wisteria, the sea.' I know he will not ask me anything about myself.

When I open my eyes again, a strand of hair falls over my face. He tucks it behind my ear and I kiss his fingers. His toes trace the arches of my feet. I sit up, unbutton my dress and take it off, draping it over the end of the bed. As I lie back down, Tim smiles at me from the photograph on my desk. Our last day together before I caught the ferry.

'Well, what did she say?' Tim asked as I emerged through the moon and stars curtains of Gypsy Rosa's booth. He was standing with his back to the railings, hands in the pockets of his cords, the sea a strip of lead behind him.

'Oh, I'm going to live a long life,' I said, 'and have plenty of children.'

'Good,' he smiled, taking both my hands in his. 'That's what you want, isn't it?'

I nodded.

We walked along the prom, coats fastened against the breeze, then he pointed out a bench, we sat down, and he put his arm around my shoulder.

'Anything else?' he asked, stroking my face with the backs of his fingers.

'What?'

'The gypsy? Did she say anything else?' He smiled and I watched the dimple appearing in his left cheek. His face was flushed pink from the cold.

'I'm going to travel.'

'Oh, well, she's right there.' The dimple disappeared again and he swallowed. 'A whole year away, Geri. I wish you didn't have to go.'

I looked down at the beach. A boy in a billowing cagoule was running, tugging at the strings of a kite that swerved and dipped then plunged onto the sand. Tim pulled me in towards him until our cheeks touched. His skin was cool. The bristles on his chin rasped a little and I shivered. Then he kissed me so gently I wanted to put my head on his shoulder and sleep.

'It'll be okay,' I said.

'Of course it'll be okay for you.' His fingers tightened around mine, pressing my signet ring into the flesh below the knuckle. 'You'll be out there where you want to be, seeing the world.' Over his shoulder I could see the row of hotels and B&Bs facing out to sea. Faded Edwardian buildings. *The Ashley, The Regal, Bay View*. Huge picture windows. Vases of silk flowers and china figurines on the sills. Signs announcing *Vacancies*. It was the end of the summer and everyone else had gone home.

He kissed me again, his fingers in my hair; stroking my ear lobes. I wanted him to get up from the bench, take me across the road and check in somewhere, lie down with me on a strange bed and make love to me before I left, but I knew he would not.

'Tim,' I said, pulling back a little and looking into his eyes. 'You could come with me to France.'

'What do you mean?'

'You're a free agent now. You've finished your degree.'

'Oh, you know I can't afford to, Geri. I'll need to save up.'

I ran my finger over his bottom lip. 'You could hitch.'

He was looking down at our hands, his voice almost a whisper. 'Is that all she said?'

'Who?'

'The gypsy?'

A seagull circled above our heads then swooped down and perched on the litter bin beside the bench. It preened its chest, feathers ruffled by the breeze, then opened its bill, squawked and flew off again, gliding out over the sea.

'She said I'm going to fall in love. I'm going to meet a man with the letters A and D in his name.'

Sanford sits up, reaches over to the desk and picks up the photograph. 'Has this guy been over to see you yet?'

'No, not yet. He's still saving.'

He shakes his head, puts the photograph back, glass down, takes my chin between his finger and thumb, turns my face towards his and starts to recite:

'That god forbid that made me first your slave...'

He clasps both hands to his chest.

'I should in thought control your times of pleasure...'

He screws his knuckles into his forehead, then holds his hand out to me. I want to laugh.

'Or at your hand the account of hours to crave...'

He takes my hand, his thumb drawing soft circles on my palm. Then he dabs at the corner of his eye with his fingertip, but there are no tears.

'I am to wait, though waiting so be hell, Not blame your pleasure, be it ill or well.'

I can feel his breath on my lips. He is staring at me but his eyes are empty. Blue marbles.

Still clasping my fingers, he stretches out on the bed again and sighs, 'My English Rose.' He pulls me towards him and I lie down. Next to his skin, mine is a deep shade of brown. Our sides touch. I can feel his heartbeat. He is hot. Except for the black tufts under his arms, his skin is soft and hairless. I have to touch it, first with my fingers then my lips. I kiss his arms, his chest, lick his nipples. He tastes of salt. Then I look up at his face. His eyes are closed and he is moaning. I imagine his letter home: *In Toulouse I met up again with the students from England. We ate couscous in the Place du Capitol, walked home by the Garonne with the moon on our backs, and I fell in love with my English Rose.*

I kiss his eyelids, his cheekbones, the tip of his nose, and he gasps. My breasts are aching to be touched but his hands are still locked behind his head. I unfasten my bra and let my nipples brush his chest. He whispers, 'My love.' Then, in one quick move, he lifts his head, releases one arm and wraps a hand around my neck, his fingers snagging the hairs on my nape. He pulls me hard onto his mouth. Our teeth clash. I draw back enough to see his head lolling from side to side on the pillow, his mouth gaping. I can count his fillings. He starts to groan, grinding his buttocks into the bed. Then he opens his eyes and sits up. Glaring ahead, he tugs at his briefs with one hand, squirming until they are round his ankles. I reach down and peel them over his feet, freeing his toes. I think this might make him smile but his eyes are closed again, his tongue curling and sliding over his lips. As he shuffles back down, his hair sweeps over the shelf behind his head and I watch the sachet of sugar flutter to the floor.

'Turn round,' said Tim, 'and close your eyes.'

I was halfway up the steps of the train but I stopped and turned back towards him. As he kissed me, I felt him slip a piece of paper into my palm. I opened my hand and looked down. It was a little sachet of sugar. He must have picked it up in the station cafe and written on it whilst I was in the toilet.

'I'm sweet on you too.' I laughed.

He hugged me, then held me hard by the elbows and looked at me. His eyes were wet, green as pond water. 'Geri, you know what the gypsy said about the man with the A and the D in his name?'

'Don't worry.' I smiled. 'It was just a bit of fun. I love you.'

'No,' he said. 'Aren't you forgetting something?'

The guard strode towards us, waving his arms, belly flopped over the waistband of his trousers. He scowled at Tim, ushered me up the steps and slammed the door. He smelt of stale sweat. I lowered the window and leaned out. Down on the platform, Tim looked smaller than before. 'What?' I said. 'What am I forgetting?'

'The A and the D. She must have been talking about me. It's my middle name, remember. David.'

Sanford is panting, his free hand splayed on his chest, then curled in a fist, kneading his ribs, edging down to his groin. I want to sit back and look at him naked, but his grip tightens round my neck. His hand scrapes up the back of my head and over my scalp, pushing the hair onto my face.

'Down,' he moans, his fingers clamping my skull. A nail breaks the skin below my eyebrow and I wince. Through the mess of my hair, I see his penis. It is thick, the tip a deep, angry pink. 'Down.'

My head is being twisted from side to side. My neck jars. He is writhing, thrusting at my face. His penis flicks across my lips and grazes my tongue. It tastes like rotten fish.

Indian Summer

ELIZABETH MORGAN

She stirred in a half sleep, aware of some unease.

She opened her eyes, and then closed them abruptly, for a strong ray of blinding warm sun shone on her face, like a spotlight. Turning from the glare she sat up and focussed on the confusion around her.

She rose from the bed, picking her way over suitcases, black plastic bags, and boxes, to a mirror standing awkwardly on the chest of drawers. Frowning, as she gave her face and chin a critical appraisal, she brushed her hair, which still fell in girlish waves about her face; the only aspect of her middle-aged self that she felt had borne the passage of time well.

The kitchen was a mess. Boxes of crockery, cutlery and saucepans, were piled high on the farmhouse table. She cleared space for a cup and quite by chance found the electric kettle poking out of a box labelled 'Bedroom'. Sorting out this shambles would take months, but there was time, no rush, no one to rush for, after all she was alone. She had been alone and lonely for eight years since David's death. The thought of him sent her scurrying upstairs to prise his framed photograph out of a box beside the mirror.

Peter and Susan were still at school when he died, but finally coming to terms with her new single life, she bought a maisonette in a leafy part of Camden Town, and began the search for a cottage in Cornwall, always the family's favourite patch for holidays.

It was now eight o' clock, the sun already hot in a Mediterranean sky. Since June, Britain had had one of those freak summers, which turned coastlines into tropical rivieras. Strolling out to the small stone terrace at the back of the cottage, she sensed a little frisson of pride as she surveyed her new home; a small dishevelled fairy tale confection of white walls, French windows, pink roof tiles, and purple wisteria growing over the back door like an un-brushed fringe. From the terrace gate you could walk across a strip of grass, dried yellow now by the sun, and along a gentle cliff slope to the beach.

She walked round to the front of the cottage. There had been a path, but it was overgrown like the garden. Weeds stood tall as bushes, and roses turned to bramble had stems thick as tree trunks. Dog daisies reared their perky heads, providing rare spots of colour in this palette of green. She leant on the gate, half expecting it to collapse. There was an awesome stillness about this place, broken only by lapping waves on the shingle down below, and the cries of birds. She would paint here. If she painted all summer she could have an autumn exhibition in London. Autumn next year, not this year.

This year - oh God!

She sat down beside the telephone and again questioned her own wisdom in buying the house. Their marriage had not been easy. When the children were young there had been a mutual focus of activity and interest. They could easily have separated later, like most of their friends. She rose and walked to the open kitchen window. Three seagulls were perched on the terrace wall. She threw them pieces of bread, and laughed at the comic tilt of their heads, pondering briefly upon the souls of dead seamen. They refused to move even after their third meal and were regarding her so quizzically, she laughed aloud. ' Thank you, Tom Dick and Harry. I think I shall like it here.'

She telephoned Peter.

Did he know of a fellow student reasonably knowledgeable about D.I.Y. who could be persuaded to spend three paid weeks in Cornwall?

At eight o' clock the telephone rang. A young well-spoken male voice asked. 'Is that Mrs Claire Hampson?'

'It is.'

'I'm a friend of Peter's – er – doing Architecture, – final year. He says you need a handyman.'

'Well yes I do, and possibly some simple plumbing and woodwork.'

'Yes, that's OK.' He laughed. 'Hands on experience you know. Architects should get their hands dirty now and again.'

'Well, if you are sure...'

'Don't worry. My father is a builder. I've always helped him in the vacations.'

'Great. I'll pay you and feed you...'

'Yep! Pete's explained all. Sounds good, so – when?'

She could not believe her luck. Even if he wanted pop music blaring all day, it would only be for three weeks. It was arranged she would meet him off the train in two days and for identification she would wear a white jacket.

'There are a few white jackets, but you look like Mrs Hampson.'

She turned. 'Yes! You must be...'

'Nicholas Groves.' He was tall and well built with a wide boyish grin, his eyes very blue against a tanned face.

'You're taller than I expected,' she said, realising immediately the foolishness of the remark.

'God! Have I got a short voice?' he quipped.

They were at ease with each other from the start, which was just as well, Claire reflected, since they were obliged to spend the next few weeks incarcerated in the cottage.

After supper she showed him all he would be required to do, then they took coffee on the terrace as the sun was sinking into the sea. Shadows of orange and russet fell over cliffs. Seagulls, their underbellies reflecting the red sky, resembled misshapen flamingos as they dived into flaming clouds.

In bed that night, the moon spreading a soft light across the room, she felt relaxed and calm, happy that someone was in the house with her, albeit a young man half her age.

During the next few days they worked harmoniously from early morning. From time to time they would both have a word with Tom Dick and Harry, their unblinking observers, who appeared to be developing a discerning taste in orchestral music as well as stale bread.

Often they would work together until midnight, she painting walls, he sawing wood or putting up shelves. Then in working clothes they would stop, sit on the moonlit terrace, stones still warm from the sun, drink wine, listen to the sea, and talk. They talked about everything. He talked about Debbie, his last girl friend. She talked about David, her marriage, its delights, its problems, her work, and the difficulty of coming to terms with widowhood.

'Don't give up, Claire.'

She smiled. 'All behind me now. I mean I don't particularly like it, being alone – but I'm accepting it at last.'

'You mustn't give up.'

'I'm too old, Nick.'

'Nonsense! You know...' He stopped. 'You only look about forty.'

'Flatterer!' She blushed and giggled like a girl, and though she could not believe him, she was pleased.

'No – really! I lived with a lovely lady of forty-two in my second year. They were all jealous of me.' He grinned at the recollection.

'Why jealous?'

'Didn't you know it's every young man's dream to make love to an older woman?'

His blue eyes looked at her directly. Delicate ripples chased up her spine disconcerting her usual composure. She smiled back at him, cheeks burning.

'So you see – Madame is the perfect age!'

They laughed.

They laughed a great deal together.

Something was happening to Claire; something was changing. The ease of communication between them, the jokes they shared, the nudging innuendo, all essential parts of life and living that she missed so much. It was like being plunged into bright sunlight after endless rain, and it felt so comfortable it made her afraid. She was relishing a friendship with someone of her children's age, without the burden of role-playing. She felt free with him, and the years between them seemed to disappear. They enthused over symphonies, operas, paintings. There was one particular oboe concerto by Corelli, which they both loved and played incessantly.

She became flirtatious and skittish. He made her laugh with his student yarns and by frequently playing the clown. They went shopping in the village, and consulted each other as couples do over cheeses, over wine, meat and vegetables.

Nick seemed to take as much pride in each completed task as did she. He had endearing habit of referring to the cottage proprietorially, 'our cottage', and 'our garden'. Claire thought how lovely it was to be an 'us', or a 'we' again, if only for a few weeks.

One evening talking about relationships, he'd said, 'It was Debbie who asked me out first. Girls don't wait about now. They make the first move.'

She laughed. 'So I've heard! Times have changed.'

'Thank God!'

'You don't mind being pursued?'

He grinned. 'Claire I love it! I'm abysmally self-conscious with women!'

'But you're bursting with confidence!'

'Superficial. It's a big con.'

'I envy girls today. We were supposed to wait to be asked.'

'Afraid of being rejected?'

'Partly.'

'That hasn't changed, Claire. We're all afraid of being rejected.'

He looked at her with that same direct gaze, which when met head-on touched something inside that she found disturbing, because she was sensing again gentle frissons of pleasure in the pit of her stomach. Her body was waking up after a long sleep.

'You're afraid aren't you?' he said gently.

She reached for the bottle of wine and recharged their glasses. 'So you've guessed my secret, young man.'

He grinned. 'Which is?'

'That underneath this incredible display of middle-aged confidence, lies a "wee tim'rous beastie!"'

'You and me both then.'

She gazed down at her glass of wine, her hand resting beside it.

'Let's drink to us then, the tim'rous beasties!'

His hand lay close to hers on the table. As he picked up his glass their hands brushed slightly.

At the end of the first week, the weather was so superb, they decided to take time off during the day to swim and work late into the evening. The first time she wore her bikini, he looked her up and down approvingly then asked. 'Do you have to work to keep yourself in such fabulous shape?'

She laughed dismissively, but was pleased he had noticed.

How she wished for the courage to touch his long lean body, stroke his tanned skin. Sometimes she would challenge him to a race down to the sea, giggling like a teenager. After a swim they would lie together on one large towel, propping chins on folded arms, eyes puckered against the sun's glare, and talk and talk. Their hands lay together always close but never really touching.

By his last day Nick had managed to finish his work, and Claire was delighted with all he had achieved. That evening she banished him from the kitchen. She wanted to make their final dinner memorable. Napkins in place, candles lit, she put on the Corelli concerto and called him in. She was to remember his look as he opened the door, tender, and warm. Then with a sweeping gesture, he produced from behind his back a huge bunch of flowers.

'Tarra! For you, beautiful lady.'

Next he placed two bottles of champagne on the table.

'For us!'

'Oh! Thank you Nick.' Quite spontaneously she pecked him on both cheeks. 'There was no need, really.'

'I wanted to,' he replied softly.

After dinner they sat on the terrace drinking the champagne.

'I'll miss you,' she said.

'And I'll miss you – very much. Talking, sorting out our problems and everybody else's, and of course Mr Corelli.' He sighed. 'You've helped me Claire.'

'How?'

'Well – I don't think about Debbie any more. She's banished! Thanks to you.'

'I'm glad,' she smiled.

They fell into a relaxed silence.

The evening was warm and almost tropical, and it was difficult to discern where the sky ended and the earth began, so perfect was the fusion as if the dark night had raised the world a little closer to heaven. Bobbing lights on fishing vessels out for the night's haul could have been mistaken for falling stars, cascading from the glowing headland.

'Lovely isn't it?' she murmured.

'Exquisite.' He turned to her and smiled. 'I'll remember this.'

She was trying to forget that tomorrow she would sit here alone.

Then he said. 'I hope we can see each other in London – I mean I'd like to, er take you out – to a concert perhaps, that is...if you'd...'

Those little frissons in her stomach made her feel slightly breathless and she did not wait for him to finish. 'That'd be lovely Nick. I'd like that too – in fact – I'd love it.'

He left the following morning.

How she cursed herself. Other women made passes. She reflected on his words over and over again. But back in London, who could tell?

Claire's close friend Margot came to stay for a few days. Margot was worldly-wise, and Claire's trusted confidante.

'So why on earth didn't you two get into the sack. This isn't the age for pussy-footing, darling!'

Claire shrugged, 'Well as I'm older, a rejection would have been pretty devastating.'

'Confidence sweetie! Claire darling you are a very dishy lady. He could equally well have thought you'd turn him down. Come on!'

Claire gave a thin smile, 'You have a very foolish friend, old fruit.' Margot put her hands on Claire's shoulders. 'It's never foolish to fall a little in love. I think you have both fallen a little in love,' she added softly.

Claire received a letter from Nick in which he told her he just met the rest of the family at a party given by Peter, and signed himself, Love Nick. PS. I miss our long heart to hearts and Mr Corelli.'

Two days later she wrote a reply ending with:

The feathers on Tom, Dick and Harry are greyer. The sea has changed colour to a dark green, and there are a few yellow leaves on the oak tree. I cannot sit on the terrace these evenings as there is a cold wind blowing off the sea.

I too remember those lengthy heart to hearts when we put the world to rights. You have described your flat to me so often I imagine you sitting at your desk writing and working.

Music remains a constant joy, especially our Mr Corelli.

Nick, I'm glad we still share him.

Look forward so much to seeing you in London.

Love, Claire.

It was during her last weeks at the cottage he telephoned.

'Claire! May I come down to see you?'

She called Margot. 'So what are you waiting for, gal?' she whooped. 'Now's your chance. I'm counting on you. OK?'

Claire bought herself a pretty silk blouse in a boutique, and had her hair done.

Waiting for the train to pull in, she could feel her heart pounding.

Her stomach leaped with butterflies like a teenager. Supposing she took the initiative? Supposing he rejected her? But why should he reject her? Surely coming here to see her was proof enough that theirs was no ordinary friendship.

By the time the train finally arrived she was in a state

of anxious expectation. He walked towards her arms outstretched, and looking even more beautiful, she thought.

She went upstairs to change for dinner. As she came into the dining room he smiled appraisingly. 'Wow! You look absolutely gorgeous, Claire.'

She was barely able to contain the excitement that bubbled within her.

After dinner she set a bottle of brandy on a tray with their coffee.

As she crossed behind his chair to fill his glass she put her hand on his shoulder and gave it the merest squeeze. 'Lovely to have you back, Nick.'

'Come and sit down,' He smiled. 'I'd like to talk to you – that's why I'm here.'

Her heart raced. Her palms were sticky. This was it. There was no point in being nervous. Even if he were to make the proposition she still had the choice. She wanted to appear relaxed so she sat on the floor.

'Well Nick, what is it?' she asked simply.

'I – I want your approval Claire.' He hesitated. 'You know – at least I think I told you, I had met your sister?'

'Sister?'

He laughed. 'Sorry, Freudian slip. Your daughter. That's a compliment Claire. You look like sisters! We met at Peter's party and since then we've been seeing a great deal of each other.'

She stared at him wide-eyed, her body trembling with shock.

Her cheeks burned. She was on a carousel, her head spinning. She could find no words, but merely nodded in response.

'She's so like you – not only physically – she laughs at the same things, and she has exactly the same look on her face when she's thinking. But most of all, she's got your warmth and energy.'

He stopped, carried away by recollections of Susan, totally unaware of Claire who was looking at him, expressionless, mute.

He laughed suddenly embarrassed by his effusion. 'If it sounds as though I'm bowled over – I am! Completely.'

'Well...I'm...I'm glad for you both – of course.'

'The thing is we want to move in together – and – because I know you so well, I would like your approval.'

She smiled back, rose unsteadily to her feet and poured herself another large brandy.

'And Susan, does she...?'

'She thought it better I talked to you, as we – you and I are such good friends. Aren't we?'

'Of course.' She said quietly.

She felt quite sick but desperately wanting to behave normally, she continued to smile, a silly plastic smile that made her cheeks ache.

'So?' he asked anxiously.

'So, why not?'

She drank another glass of brandy, and felt her legs about to give way.

'Nick I'm a little tired. I think I'll turn in.'

The room swayed, but with the plastic smile still in place she added, 'Not as young as I used to be.'

'What rubbish!' he laughed. 'Do you mind if I stay up for a while and listen to music?'

She threw herself down on the bed, and lay quite still for several minutes. Slowly she sat up and took off her new blouse. Steadying herself she crossed the room, and saw in the mirror her brimming eyes, large and round.

'You stupid, silly old woman,' she whispered. 'Stupid, stupid old woman.'

With tears rolling down her cheeks, she looked at David's

photograph.

She had never felt quite so alone, and sobbed uncontrollably.

That night she slept fitfully, her thoughts centred not on her daughter, but on herself, and the lover she, Claire, had provided for Susan.

What irony.

The next morning she tried to behave as though last evening's conversation had not taken place. They walked on the beach, he picking up flat pebbles and skimming them over the calm sea, as boys do; she laughing and making him laugh.

After lunch he drove the car to the station, and hugged her as the train approached. 'Thanks Claire – for everything, Susan's going to call you tonight about seven.'

'Fine,' was all she could say.

Without thinking she pulled out his shirt collar which was lying creased under his denim jacket, and patted it flat.

'Mothers!' he said, with a broad grin.

Back in the cottage, she poured herself a glass of wine, closed her eyes and switched on the Corelli.

At seven o' clock, the telephone rang. She could not answer it.

Tomorrow she would feel better.

Tomorrow she would call Susan.

Tonight she would call Margot, although she knew in advance what Margot would say. 'So what darling, you didn't compromise yourself! You're a big girl now, so be thankful it's stirred you into life again!'

Which was exactly what she did say.

Claire threw a jacket over her shoulders walked out on to the terrace, automatically taking a handful of bread for Tom, Dick and Harry's breakfast. Life would go on as before, but

she would never doubt she and Nick had shared something
– something?

The Dancing King

MARIA DONOVAN

Brenda is lying in bed reading a romantic novel when the knock comes at her door.

There he stands, tall, handsome and unfamiliar, dressed in a tuxedo. '*Pour vous*,' he says, handing her a rose.

'Do I know you?'

'I thought you wanted me to take you dancing.' His eyebrows flash.

Brenda takes a deep breath, shakes her head, then swings the door shut in his face and grumbles her way back to bed.

He knocks again.

Brenda bites her lip. Bother. Just when she didn't need a man in her life. 'Come in.'

He opens the door, wearing a knowing look.

'Just don't speak to me, that's all,' says Brenda. 'I'm reading.'

Loosening his black tie, he lies down beside her on the bed. Over the top of her book she can see dark trousers extending all the way down to the end of the duvet and a pair of shiny shoes.

Time passes, and the tension grows with each rasp of a page turned. Out of the corner of her eye she sees him looking at her.

He puts a hand on her arm, brings his face close to hers.

'Shall we dance?' he says. Standing up, he offers her his

hand. Brenda smiles, in spite of herself. She turns down the corner of the page. With a snap of his fingers he brings the sound of a full-string orchestra looping into the room.

Feeling at a disadvantage dancing in her pyjamas, without a shred of make-up on, Brenda keeps glancing backwards, afraid she will snag her spine on the corner of the wardrobe.

'Would you relax?' he says. 'It's like dancing with an ironing board.'

Just as an experiment, she closes her eyes and lets herself be moved. His hold is firm, his footsteps certain. It's like floating, another state of being. He doesn't push or wrench.

'You're good at this,' she says.

'Only the very best for you, my darling.'

She opens her eyes.

He's wearing a smile of the deepest self-satisfaction. Surprisingly, she finds this quite endearing.

At last she begins to grow sleepy. He sways with her towards and away and towards the bed, with the subtle advance of an incoming tide. She remembers the light going out and the sound of him slipping off his tie.

In the morning he's gone; no need for Brenda to worry about her morning breath or what to say at breakfast. The sheet on his side of the bed is quite smooth and there isn't a dent in the pillow, as if he's never been there. But the rose on the bedside table is drinking from her glass of water.

The next evening she goes to bed early, unfolding the corner of the page she turned down last night.

'Hello there,' he says.

'Woh!' The book flies up in the air. 'What are *you* doing here?'

He shrugs. 'You called me.'

'I did not,' she says, indignantly.

'You must have.' He smiles gently. 'I'm here, aren't I?'

A few nights later, despite her best intentions not to care what he does when he's not with her, she asks him where he lives.

He takes a drag on his cigarette and blows out smoke before answering, 'The shed at the bottom of the garden.'

'There is no shed at the bottom of the garden,' says Brenda.

'Not at the bottom of *your* garden – no,' he says, teasingly.

The next day she looks out of the bedroom window. The shed belonging to the house next door is quite close to her fence. Brenda turns back to make the bed; there is just a slight crease in the sheet where his body has lain and she hesitates before smoothing it away.

'I wonder if you could help me,' Brenda says to her neighbour. 'I've lost my kitten and I think it might have accidentally gotten into your shed.'

'Nah,' says the neighbour. 'Door's been shut for days. I've had the flu.' He waves a snot-frozen hanky.

Brenda stands firm. 'I thought I heard it crying in there. Perhaps it got in some other way?' The neighbour is sceptical but gives Brenda the key so she can have a quick look and set her mind at rest.

Down the garden path she goes, her heart leaping. The shed door is secured by a large, well-oiled padlock. The key slides in and turns easily.

Inside the shed it is dark and smells of old garden tools, clay pots and compost. There's no bed, other than a folded-up canvas sun-lounger, and no clothes or shoes or other things. She does find a blue-and-white striped mug hanging on a hook, with a stain of old coffee inside. The windows are jammed with dirt and cobwebs.

'No sign of the cat,' she tells the neighbour. 'Thanks.'

That night her lover does not appear. She curls up in the bed to have a good cry, then reads herself to sleep. In the morning she finds she's slept on her book and buckled its pages.

'Where've you been?' These are the first words out of her mouth when she bumps into him outside Woolworth's.

He hasn't been round for days. Relaxed but friendly, she'd said to herself, that's what I must be next time I see him, whenever that might be, relaxed *and* friendly. But she hears herself saying, 'Where've you been?' instead; and within two minutes they're having a row and she's shaking.

Later, she feels so sorry for misjudging him. He'd wanted to see her, of course he had. The truth was he'd been on his way over to her place the other night when he'd noticed a woman about to give birth in the doorway of Marks and Spencer. By the time he'd had a chance to call it was already very late.

'What did she have?' asks Brenda.

'A boy, a ten-pounder. Really quite something. She's calling it after me.'

He even has a creased Polaroid to show her, of a sweaty-haired woman lying back on her pillows with a tired smile, and himself standing up, wearing a wide grin and a green hospital gown, holding a new baby in his arms.

Later, after sex (forgiving, tender, urgent), while they are mid-snuggle, she mumbles to him in a sleepy and contented voice, 'You can always call. I don't mind if it's late. I lie awake anyway, reading.' But just as she falls over the rim of sleep she thinks: isn't it odd that I don't even know his name? And now he's given it to someone else's child.

That summer, they go on holiday together for two weeks, driving and dancing around Scotland. They laugh at each other's jokes. Sometimes they get lost.

'It doesn't matter,' says whoever's at the wheel. 'We're bound to end up somewhere in the end.' They dance during the day among the heather and look out for hotels with ballrooms.

She hears him whistling in the bathroom when she wakes. He gets up early to shave so that his chin will be smooth when he kisses her. While he's doing that she chews gum and applies subtle touches of make-up. When she hears him pull the plug, she wraps the gum in its silver paper and hides it under her book. He finds her smiling sweetly, eyes closed, ready to be woken with a kiss.

Sometimes though, at dinner, they don't have much to say and she glances about, wondering if she would prefer to be talking to someone else; but then she looks sharply at him, wondering if he's thinking the same thing. Given the chance, they take to the floor and glide until she is happy again.

He moves in with her. When the first night comes when neither of them wants to dance, it feels as if something has ended. Brenda reaches for her long-neglected book. But he says, 'I need to go to sleep now. Got an early start.' She puts out the light, but then lies awake, wondering whether to cuddle up to him; for the first time the bed feels too hot with him in it.

To show her adaptability she buys herself a torch for reading in bed when he wants the light out. In the winter she changes this for a lamp on a headband, so she can keep at least one hand at a time under the duvet. He laughs at her. Without speaking or looking up from her book, she brushes her icy fingers along his thigh. He stops laughing and yelps.

Some time later, he's calm enough to try sleeping. He turns on his side and puts his back to her, mumbling, '*And* you've got a cold bottom.'

But she's always had a cold bottom; he's supposed to like warming it up.

Around Christmas time he goes out a lot without her; she accuses him of dancing with someone else.

'You're paranoid,' he says, fumbling with his black tie.

'Here, let me.' She nips at his fingers till he lets go of the strip of silk and allows her to knot it for him.

He kisses her on the cheek, saying, 'Don't wait up.'

In the week before Valentine's Day, he disappears. It doesn't look, at first, as if he means to stay away. His razor is left un-rinsed in the bathroom; his shirts are on a hanger, waiting to be ironed; his socks are strewn across the bedroom like the droppings of a large and restless herbivore.

When all the socks have turned quite stiff, she puts them in an old pillow-case. But the laundry basket is never empty while they are in it.

A month later, opening the bedroom window, she extracts a corrugated sock and lobs it onto the roof of next door's shed. Soon the pillowcase is empty.

That night, to distract herself from saw-edged emotions which are trying to cut her in half, she browses the half-read pile of books by her bed. Every time she feels like crying she makes herself read another sentence.

One evening, when she can think about signing up for contemporary dance classes without weeping, he knocks on her door.

'I've got my dancing shoes on,' he wheedles through the

lock.

Brenda says nothing. At last he goes away.

The next evening she is tensed for his return. Tap, tap, tap. He calls to her through the keyhole, 'Let me in.'

She turns out the light and says nothing, even though she wants to yell at him. Or weep and open the door.

On Saturday he comes round at midnight, drunk.

'Go away!' she shouts.

All is quiet. Brenda wonders if he is preparing to climb the drainpipe and try to get in at the window. She stays sitting up in bed for some time, straining to hear. But there is nothing.

The summer comes and the evenings are so light and so sad. She reads and reads and reads. How glad she is to have the big cool quiet bed to herself. But her feet twitch and, having turned out the light, she often hears music coming from the garden of a house close by, a deep familiar voice, and twirls of carefree laughter.

These sounds are just loud enough to keep her from falling asleep.

Some Sort of Twilight

CAROLYN LEWIS

Even the envelope looked posh. It was sitting on the table on top of the rest of the mail that Mum had picked up from the mat. She never opens anything in the morning unless it's urgent. She says that she's got enough to worry about, just getting to work on time without having to think about the gas bill or reminders from BT. So the envelope with *Air Canada* printed in bright red letters looked really out of place on our table.

Mum had put the envelope next to the salt and pepper pots she'd brought back from a day trip she took with her mates from work. They went to Porthcawl, 16 of them in a coach. She said the salt and pepper pots reminded her of me, when I was a baby, two fat faced cherubs, one with *Salt* and the other with *Pepper* written on their stomachs. They look really tacky.

See, that's what I mean, the envelope looked wrong in our kitchen. It looked glossy, from another world, a world we don't live in. All the things we're not.

This business of me living with Mum and Dad living in Canada and him sending me stuff gets really complicated at times. I get home before Mum most days and, looking at the envelope, knowing she's placed it on top of the pile, knowing what it was all about, made me so uncomfortable.

I was glad the house was empty, glad that I didn't have to

say anything to Mum. We get on all right most of the time but whenever something from my Dad arrives, there's this whole area of difficulty we have. Whatever he sends, we both know it's there and we both ignore it, we talk around it, over it, like it's a bomb or something. After a while, Mum will ask me, 'What did you get from your Dad?' and then I know it's ok to talk about it.

I got a can of Coke from the fridge. Mum writes notes for me, things she wants me to do when I get home. One was stuck to the fridge door. *Peel potatoes and carrots. Lay table.* Usual stuff. Sometimes she'll write *Wash a lettuce, prepare salad.* Then I'll know she'll be banging on about another diet. That's when she'll put all the biscuits in the freezer. No diet today though: she'd taken out four sausages from the freezer. They were lying in a bowl on the windowsill.

I picked the envelope up. I could feel edges of different sheets of paper inside. Airline ticket, luggage labels, notice of time to arrive, bumf on passports, everything for my trip to Toronto. I didn't want to open the envelope. I liked not seeing what was inside. Although I did know.

I also wanted Mum to know that I wasn't too bothered about opening it. Not that big a deal. Flying. To Canada to see my Dad. Been there, done that.

I drank the Coke and began to peel the potatoes and carrots. Mum would be home about six o'clock, she wasn't on late shift this week. Just gone five now, enough time for me to get out of this disgusting uniform. Lay the table first, how long does that take? Five seconds. Ok, computer, here I come. See if there are any messages from Sarah or Emily.

Only message I had was from Dad. He wanted to know if the ticket had arrived. Well, it has. It's sitting on the kitchen table but I don't want to let him know just yet. I'll wait until Mum gets home. Not sure why I'm doing this, what difference will it make? Somehow it just does.

That's the front door. I know the words that will come out of Mum's mouth, they're the same nearly ever day. Yes, here they come. 'Christ, I'm knackered. My feet look like they've been boiled.' My Mum. She works in a car rental office at the airport. She hates it, loathes the job but she's 49 and she says that she'll never get another one. I don't know if that's true but she says we live in an ageist society and once you're fifty you're on the scrap heap and she's not going to tell anyone. How will that work? I mean, there's PAYE, tax codes, personal pensions, all that stuff. How wouldn't they know?

'Hello, Hannah? You upstairs?'

Where else would I be?

'Yeah, only going through my schoolbag, checking homework, down in a sec...'

'Right, I'll put the potatoes on, bangers and mash for tea, ok?'

'Yeah, fine.'

I can hear her rattling around in the kitchen, I can hear the sound of a tap running. She'll be up the stairs in a minute, to get changed; she hates her uniform too. It's almost as bad as mine.

Here she comes. She rattles the handle on my door as she goes into her bedroom, she does that most days too. Just to let me know that she's home.

She didn't come in, she must have been standing outside my door. 'That's it, diet on Monday. Button on my skirt popped off. Spent all day yanking it up.'

I heard her bedroom door close. The house was silent again. Mum in her bedroom and me in mine.

Tea was ok, pretty much the same as always. Mum was going on about her job as usual. She doesn't want me to agree with what she says, she says she just wants me to listen. `...so, when I realised that the Mondeo had a full tank, I said he could have that one for the same price.' She was quiet for a moment, then she cleared her throat. I knew something was coming. Dad used to say that she was sharpening her voice.

'Hannah? That new bloke, Martin, well he's asked me out again. What d'you think?'

'Muuum! We've been through this a zillion times. What's to think about? He's divorced, you're divorced, he's got a son, you've got a daughter, you both live in the same city. Why not?'

Mum twiddled with her fork, there was a piece of sausage left on it. If I know Mum, she'd be thinking about leaving it, that would make her feel virtuous. Never mind that she'd eaten all the mashed potato.

Her head was bent over her plate and I could see fine, grey hairs peeping out between the dark brown.

'Wish I was your age again; everything is so easy with you. Just make a decision, do it, that's it, piece of cake.' She still had her head down, obviously thinking about that last piece of sausage.

All of a sudden I felt really mean and I leant over to touch her arm. 'Mum, it *is* that easy. Go out with this, this Martin. He seems like a nice enough bloke. If it doesn't work, if he doesn't float your boat, then you don't go out with him again. Easy peasy.'

'But we work together, what about that?'

I watched as she put the sausage in her mouth. 'No big deal, if it works out, you have passionate sex in the back seat of a car and, if doesn't work out, ignore each other. See, sorted.'

She chewed slowly and lifted her head to look at me. 'Is everything that easy for you? That sorted?'

I shook my head, thinking of the envelope from Dad. `No,

but this isn't such a big deal for you either, Mum. Go on, go out with him, you could do with a night out.'

She smiled at me. 'Well, I'll think about it. I'd feel better about myself if I could lose a stone, or four! Ok, Hannah, get yourself upstairs and make a start on your homework. I'll sort this lot out.' She jerked her head towards the plates. Neither of us had mentioned the envelope.

I can hear the theme tune from *Eastenders*. I've checked my computer again but there are no more messages, just the one from Dad. *Hi Hannah, just checking to see if the ticket has arrived yet. Let me know - ok? We're all looking forward to seeing you. Love Dad.* There were four x's and underneath Dad had written, *one from each of us.*

Yeah, right. One from Dad, one each from the twins, Josh and Cort and one from Patti, Dad's wife. That still sounds weird. Dad's wife. I've just noticed too that he's sent this from his office, not from his home. His office is amazing, a real skyscraper. Dad took me there once, I think it was the first time I'd gone to Toronto. I was about nine years old. I'd never thought about the meaning of the word, *skyscraper.* I'd asked Dad, `Does this really scrape the sky?'

When he left home, when he left Mum and me, that was hard and the fact that he'd also gone to work in Canada somehow made it a lot worse. He came back, flying over just to see me, two or three times a year. We did the stuff that fathers do with their kids when they don't live at home any more. We did the cinema, the zoo, the trips to restaurants and he bought me some pretty amazing presents.

At first I didn't realise what it must have done to Mum, me coming back here, my hands full of the latest presents: top of the range Walkman, Gap sweatshirts and Nike trainers. She never said much when Dad brought me back. She just said, 'Thank you, it looks as if Hannah's enjoyed herself.' All that politeness, the stiff smiles, all that hovering in the doorway like Dad was an uncle we only saw once a year. Actually, come to think of it, it soon became once a year.

When Dad phoned to say he'd got married again, he said things like, 'It was a pretty fast decision, that's the way Canadians do things. We decided to just go ahead and do it.'

I can remember putting the phone down very quickly. It had to be quick because I wanted to say to him, 'But *you're* not Canadian, you're my Dad. You only live over there, it doesn't make you into a Canadian.'

It wasn't the only quick thing the Canadians did either. Six months later, in another phone call, he said, 'Guess what? Patti's had twins, boys. We're calling them Josh and Cort. What d'you think? You've got brothers now.'

Dad sent tickets over that time too. I was nervous about seeing Dad with the boys. He'd emailed and phoned and everything but I hadn't seen him since he'd become someone else's Dad as well as mine.

That was such a strange visit. Patti was quiet the whole time and the boys, well, they weren't. They yelled and yelled. Screamed. Both of them the whole time I was there. When Josh was asleep, Cort yelled and when he stopped, Josh started up again. It was murder on the eardrums.

Dad and I went out a lot. We walked around looking at the buildings. Dad called it *downtown.* We shopped in Eatons, we ate huge sandwiches and we sat for ages on the benches overlooking the harbour. Dad messed about, he pretended to be a lighthouse, holding an ice-cream cone in his hand; he said it was the light.

Dad knew I wasn't comfortable in their home. It's in a block of flats, *apartments* Patti calls them. The one they live in is bigger than our house though. Every room is pale, as if the sun has bleached all the colour out of everything. Patti says the wood is blond. She keeps the sun out all day by pulling these huge blinds down over the windows so you stumble around in some sort of twilight. Totally weird.

When I went last year, the boys were two years old and that's why I'd gone, for their birthday. Patti had dressed them in identical outfits: dungarees in a check pattern, she called it *plaid.* Their wispy hair was gelled back and they had dark blue, suede boots on. They'd stopped yelling though. In fact they hardly said a word, neither did Patti, at least not to me. I thought that, perhaps she'd left the blinds up and the sun had bleached them all.

She said she had a headache when Dad suggested a trip to Jellystone Park. I know Dad only suggested it for the twins. Patti said she didn't think the twins should go either. Can't remember why. Dad didn't argue or try to change her mind.

In the end Dad and I didn't go there either. We went to Ben and Jerry's, the most incredible ice-cream parlour you've ever seen. Buckets and buckets of the stuff. We were sitting in one of the booths, licking away at one of these humungous ice-creams when Dad said, right out of the blue, 'Patti wants another baby, she'd like a daughter next time.'

'Oh, right.' I relied on my mouth to work because my head couldn't cope with that.

Dad was digging the spoon right to the bottom of the dish. 'I don't want another baby, another daughter, I've got one already.' He leant over and touched my arm.

'Anyway,' he said, 'three kids are enough, actually they're more than enough.'

I knew that Dad paid the mortgage on our house at home and Mum paid the rest of the bills and when Dad wanted me to go to private school, he paid all the fees for that too. But what I didn't know was what to say to him then. This seemed to me to be private stuff, behind closed doors sort of stuff.

Dad had pushed his ice-cream away. 'Three is enough, ' he said it again but this time it sounded like he was saying it to Patti only she wasn't there. 'Ready to go?' he half rose from his seat.

'Dad?' I wanted to stay a bit longer, just a little while before we had to go back to the boys and Patti and, anyway, I hadn't finished my ice-cream. He sat down again.

'Hannah?'

'Dad?'

We were falling over ourselves to be polite. Dad smiled. 'You first.'

Everything I'd wanted to say to him ever since he left, all the words bashed up against each other inside my head. It wasn't a couple of days of words, it was years of unspoken words.

He said my name again then leant over the table, putting his head close to mine.

Suddenly I thought of Mum, I thought about her sitting in the lounge at home, watching the television, drinking the one glass of wine she allowed herself each night.

'Do you ever think about Mum?' That wasn't what I wanted to ask.

Dad looked a bit surprised. 'Your Mum? Well, sometimes I do. Why do you ask, she's all right isn't she?'

I nodded, 'She's fine.' I dug another spoonful of ice-cream out of my dish.

Dad watched me for a while, he must have been waiting for me to say something else.

I couldn't look at him. 'Do you miss us, Mum and me?'

He didn't speak for a while and I kept on digging more and more ice-cream out of the glass sundae dish.

'I miss the early years, Hannah. The years when you were small, before things went wrong. I get a reminder of those years now, with Josh and Cort. The times I had with you when you were small are very precious to me.'

I didn't want to hear about Josh and Cort. I pushed my ice-cream away.

When we got back that day, I felt even more uncomfortable around Patti. She's a tiny woman, really thin. Her wrists are about the size of birds' legs and she's got long fingernails. She always shrieks if she touches anything that might break them. I'd been chewing my nails then. I was only twelve and my nails were really gross at that time. I'd also discovered a shop selling second-hand Doc Martens and I was wearing my favourite pair: they were dark purple and I'd bought pink Lurex laces to go with them. Mum said I'd been a bit late with the Gothic look.

The whole time I was with them, Patti skirted around me like I had some sort of force field. She wore shoes with kitten heels and they went *clack, clack* whenever she walked across their blond wooden floor. My DM's left scuffmarks, she rubbed at them when she thought I wasn't looking. She didn't have a clue how to talk to me. 'How are things at school? What do you want to do when you leave? Have you thought about University?' I mean, come on. I do want to go to University. Wonder what she'd say if I told her I liked the sound of the one in Toronto? I was as glad to go as she was to see me go.

Dad's been over since. We went to see *Starlight Express.* I didn't have the heart to tell him that we'd been before, twice. After the show we went to a restaurant and I asked about the boys, about Patti.

'Fine, they're all fine. They send their love.' He took some pictures out of his wallet and handed them over to me. The twins' faces stared out from the photo, the parting in their hair was so straight I wondered if it had been done with a ruler. As Dad put the photos back inside his wallet, something on the other side caught my eye.

'Wait, what's that?' I tugged at the corner of the photo I'd seen. It was one of me. I'd been about six I think. A school photo: tie with a huge, lopsided knot. Navy cardigan and a bright, white blouse. My face all covered in freckles and my hand trying to cover the gap in my front teeth.

'I carry that one with me all the time.'

'Have you got one of Mum?' The words felt hot in my mouth.

'Your Mum? Well, no, I haven't.'

'Why did you leave her, Dad? ' My mouth felt burnt, as if I'd swallowed hot food.

'Oh, Hannah, not now.'

'When then? I've never asked you before, not once.' I could feel stupid tears and I kept on blinking to get rid of them.

'Has your mother put you up to this? Has she been talking to you?'

'No, she hardly ever mentions you.'

There was silence after that. We both stared over each other's shoulder, hoping no-one in the restaurant noticed we weren't talking. A waiter came over, asking if everything was all right.

'Yes, thank you.' Dad's voice was clipped.

He sighed, 'Look, I won't bore you or insult your intelligence by telling you that sometimes things between two people don't work out.' He stopped and looked at me. 'Are you sure you really want to know?'

'Yes.'

He sat back, I felt a sort of tingling in my scalp.

'Your mother and I drifted apart.' He gave a brief laugh. 'I sound like a cliché don't I?'

Well, yes he did.

'She hadn't done anything wrong and actually I hadn't either but the marriage was dead in the water. My job was taking me all over the place, I was working longer and longer hours. I hardly ever got home and, when I did, there was nothing to talk about.'

'There was me, didn't you talk about me?'

His voice was soft. 'Of course we did. You held us together for a long time.'

'What, like cement?' I couldn't help it.

He frowned. 'You started this, you wanted to know.'

There was another silence, this time we both looked at our hands. Dad tugged at his wedding ring. He and Patti wore matching bands. The noise in the restaurant flowed around us while we sat not saying a word.

Dad waved at a waiter. 'I'll get the bill, it's getting late.'

So that was it: the reason my parents divorced, there was no reason.

In the car going home, Dad kept turning his head to look at me. I saw his fingers drumming on the steering wheel. 'Hannah?'

'What?' I'd had enough talking.

'Do you remember me saying that Patti wanted another baby?' His tone was light, almost teasing.

'Yeah, I do, why?'

'She wants a daughter...'

'Yeah, you told me that.'

From the corner of my eye, I saw his head turn towards me again.

'Look, Hannah, help me out here.'

'I don't know what you want me to say, Dad.' I felt very tired, I just wanted to go home.

He swallowed, 'She loves the boys, we both do, it's just that she says she'd like a daughter'

'What has this got to do with me?'

'I'd like her to get to know you properly. Let her see what a great girl you are, what a great daughter.'

'Why? I'm not her daughter, I'm yours and Mum's.'

'Yes, of course.' He swallowed again. 'Look, Hannah, what I'm trying to say is that I'd like you to be friends with Patti, a sister to the boys. Spend some time with them. I'm away a lot, travelling all over the place and I'd like to think of you all getting along when I'm not there.'

'Oh, Dad, I don't know.' *Spend time with Patti? Me?*

'Please, Hannah, do it for me. Look, I'll level with you.' He stopped talking and glanced at me before he spoke again. 'Things are not that great right now and I really could do with your help. Another child, well that's not something I'd planned for.' He didn't say much after that except to ask me if I'd at least think about what he'd said.

I could hear the theme tune from *Eastenders,* the programme must have finished.

Sitting on the bed, trying to look over my school books, none of it made any sense. My head was full of Mum, tickets, Toronto, Dad. I knew what the latest ticket was for, it wasn't only about going over there on a visit. I knew what Dad wanted. More cement, more keeping things together. Playing at Happy Families, being the daughter.

I got up and walked over to the computer and typed in Dad's email address. If I send this message to his office he'll be on his own when he reads it.

I went downstairs and asked Mum where she'd put the button from her skirt.

'Why?' She was sitting in the armchair, her fingers laced around a glass of wine.

'Thought I'd sew it on for you, ok?'

'Guilty conscience or something?'

'Don't make it into a big deal, it's only a button.'

Before I went upstairs to get the button, I poured Mum another glass of wine.

Florentine Spring

ELIZABETH MORGAN

It was May and it was hot; an exhausting heat.

In England we'd had rain for weeks. Here, in Florence the grass was beginning to shrivel with thirst.

Unusually the café in the square facing the Uffizzi had few clients. I found a raffia chair in the shade under a parasol, marooned in a sea of empty tables.

I had chosen to come to this city alone. I wanted to be alone, to clear my head, to focus my energies on something new. Florence with her compelling timeless collections would always demand total immersion from the spectator, and therefore seemed ideal.

This was my second day. Already I had queued to see Michelangelo's David, and like everyone else had gazed in wonder at the genius of his creator.

It was about three thirty in the afternoon. I had been in the Uffizzi gallery since mid-morning, and sated with beauty, was now in need of a restorative cup of good Italian coffee. From afar the waiter appeared with my order. Weaving skilfully between the endless maze of tables he finally placed the delicious brew before me. I was about to put the cup to my lips, when a voice in heavily accented English asked, 'Please may I join you?'

Annoyed at this interruption I turned and saw a pale, quite unappealing man of about forty hovering at the table behind me. I noticed his spectacles had particularly thick lenses, a far cry from the mythical Italian Lothario. His shoulders drooped, and there was something pathetic about his demeanour. which perhaps under normal circumstances would have softened my attitude towards this intruder. But not today.

'No!' I snapped. 'I wish to be alone. There are plenty of other tables'. My hand swept imperiously over the surrounding empty spaces. He sighed. Turning away from him, I drowned my lips in steaming froth. He remained standing behind me. I could feel his presence. Persistent. Immobile.

'Please English lady, it is only to practise my English. I ask you again, please let me sit with you?'

I continued to drink my coffee, determined not to face him.

'Please,' he implored. 'You see I love your country. I love your language. I am Dottore of Physic. I teach at the Lycée.' He used the French word. 'I have little opportunity to speak English.'

He edged nearer. It was possible that this thin pasty man with thick glasses was telling the truth. I could imagine him as a youth. The puny little school 'swot'. Perhaps that is why I relented.

His hands were pale and delicate, certainly strangers to physical work. His voice too was quiet, almost diffident. He said his mother, now retired, had been professor of English at the same high school. He had been married to a Russian girl whom he knew had married only for a passport. Six months ago she had left for a two week holiday in Russia, ostensibly to see her parents, leaving him to care for their little daughter to whom he appeared quite devoted. He was still in love with his wife, he said, and was constantly begging her to return. Meanwhile a Dutch au pair had been enrolled for baby minding.

I was due to spend two weeks in Moscow the following month, so not unnaturally he asked me whether I could post a letter to his lost love who was living in Minsk. It would have been churlish to refuse. He said he would give it to the receptionist at my hotel.

Our desultory conversation over more coffee, ranged from painting and sculpture to theatre. He told me his name. I felt obliged to tell him mine.

'There is a beautiful Roman theatre just outside the city. Only fifteen minutes. Have you seen it?'

I had not.

'Please let me take you there.'

It was only 4.30.pm. 'Thank you , but I can surely take a bus?'

'That is not necessary. I have my car just around the corner.'

I knew about the average Italian male's interest in foreign women whatever their age and shape. I was not going to be one of them, therefore I said nothing, ignoring his suggestion.

'Please. It would make me happy to show you the theatre. Afterwards I shall drive you straight back to your hotel. Please.'

Again I could see the young boy put upon by his peers,
Again I relented.

'Very well. But there's just one thing. Do not imagine I am here for any kind of adventure, an *aventura*. I am happy to speak English to you, and thank you for offering to show me the theatre. But expect no more. No more!' I emphasized.

What was I thinking about? For all his pasty vulnerability he would certainly be stronger than I.

He gave a little smile, revealing teeth that were small and neat, halfway between child and adult.

'Please. I know the reputation Italian men have. Do not worry. I am not like them.'

Courteously he opened the car door for me.

He drove carefully, and continuing that special ritual of aimless conversation between strangers, fifteen minutes later we arrived at the site. Fortunately for me, my escort knew his history. Every breath of the theatre's life, every monument and altar, was explained in fascinating detail. Once I fancied an arm round my waist, but I quickly moved out of range. An hour later he suggested an ice cream at the small restaurant close by. I felt a sense of relief when the restaurateur appeared to know him and waved a greeting. Somehow it made him less of a stranger, less of an intruder.

I thanked him for the delicious *gelati*, the guided tour, and politely requested that perhaps he could now take me back to the hotel.

'Of course,' he smiled. 'But I would like to show you our new football stadium where the World Cup will be played.'

I laughed. 'Sorry but I have no interest in football.'

'Don't worry. It is on our way back.'

I felt trapped. Yet nothing out of the ordinary had happened. Events had followed in a completely natural sequence.

We skirted the stadium, to which, as foretold I remained indifferent.

He continued the drive into the city through a green suburb of luxury apartments. Suddenly he turned a corner and slowed the car to a halt outside an impressive façade.

'Why are you stopping?'

He smiled ingratiatingly. 'Please, I would love for you to meet my little girl. She is with the au pair right now.'

This was a step too far.

'I'd love to meet her. Do bring her out. I shall wait in the car.'

He looked at his watch. 'It is near her bath-time. Maybe

she is already in the bath.'

It was six-thirty. I remembered my own children's bath times.

'Please come in. Just for a minute. I shall get you back to your hotel very quickly. Please!'

The estate seemed to be out on its own, away from central areas. There were no names to commit to memory. Each tree-lined avenue was like the last. I saw no cars, no taxis, no shops. If a stranger, anywhere, had invited me into his flat, I should have declined the offer in no uncertain terms. Yet, this was exactly what I was about to do. Had I taken leave of my senses? My friends had joked about the holiday. 'The Florentine Spring of Mrs X', they had teased, wishing me an encounter with a Warren Beatty look-alike. At the time no one had mentioned the story's grisly ending.

How easy it is to become involved unwittingly in a web of sequential circumstance. Somewhere at the back of my head a small frisson of unease was beginning to surface.

I followed him into the marble atrium of the sumptuous block. The lift was out of order. I remember jabbering nervously about his little girl as we climbed the marble staircase to his apartment on the second floor. He said nothing. It was all deathly quiet. No one came. No one left. Apartment doors were hermetically sealed to the outside world.

He unlocked the door. There appeared to be no one there. I stood in the hall.

'Your little girl? Where is she?'

'She must be out with the au pair. Look. Come and see!'

Through an open door I saw a child's nursery. Toys were grouped in an unnaturally orderly fashion. Either the au pair was fastidious to the point of obsession, or they had not been played with for some time. A second later I noticed his framed Doctorate in Physics diploma, hanging in a central position on the sitting room wall. I was ashamed of myself for being so suspicious. This shuffling academic with the thick spectacles appeared to be telling the truth.

'I'm sorry to have missed her.' I looked at my watch. It was now seven-o-clock. 'I really think I should be getting back.'

'Yes, of course, but please one thing. Would you stay with me while I try to ring Marianna in Minsk? I always speak to her in English and you will give me confidence. I really want her to come back. Please sit down.'

Once again he looked pathetically like the bullied school 'swot'. I had no choice.

I sat at the large table in the living room. It was covered in deep red plush. The furniture was altogether too heavy and ornate for the light airy feel of the apartment.

He was at the hall telephone and seemed to be having difficulty getting through to Minsk.

I looked round the room. There was no balcony. I had seen him lock the front door. There was no way out.

'Yes I know. Sorry to disturb you,' he was muttering. 'Look I know – I know, but when are you coming back?' His voice sounded sharp, urgent.

After a moment or two he sighed, put the receiver down and walked into the living room. Having fulfilled my duty, I rose from the chair ready to leave.

'She was in bed with somebody. My wife!'

'But – you can't possibly know.'

'I heard a man's voice.'

'You could have been mistaken.'

He shook his head and the shoulders drooped even more.

'Please will you have a coffee. I make good espresso.'

If only I had insisted upon leaving at that moment.

The coffee, thick and black, was served in two minute

cups. We sat primly at the dining table, facing each other, drinking our coffees.

Suddenly he broke the brief silence. 'I have done something terrible,' he blurted.

A dozen things went through my mind, from pupil seduction, to wife beating. Determined to be cool at all costs, 'Have you killed someone?' I asked, far too lightly. Hardly had the words been uttered, I realised how dangerously provocative my question had been. Here I was, trapped with a stranger, in an apartment somewhere in Florence where no one would ever find me.

'No! Of course not,' he replied indignantly.

He picked up a spoon and stirred his coffee.

'No, I have not killed anyone,' he said quietly. He looked up from his cup. His small close-set eyes stared at me, unblinking through those thick lenses.

'I have made love with my mother,' he said.

His gaze fixed, he watched and waited for a reaction.

Like salacious telephone calls I knew that the more panic and horror caused, the greater the sexual excitement. At all costs I had to be calm, despite the fear coiling round the pit of my stomach.

Be grown – up. Don't react! Instructed a voice in my head.

With sickening realisation, I knew there was only one course of action. I would have to play act a blasé therapist, if only to give me time to think.

'Uh-huh,' I replied with as much *sang-froid* as I could muster. 'It was practised in parts of Britain up until the last century. In my own part of Wales I believe it was quite common for a boy's first experience to be with his mother.'

He snorted. 'But I am still making love with her. Of course she is old now, but she still gives me pleasure, as I give her. Even this morning.' He gave a little laugh.

Be calm! Be calm! Remember you have heard it all before, urged the voice.

'And your wife; did she know?'

'A little – not all. My mother did not like her. Anyway it was difficult. I love my wife but I cannot, how do you say – come – unless I think of my mother. You know, I could never make love to anyone without thinking of my mother.'

'Have you – er – had help? Spoken to anyone?'

'When I was at university. The psychiatrist said it would be all right, that I would get over it especially as I had a girl friend. But she did not understand that I was still making love with my mother, nearly every day.'

Where was the child? Where was the au pair? Where indeed was Marianna? And where was I?

Talking was making him more relaxed. The more he said,the more my head reacted to each new disclosure, and the more I had to pretend.

'My mother invited me you know.'

'Sorry?'

'I was eighteen – doing my army service. She picked me up for a picnic in the country. She was not wearing panties. I saw her sex. She invited me to touch her.' He paused, waiting I supposed for a reaction. I said nothing.

'My mother is a widow. I am the only man in her life since my father died when I was very young. She is so beautiful. Fantastic legs!'

The woman was a monster. Even Jocasta sinned by accident.

'Her shoes! High pointed heels.' He stopped and leant across the table towards me. 'You know,' he chuckled, 'I have a suitcase full of her old shoes in the garage. I look at them every day.'

'But your wife?' I insisted, making a feeble attempt to bring this twisted mind back to reality.

He laughed. 'She hated the shoes.'

'Does that surprise you?'

Ignoring my question he became increasingly animated as he recounted a visit to a Beatles concert in London.

'We stayed in a hotel in Highgate. My mother looked wonderful in short mini skirt and high heels. The landlady thought we were lovers – well, we were.' He laughed. 'But my mother is very noisy when she has orgasm, and the landlady asked her in the morning if she had been ill during the night. We had so much fun!' He laughed heartily at the memory.

I had to get out of this apartment before he thought of something else.

I rose from the table. So did he. 'You know, your hair reminds of my mother's when she was younger. Your legs too.'

With a sickly grin, displaying those abominable teeth, he moved around the table towards me. This was it. My heart thumped, my palms were damp. Despite the paralysing fear, I had to think quickly.

No way out! No way out! the voice repeated in my head.

I had created a short distance between us, but not enough. His hand stretched out to touch my hair. I could feel his repellent glancing stroke.

Think! Think!

Moving out of the living room and out of arm's length, I said, 'I'd love to see your little girl's nursery again. It will remind me of my own children.'

The sickly smile reappeared. 'Of course.' He did what I'd hoped, and led the way. There was a key in the nursery door. Could I lock him in? I was frantic now. But what then? I could climb down from the living room. Climb down? How? With what? Of course, the bathroom! Smash the window and climb down the drain pipes; much easier. Smash it with what?

Get out! Get out! the voice persisted urgently. There was only one way to leave this flat, and it would have to be, could only be, with him.

Keep him talking that was it. Get in the car. I'd be safe in the car while he was driving. But it was becoming all too clear this Ancient Mariner was nowhere near the end of his tale. Even when switching verbal gear to his child, within seconds he had reverted back to his odious mother, gabbling on about her breasts, her thighs, her panties her shoes. The sickly smile was becoming a leer. He moved towards me, recounting how his friends at University would come to parties at their house, and how he hated one of them for sleeping with his mother afterwards. Lying in the next room, he heard them and was consumed with jealousy. Again the leer and the outstretched arm to touch my hair. The smaller space of the nursery made me even more defenceless. I had been so stupid. Why had I led him in here? *Be calm! Be calm! Think!* urged the voice.

My watch read 9.30pm. It was already dark outside. I took a chance.

'Look why don't we continue talking in the car? I'm so hungry aren't you?'

'Sure,' he beamed. 'I take you to a good place for the best pizzas.'

'In the city?'

'Sure! Not far from your hotel. Come on!'

I needed no second bidding. My legs trembled as he brushed past me to the front door, again briefly touching my hair with his hand.

At last, shoes skidding, heels clattering, I rushed down the marble staircase into the real world, the world I knew.

'Please get in the car.' he whined,

Anything was better than incarceration in that hateful

apartment with this maniac. He drove recklessly, tyres screeching, through silent empty avenues, each apartment block a clone of its neighbour. My mind was trying feverishly to formulate an escape route. The only possibility now was to jump from the car. I waited for his maniacal driving to bring the vehicle closer to the pavement. Too late. Without warning we were joining the mindless cacophony of wild city traffic. He took the fast lane. I held on to the seat belt for dear life. He was driving like a madman, and jabbering incessantly about his mother. He laughed. He became exhilarated, assaulting me with graphic descriptions of mother and son posing as lovers; of drunken nights in Rome; of mother teetering around the Trevi fountain in spiky heels; of making love under park benches; of having to tie a scarf around her mouth to subdue her phenomenal orgasmic responses. This hateful homunculus was using me as a masturbatory punch-bag. I was frightened now. The noise of claxons, drivers yelling abuse at each other through open windows and the suffocating smell of burning tyres, turned the highway into a bumper car spectacle. Suddenly he swerved into the nearside lane leaving screeching brakes and panic in his wake. He jerked the car to a stop. 'I have to buy some chocolate for my mother. I go to her favourite shop, right here. Wait.'

He slammed the door and barged through shoppers crowding the pavement . I counted five, and leapt out. I had to get back to the hotel, somehow.

I spotted a taxi, and waved frantically, but was ignored. I ran as quickly as ambling pedestrians would allow, to a 'Taxi' sign. Out of breath I leant against the rail. Would he pursue me? My eyes scanned the hurtling traffic for a taxi, but there was none. A car pulled up. A man with a gnarled face poked his head out of the window. 'Give you nice ride, Senora.' I gestured him away, but within a few moments I was aware of a male hand rubbing my thigh, and a body pressing into me. I grabbed the hand threw it off my thin cotton dress, and turned to see a toothy male leer. 'I give you very good price nice lady.' His foul breath reeked of Chianti and garlic. Moving away quickly, I realised I had been waiting in line for a different clientele. Panic took over. If I fell, if I were to be knocked down, even if I found a cab, could I be sure of getting back to the hotel safely? Anything could happen and my family might never know. I was more vulnerable now than I had been with the crazed Dottore.

I continued walking, being pushed and shoved along the pavement of this bustling seedy suburb, when his car drew up alongside the kerb. He smiled. 'Sorry I keep you waiting so long. You got fed up, yes? Come on. We go for pizza.'

The very sight of him was repulsive, but the circumstances gave little choice. At least I knew this monster and where he taught.

'Well if you don't mind I'm not hungry now. Would you drive me back to my hotel?'

He shrugged. 'As you like. Please get in.'

Again he drove like a maniac. I just hoped it was in the direction of my hotel. Judgemental one is supposed never to be. We are conditioned. Live and let live, the modern slogan for life. My head was swimming, confused, fearful.

The hotel was in a quiet side street. We pulled up outside. He turned off the engine, and I attempted to unlock the passenger door, but failed.

'Just one moment,' he said. It was the same quiet voice I had heard in the piazza that afternoon. Was it quiet or simply sinister?

'Would you let me out please?' I asked as reasonably as possible.

His hand was on his trouser zip, gently massaging his groin.

'Look, all this talk about my mother has made me very excited. Do you mind if I touch myself?'

'Don't you dare!' I hissed. I'd had enough of playing the psychiatrist. 'Let me out or I shall call the police. Now!'

He complied, and I ran into the hotel.

For twenty minutes I stood under the shower, attempting to wash this encounter out of body and mind. But it was not going to be quite so simple.

At 8.30am the following morning I received a call from him. Then another just as I was going out. Three more messages were awaiting my return in the early evening. Therefore I decided to leave for Siena earlier than scheduled. Florence was turning sour. This had not been the immersion I had planned.

Within hours of arriving at my hotel in Siena, I received four calls from him. The booking receptionist in Florence had obviously passed on the name of my new location. Heaven knows what story the deranged Dottore had fabricated.

Thereafter he tried to contact me five or six times each day.

The holiday was turning into a nightmare.

Siena is no distance from Florence. He could turn up at any time. I gave the manager instructions to tell any callers that I had left.

Frankly I was never so happy as when I finally boarded the plane in Pisa, privately vowing never to return.

Within a week of being home I received a long five-page letter in very good English. The Florentine hotel had given him my home address presumably on yet another elaborate pretext. His writing was very small and round, displaying obsessively meticulous care, with not a letter misplaced. Not surprisingly it was five pages of his mother, sex and her orgasms, plus a few lines in which he quoted his wife's last communication.

It was somewhat alarming that he seemed to regard me as a friend who could help.

I did not reply, nor have I ever revisited Florence.

Love the One You're With

KAY BYRNE

It was like one of those rare configurations of planets when horoscopes forecast career upheavals or dizzy new romances for all and sundry – even the housebound old ladies who read them so avidly.

You see, I had just realized that if I played my cards right, I could sleep with a different man every night of the week to come.

What's so amazing about that, you say? Any slapper can go out and get laid. As my friend Tony puts it: 'There's no such thing as an ugly woman.'

But I am far from being your typical slapper. I'm an assistant curator at the town museum with two degrees, my own house, and the obligatory cat doled out by God to all spinsters.

So I am not planning to let down my hair in some sleazy singles bar. In fact, all the men I am hoping to bed this week are already in my life ... or have been ... and the stars have conspired to deliver them all to my door, one by one, from Monday to Friday.

First there's Richard. I lived with him for four years. We were in love but he was a control freak, always chivvying me to do things. In the end he acted so much like my dad that sex with him began to feel like incest and I went right off it.

Dean was the one after Richard. He was moody, but such a gorgeous hunk I put up with his mammoth sulks. We played a game of tit-for-tat infidelity until we had hurt each other so much we couldn't feel any more.

Kevin came next. He was ten years younger than me and I went out with him for ten months. My friends took the piss, but they could say what they liked because he made an impressive Omelette Arnold Bennett and rogered me vigorously on his cream leather settees.

That's Monday, Tuesday, Wednesday taken care of. Thursday belongs to Paolo, a beautiful olive-skinned opera singer I met one heady day last summer. We went out on a few dates but then he went off touring. His real name is Paul and he was born on the most notorious council estate in town but he has adopted a sexy Italian accent to match the Mediterranean good looks, about which he is entertainingly narcissistic.

On the first night we spent together he stroked my shoulder in sensuous appreciation. 'Your skin is so smooth and silky,' he murmured. 'It reminds me of my own.'

And Friday? That's when I'll see Bob, boyfriend of the moment. Not very tall, not very good-looking, not very rich, not very ambitious. It's easier to describe what he isn't rather than what he is. He's not Mr Right, but he'll do for now. He says he is away on a course all week and will be back on Friday. No doubt expecting me to be all sex-starved and mad for it. Ho! Ho!

What's with the disapproving look? What you don't know can't hurt you, as my grandmother used to say. I've got a packet of condoms. Besides, how many chances does a girl get to collect five scalps in one week? It'll be something to tell my grandchildren.

So Monday comes around. I spent all Sunday exfoliating, shaving, plucking, waxing etc. I started that lark after I discovered that the geeky engineers who kept a league table of totty at the university I attended referred to me as The Gorilla. Well, it was the Seventies. I'd read Germaine Greer, and I wasn't going to shave my legs for any man. Or wear a bra, although I didn't realize that I had unwittingly played into their hands on that one.

Richard lived two hundred miles away but was calling in to see me on the way back from a seminar; ostensibly because he was delivering a rare book on Egyptology that he wanted me to have. He was generous, but I knew his real motive was to present himself to me again in the hope that I would see the light and marry him. Part of me was curious to see whether anything of the sort would happen. At 34 I was fighting an irritating and out-of-character urge to have babies.

I hadn't seen him for a year and I thought a few drinks at my local would help break the ice, but on the way to the pub he confessed that he had given up drinking. As a social worker who had gone into drugs and drink counselling, he said he had been shocked by the consequences of substance misuse, as he put it.

'Don't worry. I'll have a soft drink,' he said loftily. At the bar Tony, the landlord, whom I quoted earlier, looked inquiringly at me and then at Richard as he pulled my pint. I made the introductions.

'I hope you'll be a good influence on her, mate,' says Tony. 'She's in here every night knocking 'em back.'

'So! Your name is Drink Too Much! You really should cut down a little!' said Richard, lapsing into a Monty Python routine. It gave me a pang of nostalgia for our shared past, until he followed it up with a serious lecture about the dangers of alcohol abuse. I hastened to the bar for re-fills.

'So, are you seeing anybody at the moment?' He was nervously shredding a beer mat as I sat down again. I noticed that his hair was receding fast.

'No. Well, yes.' I quickly corrected at the flare of hope in his eyes. 'But nobody serious,' I added, just to keep the interest going. 'Are you?'

'I'm doing alright,' he said mysteriously, gazing longingly at my pint.

By the end of the night Richard had succumbed to the booze and was incredibly pissed, having been off it for so long. He sang along loudly to the cheesy old numbers on Tony's beloved jukebox. I, meanwhile, had recollected why he was not the one for me, but thought I'd sleep with him anyway; otherwise I wouldn't make my record.

Once we were in bed, the only way I could go through with it was by being on top. I rode him at a gallop, hoping he wouldn't notice that I was gritting my teeth because it still felt like I was fucking my dad. I needn't have worried. His gaze was focused on the rapidly-gathering momentum of my bouncing boobs, and he smiled beatifically like a soul who has just seen the gates of heaven.

I spent a sleepless night wondering what the hell I was doing. I even felt guilty about Bob, but Tuesday eventually dawned and it was out with the old and in with the new. I left Richard in bed nursing a pig of a hangover and escaped to work. I had an uneasy feeling that I had opened a can of worms, but I put it to the back of my mind as I contemplated the night ahead with Dean.

Ah, Dean. He was the one I still dreamed about. In those dreams we were always back together and it was wonderful. Now I was going to see him again. He was back in town for a job interview.

'I'm sick of London,' he'd told me over the phone.

As soon as I got home from the museum I swapped my sensible suit for a slinky top and figure-hugging pants, tousling my usually sleek dark hair and dabbing on his favourite perfume.

I had bought lots of delicious food too so that I could cook him an intimate little supper *à deux*, but when he rolled up at 7pm the first thing he said was, 'Come on, let's go to the pub, I'm gasping for a pint.'

He hadn't changed a bit. Still drop-dead gorgeous. On the way to the Cherry Tree, he picked me up and swung me round, pressing his nose into my neck. 'Mmm, you smell as good as ever.'

The interview had gone well and he was in an ebullient mood. I tried to suppress a smile of delight.

The pub was already pretty full when we got there. Tony was watching some football match on the giant television screen and barely looked at us as he poured our drinks.

'France have scored already, mate.' He said to Dean, ignoring me.

'Christ, it's the England France match,' said Dean. 'I'd forgotten about it, what with the interview.'

He plonked his delectable derrière on a bar stool and stared at the screen.

Three hours later I managed to drag him out of the pub. He had hardly spoken to me all night, and it was too late to cook.

'I was going to make you some food,' I explained.

'No worries, beer is food,' Dean slurred, stretching out his six foot four frame on the sofa.

I went to the kitchen to make some strong coffee. I wasn't going to let him slip away that easily. But when I got back he was already a goner, snoring in that foghorn-like way I had forgotten about. I pulled off his boots and left him to it. There was always the morning.

He was already in my bed when I woke up the next day.

'Sorry, Noodle,' he said, using his old pet name for me. 'Hope you don't mind. That settee was killing my back.'

Mind? No, I decided to be big about it. He was lying on his back, one hand behind his head, the familiar musk of his sweat undoing me. I propped myself up on my elbow, allowing a nipple to escape the covers. He didn't seem to notice.

'Fetch us a cup of tea, love.'

I ignored his request, asking instead why he wanted to come back to boring old Bridgetown.

'I thought you loved London,' I said, wriggling closer to that divine body. 'Well,' he paused, looking a bit sheepish. 'I've met someone. And she's pregnant. It's all happened so quickly.'

'Pregnant?' I echoed stupidly.

'Oh, it's OK, I really like her. We might even get married. But neither of us fancied bringing up the baby in London, it's no place for a kid, is it?'

I could only shake my head. Dean glanced at the clock and jumped out of bed. 'Christ! Is that the time? I'm going to miss my train.'

After he had gone I sprawled back on the bed to contemplate the state of my project. Only two days in and things were going horribly wrong. Apart from my record attempt already being in ruins, the news that Dean was going to be a Dad – with someone else – was like a blow to the stomach.

Richard rang just as I was leaving the house.

'Thanks for a lovely time on Monday. Sorry I got in a bit of state,' he said.

'No problem.'

'I can't really remember much after we left the pub. Did we... ?'

'Did we what? Have sex, you mean?'

'Well, it's all a bit of a haze.'

'No. We did not. You passed out, actually.'

'Oh. I must have dreamed it then...'

I still felt down when I got to work so I decided to call Bob. He had switched off his phone so I left him a message and sent him a text as well. I kept checking my phone all day but he never got back to me. Bastard.

Kevin had told me to meet him in town that night at a new bar where the in-crowd had taken up temporary residence. He was like that: he had to have the flashy car, the Armani suit. I turned up in my jeans just to annoy him.

'Oh, for heavens sake! We'll never get into the club now,' he said, stirring his White Lady rather petulantly.

I laughed, feeling quite fond of the young whippersnapper. Tonight would be good. Kevin wouldn't let me down.

'We can always go to Boggles. They let anyone in.'

His face was a picture. I knew he wouldn't be seen dead in a place like that. Kevin had been away for the last six months at the New York office of the advertising agency he worked for. He was full of tall tales about the champagne lifestyle and the women who were just falling over themselves to bed a dashing Brit. Which I knew probably meant he wasn't getting any.

He lived the life but he didn't look the part, unfortunately, being decidedly challenged in the height department. I could see he was wearing his Cuban heels tonight.

Two drinks later, they were his undoing. He jumped down from his bar stool to go the loo and went over on his ankle. It started to swell straight away.

'Ow! Ow! It's agony,' he wailed. 'Call me an ambulance.'

'Don't be ridiculous. You just need something cold on it, like a bag of frozen peas.'

'You know I hate vegetables.'

'Well, I've got some back at my house. Come on, I'll hail a cab.'

There were no taxis to be seen so I dragged him, protesting, onto a number 9 bus which soon had us at the end of my road. The driver watched impassively as Kevin hobbled down the gangway, moaning theatrically. It had started to rain and he was soon complaining about that too. It was only another two hundred yards to my house but as we reached the Cherry Tree he stopped dead.

'I'm not going another step further.' He sounded determined. 'Come on. I'm going in here to call a cab home. You can buy me a stiff brandy to dull the pain.' Tony raised a sardonic eyebrow when I walked into the bar, half carrying my ailing toy boy.

'He fell off his bar stool,' I said glumly, ordering the brandies. 'I can't seem to organize a decent night out any more without something going wrong.'

'You should try staying in more often, then.'

That's exactly what I suggested to Paolo when he showed up early the following evening for our get-together. They say that most accidents occur in the home but I thought it would be a safer bet tonight. My plan was in tatters and I was pinning all my hopes on the lovely Paolo to rescue something from the wreckage.

'And what exactly have you got in mind?' He breathed seductively in my ear as we miss-kissed the continental way.

'Fish and chips and a couple of cans?'

'Perfect!'

The Italian act wore a bit thin at times and I knew it was a relief for him to revert back to type. He had just spent four months touring Europe with some crappy youth production and must have been gagging for a decent pint when he got back.

It wasn't long before there were fish and chip papers strewn all over the floor and we were halfway down the bottle of Limoncello he'd brought me back from Italy. It was making him wax lyrical.

'Ah, *bella ragazza*, how I've missed you,' he sighed, stroking my bare leg with greasy fingers.

'That's disgusting. You're covering me in chip fat.'

'Why don't we take a shower together then?'

Now we're cooking! I thanked God for my power shower and led the way upstairs. He undressed me slowly, with a light but lingering touch, and by the time we turned on the water things were already pretty steamy.

At last. Something was going right.

We were well into his favourite soapy tit routine when I noticed a strange look come over his face. Hesitant, diffident ... not like Paolo. I sensed trouble. 'What is it? Come on, spit it out.'

'I was wondering if you would like to do something special for me, *bellissimo*.'

A blow job? A spot of spanking?

No, he wanted me to do something called Golden Rain. 'Golden Rain? I thought that was the name of a firework.'

'No, *cara mia*, it's when you piss on me.'

'Pardon?'

When it finally dawned on me what he wanted me to do I tried to hide my horror. What a weirdo. How could he possibly find that a turn-on? But how could I refuse without jeopardising the entire evening?

I gave him the nod and he crouched in the bottom of the bath and waited for the rain to fall. And waited... and waited... and waited. My bladder just wasn't playing ball. No matter how hard I tried, I could not squeeze out a drop.

'Sorry, Paolo, I just can't go...'

He scrambled to his feet, looking anywhere but at me. All I could see was that his erection had shrivelled away... and so had my evening's entertainment. After Paolo's premature departure, there was only one thing for it. I headed for the pub.

'Christ, I need a drink. I've just had the most embarrassing experience.'

I pondered briefly the wisdom of telling Tony, but pulled back from the brink. 'Not with a bloke, by any chance?' he asked.

I screwed up my face and laughed.

He shook his head in mock disapproval.

'Have they got any idea what you're like down at that museum?'

No, they hadn't, thank goodness. And neither had poor old Bob. I felt an uncomfortable mix of guilt and annoyance as I contemplated the past four days. I had been spectacularly unfaithful to my boyfriend in thought, word and deed ... and for what? A series of disappointments and some of the ghastliest sex I'd ever had. The only thing I'd achieved was going to the pub a record four nights in a row. I downed my drink. Tony was singing along to the song on the jukebox and the lyrics seemed to be telling me something.

Don't be angry, don't be sad
Don't sit crying over the good times you had...
...If you can't be with the one you love, honey
Love the one you're with[1]

Love the one you're with. That would be Bob. After the debacle of the past week, I was seeing him in a new light, and felt a rush of eagerness to be with him again. But then I remembered that I hadn't heard from him all week. I checked my phone again. Nothing. He was probably too busy shagging all the women at his conference. I jumped off my bar stool and slunk home.

The next morning when I got to work I rang my best

---

1. From the song 'Love the One You're With' by Stephen Stills (Atlantic, 1970)

friend Cath. I needed a debrief. I gave her a rundown of the past four nights. I made it funny and she laughed in all the right places. But when I'd finished she said:

'I don't know why you're messing about with all those losers. You've got a perfectly good bloke in Bob. Don't you think it's time you settled down and thought about having a family? Otherwise it's going to be too late.'

Cath had just got married to Mr Perfect and was trying to get pregnant herself so she would say that, wouldn't she?

'You've turned into a right boring bastard,' was my riposte.

I was nervous as I got ready to receive Bob that night. I'd finally had a text off him saying he would be back around eight and would come straight round to my house because he was missing me. That sent me on a long guilt trip. What if he could see in my face what I'd done? I lit candles and opened a bottle of his favourite red wine to breathe.

He arrived, bearing gifts, at nine. By which time there was a bit of a dent in the wine. 'Sorry, gorgeous. There was an accident on the motorway and my phone's dead so I couldn't ring you.'

He was smiling and looked unexpectedly handsome in his white work shirt and smart suit. I hugged him and buried my head in his neck, trying to hide my treacherous face.

'Hey, don't you want to see what I've got you?'

It was a beautiful and intricately carved wooden love spoon. He was watching me to see what my reaction would be. I normally discouraged any signs of...soppiness, for want of a better word, so he looked relieved when I burst into tears. He dumped his bags, flopped on the settee and reached for the remote control.

'Don't turn the bloody telly on. I haven't seen you all week. Why didn't you ring me anyway?' I demanded.

'I was trying the "Treat 'em Mean, Keep 'em Keen"

approach.'

'What?'

'My mate Neil says it always works for him.'

He laughed as he saw my outraged expression.

'You swine!' I battered him with a cushion, but he grabbed me and tickled me into submission.

'I was only joking. I didn't have time to phone. They kept us working until ten every night and then there was a rush for the bar. I know you'll understand that,' he teased.

I felt myself relax.

Later on, long after the wine bottle had been emptied and we were entwined on the sofa together, I considered making a full confession.

'Have you been a good boy while you've been away?' I asked, half hoping he would admit to sins greater than my own.

'Too bloody right I have,' he mumbled. 'It was like a boot camp. You wouldn't believe...'

He was dozing off, his head on my shoulder. I stroked his hair, trying to make sense of the strange mix of emotions I was feeling – guilt, delight, relief, and a something I could only identify as an excitement about the future. Our future, maybe. Mine and Bob's.

I jumped up and went into the kitchen to get some food, watching him through the doorway as I spooned out olives and hummus and cut up pita breads. My non-record breaking attempt at infidelity had been a farce and a let down, but at least it had shattered a few illusions. The grass wasn't always greener on the other side, type of thing.

The cat had jumped on to Bob's lap and was kneading his chest, purring loudly. 'Somebody's missed you,' I observed.

'Yes. This cat is very discerning.' He preened himself, grinning. 'And you, have you missed me?'

I made him wait for a few seconds. 'I hate to admit it, but I have.'

I realised it was the honest answer.

Prudence

MELANIE MAUTHNER

When I was evacuated to the island in the year war broke out, I was convinced that my mother had crossed over the water with me even though I knew, because my aunt kept reminding me, that she had remained in Liverpool. It was only children they sent to safety, Aunt Prudence explained.

I had just turned six and because my mother gave me a squirrel to replace my furry owl, which next door's dog had torn apart and strewn all over our lawn, and a small photo album so I would remember her and Father and Victor, my brother, by the time I came home, I imagined she had followed me and found her place too, in my room overlooking the small garden.

Aunt Prudence ran a boarding house on the Isle of Man. It was set back from the promenade in Douglas and she made her living from families on holiday who returned to the resort year after year. Prudence had married a Frenchman, although she was a widow by the time I went to live with her, and she had a way of holding herself erect and peering over her glasses so that she seemed very tall and much older and more elegant than my mother. Her black hair was curled in waves in the style of the day and she wore mourning clothes only: grey and lilac and black.

In the summer when I arrived, she greeted me off *The*

Mersey wearing a cream dress. Later, I realised this was to celebrate my arrival, for in the four years I lived with her, I never set eyes on that dress again.

My mother had packed a small suitcase, so that I would not be burdened, she said, made of brown leather, one that hadn't sold in Father's shop. Business was slowing down with predictions of war and my mother started to sell the blackberry jam and apple and blackberry pies that Father made in order to raise a bit of spending money as she called it. My mother had never worked, there was too much to do she claimed, especially after we moved to the big house in New Brighton, on the Wirral, on the other side of the river.

There were two storeys and a rose garden at the back: they were Father's roses. In the veranda that separated the house from the garden, he grew tomatoes in pots, yellow and green ones, cherry and beef. He watered them everyday, sometimes twice a day when the sun shone. Our garden faced west and the afternoon sun lit up the tomatoes and made their aroma pervade the whole house.

I never knew what Mother spent her time on. My brother Victor had left home by the time I started school and so she only had me to look after. The piano teacher came to our house and she served us tea in the parlour where I played and practised. One afternoon after Miss Healey had left and I sat on the stool, swinging my legs under the piano, Mother circled the door and loitered with the tray and the tea things instead of walking straight to the kitchen as she usually did.

'How did you get on, puss?'

'Scales, *Twinkle Twinkle Little Star* and more scales,' I pouted, staring at her shoes on the mat. I loathed my weekly class and wanted to do ballet instead but she wouldn't hear of it.

'Can I go out and help Father in the garden now?'

'Not just yet, Shirley. I'm sure Miss Healey gave you some exercises. Another fifteen minutes or so and then you can go out.'

I pursed my lips and pinched the skin of my wrist and swung my legs high until they crashed into the underbelly of the piano. A loud bang sounded and her sharp voice trilled, 'That's enough Shirley! Stop fidgeting and get on with practising!' She frowned and the tray trembled in her hands.

She turned to the door and whatever had made her hesitate remained unsaid. That was the first time she had raised her voice at me. After that, she took no interest in my piano playing except to tell me how lucky I was because Aunt Prudence had one in the boarding house and was looking forward to my visiting and tinkling to bring some life back, now that the holiday-makers had stopped coming.

The piano in Aunt Prudence's house had lain untouched ever since Claude her husband had died, long before I was born. She set out to find a tuner soon after I arrived and then forgot about it, so I had to find other ways of occupying myself. I had learned how to swim in New Brighton Lido and Aunt Prudence took me to the beach on the front and sat under her parasol while I ducked and somersaulted in the shallows.

'Careful, Shirley, not too far out! Stay near the sand.' She waved at me, beaming.

Her summer lilac dress undulated in the salty breeze and her hat, in the shape of a swimming cap, kept her hair in place. I still felt convinced that Mother watched my every move and looked out for me even though she hadn't come and visited me yet. War was brewing, Aunt Prudence explained, when I asked her why Mother in her letters never referred to making the crossing.

'You'll see her soon enough, don't fret now pet, there, there,' and she kissed my forehead.

I prayed every night, to Mother and the Lord, clutching my squirrel, as I knelt by the side of my bed. Aunt Prudence put me in the box room next to hers on the first landing. In the mornings, she called me into her room and we sat by the window overlooking the sea, while Nell, the skivvy, brought us our porridge. Aunt Prudence kept her on even though the one or two families staying there that summer turned out to be the last guests for many years. She read out snippets to me from the morning paper or we listened to the wireless together. If there were a letter from Mother, she would read it out loud once in a while. Mother would send me a picture postcard occasionally and Father would sign his name at the bottom with lots of 'xxx' marks. Mother never did.

Aunt Prudence saw how I was a shy, reluctant reader and so after breakfast she made me read aloud to her. Mother had let me choose two books: there was no room for any more in the suitcase. I had carried down my two most favourites from the shelf, *The Eskimo Twins* and the illustrated *Alice in Wonderland* that I had won in a beauty contest at the age of two. Mother was proud of me for that.

'Maybe you'll work in fashion or as a glamour model,' she said twitching her eyebrows up and down in barely contained excitement.

Mother was already dowdy and plump by the time I came along, a late and unexpected occurrence, and she always seemed old to me though she was probably only two or three years older than Prudence.

'That's a good girl, Shirley,' Aunt Prudence encouraged me when I read a whole sentence without stumbling. 'Very good. Carry on,' she said glancing over her shoulder at me sideways.

As she spoke she filed her nails and rubbed cold cream into her fingers to keep the cuticles soft. She clasped her pink, dangling, amethyst earrings and sat at her dressing-table with her back to me while she adjusted them.

'Keep going, dear, till the end, there's time. I'm not going to leave without you!' And she laughed, a rolling affectionate chuckle, similar to Father's. She was, after all, his sister, although that was the only shared trait I detected.

When I finished the page, she bade me get dressed and then we set off for one of our round-the-island drives in her dark green MG. It had been Claude's and after he died, she had mastered basic mechanics from one of his French specialist magazines so that she could look after it herself. I sat in the front next to her, and with the windows down, her large scarf flapped in the wind. We drove along the coastal road over the cliffs. I revered her for Mother could not drive, only Father, and he only let me sit in the front on those rare occasions when Mother stayed behind. On Saturdays I accompanied him to towns outside Liverpool, like Preston or St Helens, where he purchased leather from wholesalers. Often we would be gone for half a day and as a treat, he might drive on to Southport to call in on Aunt Margaret, Mother's sister, and my cousins Paul and Brendan, who were just about my age. After the war I discovered that they too, 'the boys' as they were known, were evacuated later on in the summer, to Wales.

By the sea, Father would buy us each an ice cream, and then suddenly it would be time to drive back to the city because Mother, he said, was expecting us for high tea. More often than not, we would get home before her. We pulled into the gravel drive, avoiding the rhododendron, and he parked in front of the garage. It was too full of his jams and preserves and provisions for the day war did break

out to be ever used as a garage. He kept his rose clippers
and his gardening boots and heavy clothes in there too. If
we were back first, he would take my hand for a wander
through the rose bushes. He knew when they were going to
bloom, or droop, or die if the rains were poor. He pointed
out the soil and the weeds by the roots and how to protect
them from snails. And if Mother was running very late, he
would unravel the hose pipe and let me shower the shrubs
and then spray the tomato plants with care, for she hated
to find pearls of water on the glass panes of the veranda.
Sometimes Mother returned after we had finished our ham
and hardboiled eggs and crusty white bread and fairy cakes
and I might even be in bed.

Not so with Aunt Prudence, who never failed me. She
always kept her promise even if she changed our plans
slightly. So if it rained on a Sunday morning or the wind
swept across the island in gusts or she felt tired after a fretful
night's sleep, then we postponed our drive and went to
church instead. We both adored hymn singing and during the
talking sections, except for the prayers, she held my hand
and smiled at me and I cherished those moments with her
just as much as the island jaunts. When I asked her whether
I would still be able to learn passages for my confirmation,
she threw her head sideways and laughed behind her hands,
incredulous.

'Who put that idea into your head, dear? That's years
away, you've plenty of time yet.'

And when I insisted, she reassured me and said it was
never too early to prepare for anything and so she selected
special lines from 'The Song of Songs' for me to read out
and learn off by heart:

The Flowers appear on the earth;
    the time of the singing of birds is come,

and the voice of the turtle is heard in our land.

Anything rather than those ridiculous rhymes that she mocked, the ones I parroted from elocution class, which she banned me from mouthing during my entire stay. Lines like 'how now brown cow'. Instead, I tried to mimic her rounder vowels, for her accent had softened compared to Mother's or Father's, as a result of the time she had spent abroad, the year in France when she had met Claude.

One afternoon towards the end of the summer, she whisked me to a concert in Douglas because it featured Dvořák, a composer she loved whose music Claude had introduced her to on the continent. And the next day she announced that the time had come to hire a piano tuner in earnest, even if it meant sending for one from Liverpool. Overnight she decided that however long I was to live with her, she wanted me to carry on receiving lessons. Mother, she told me, had written mentioning this fact expressly. I kept silent and then gazed up at her, and twirling my bleached plaits, nodded with glee.

'Yes, yes, Auntie, I want to play again!' I clapped and jumped, for I wanted to please her.

In the same letter, Mother wrote to say that she was cancelling her crossing, the one she had booked for the August Bank Holiday. Prudence paused as she took a sip of her tea. Mother had planned to bring more of my twin books across: *The Swiss Twins, The Chinese Twins* and *The Favourite Wonder Book*, a new school uniform and blackberry jam and pocket money. And she wanted to see me before school started. But she wasn't coming. I sat at the round breakfast table, dropped my porridge spoon onto my dressing-gown and squinted at Aunt Prudence. She leaned back, pushed her glasses along her nose and met my eyes.

As I started to whimper, Aunt Prudence stared out to sea,

immovable and suddenly pale.

'Come here, pet,' she crooned and I climbed into her lap and almost strangled her as I flung my arms around her neck and burrowed my head in her bony chest beneath her silk gown.

'There, there,' she purred, stroking my unbrushed hair away from my eyes. She rocked me gently and my legs hung on either side of her hips. I howled into her and she soothed me with a lullaby I had not heard for years:

'Rock a bye baby on the tree-top.

When the wind blows, the cradle will rock.

When the bough breaks, the cradle will fall

And down will come baby and cradle and all.'

I sucked my thumb and shut my eyes and breathed in her lily of the valley talcum powder.

We stayed like that until Nell entered with the tray to clear away our half-eaten breakfast.

'Leave it, don't bother with it now. Come back later.' Nell demurely exited and trod back downstairs.

The morning sounds of the house echoed Prudence's lilting voice as she cooed another lullaby. Coal unloading into the cellar, milk bottles collected. Eventually, the day began. I started to attend my new school, and the following month, war broke out. At the end of the year, another letter postmarked from Liverpool reached us. It was a brief note from Father writing with news. He was spending his first Christmas of married life alone. Victor, my brother, had been called up and was rejoining his regiment. Father had wanted to bring us a turkey, but could not face a winter crossing. Mother had fled to Southport to help her sister out with the allotment. There was a lot of worry even before rationing came in and it was the only way to survive, I later heard. She stayed with Aunt Margaret the whole time I was away.

This last piece of news I only discovered from Father when I returned home and saw him again at the end of the war. By then I was ten and he had wanted Prudence to tell me everything in that letter. She never did.

After I crossed back to the mainland from the Isle of Man, and went to my new school in Huyton, just outside the city, Mother came back from Southport, and Prudence opened up the guesthouse again. I spent every summer after that on the island helping her with the accounts, 'earning my keep' Mother called it. Business slowly picked up for Father and Victor came home. Only Mother seemed changed, more harried and taciturn, even after church. Prudence came across the water for my confirmation. And soon the time came when I left school and Prudence found me a position in one of the big houses in Douglas. I continued to pray for Father and Victor and Mother, yet I was never sure whether she kept on praying for me.

Wood

DEBORAH DAVIES

Briefly she's alone, and watches the waiter bring two steaming platters of food to the next table. She smells liver and onions. She picks up a laminated menu and tries to concentrate on it. The liver-and-onion people have fallen silent. They seem to be mesmerised by their food. Without moving her head she can see that the woman eats by shooting her tongue out toward her fork and then reeling in little teetering mounds of food. She remembers liver days when she was a child. The backs of her bare legs stuck to the plastic kitchen seat as she tried to cut the offal into small, grey triangles. She remembers posting them in through her lips. The liver crumbled like sour dust in her mouth. Suddenly she wants to eat thin slices of cucumber and ripe tomatoes; maybe cold smoked fish and wobbly mayonnaise. The odour of next doors' food is the colour of gravy. She looks around for another table.

There is something lumpy and not quite dry stuck on the menu. The words 'Go on, indulge Yourself' are partially obscured by what looks like a smear of French mustard. She puts the menu down. He is threading his way through the tables carrying two large glasses of white wine. He sits down. 'I hope this won't be too dry for you', he says and takes a sip of his. He follows her glance to the half-eaten plates next to them. 'Want to move?' he says. They find an alcove by a deep leaded window. She can see primroses and pansies in the tubs outside. They look freezing, though the sun is shining. Her glass of wine is misty. It gives out a lemony glow.

There's nothing on the menu she would like to eat, but she settles in the end for a dish called calypso chicken. He says she obviously likes living on the edge. 'I'm not sure if that's true of me,' she answers seriously, and pours herself some iced water. The ice cubes sound inappropriately musical as they splosh into her glass. 'Or could it be you just don't know yourself very well,' he suggests, and finishes off his wine. When her glass is empty he goes to get two more without asking. She wonders if he's trying to get her drunk.

The calypso chicken is disgusting. The meat is wet and resists her knife. When she does manage to cut into it the incision looks surgical. He stirs her orange sauce with his fork. As it cools its solidifying. 'You can't eat that stuff,' he says, 'try mine.' She's embarassed to eat from his plate. He has some sort of beef pie with an exaggerated puff pastry crust. 'I'll feed you,' he says, and holds out a tiny new potato, spiky with parsley. She opens her mouth reluctantly. As it touches her lips it tastes earthy. 'There,' he says, 'That wasn't so hard, was it?' She has never felt so aware of her mouth, her lips before. 'More?' he asks, and she nods. This time he offers her a piece of beef. She shuts her eyes as she opens her mouth. She feels like swooning. He wipes her lower lip with his napkin. She wants to rest her head on his shoulder.

The liver-and-onion couple walk past. The woman says something to the man and he nods. She thinks they are both looking at her unpleasantly. 'I think we should have coffee now,' she says when the couple have disappeared. She sits up in her seat and places her forearms on the table. 'Okay,' he says. Alone again, she closes her eyes. She can see herself standing on the bank of a vast river. She has an irresistible urge to sink up to her neck in the dark, fast-flowing water. She senses the sun on her face. Through the window she sees the flowers have stopped shaking. The light looks stronger. When the coffee arrives she briskly pours and asks if he would like milk. 'Are you always mother?' he asks. Her hand is shaking as she holds the jug. 'I don't know what's the matter with me,' she says, and tries to smile. 'Could it be sexual tension?' he asks. She looks at him. He's smiling at her. 'Definitely not,' she says, and drinks her coffee, even though she doesn't want it.

They sit in his car. He has one of those wooden seatcovers made of beads. 'Do you find that comfortable?' she asks him. For a moment he doesn't realise what she's referring to. 'It's just that I've never understood them,' she says. She thinks about the way her family laugh at things like that. She asks if he bought it himself. He starts the engine. 'This car was my ex-wife's,' he says. His face looks stretched as he turns in his seat to reverse, 'It was part of the deal.'

They drive out of the car park, and she wonders where they are going. 'I thought we'd go to this beautiful place I know,' he says. Secretly she looks at her watch. He glances at her. 'It won't take long,' he says, and gives her the lightest touch on the thigh. 'What do you think?' She feels as if the touch has pushed her back into her real life; suddenly she can hardly believe she's sitting in this car with him. She thinks about her empty house, and calculates how long it is until the children come out of school. It seems impossible that it's all still there, while she's here. She looks out of the window at the speeding hedges. 'I think that would be lovely,' she says.

They travel for about half an hour. All the time they don't speak. She watches his hands on the steering wheel, and tries to imagine them touching her. His skin is dark compared to hers. She wonders what his brown hands would look like against her skin, she leans her head back and imagines them pushing her legs apart, his fingers inside her.

They drive into a car park with stone posts. Beyond the posts she can see the beginnings of a beech-wood. 'How do you know this place?' she asks. He says he used to bring his children here when they were little. 'That was all a long time ago,' he says. There is one other car parked. Its windows are steamed up. They both look. She can see the back of a woman's head pushed against the glass. As the woman moves she leaves a feathery shape in the steam. Through the wiped area of the window she sees the woman's bare shoulder and looks down at her own lap. 'Someone's having a good time,' he says. She turns to look at him. He is smiling, and frankly watching. She waits for him to do something. He suggests they get out of the car. He goes and opens the boot. She stands on the brimming edge of the wood. She can see deep into its green heart. It looks like a place she might have read about in a book. Thousands of branches bend down and nod. Thin columns of sunshine flash on and off through the new, translucent beech leaves.

Everything is quivering, although she cannot feel a breeze. The forest floor is smothered with bluebells. She can smell the wood's cool breath, ferny and sharp. Overlaying it all is the perfume of bluebells, so powerful is seems to be filling up her throat. 'Shall we walk?' he says, appearing at her side. He is carrying a small blanket. She's not sure whether to say something about it. They walk along a path. Wood anemones gleam in white clumps amongst the bluebells, accentuating their colour, making it purple. 'I don't know the names of many flowers,' he says. 'Didn't you want to tell your children when you were here all that time ago?' she says. 'Perhaps I knew then,' he says, 'Perhaps over the years I've forgotten.' 'I can't imagine doing that,' she says. 'Believe me,' he says, 'It happens.'

He holds her hand. His feels warm and dry. He gently pulls her round to face him and kisses her cheek, then her closed eyelids, then her lips. He is still holding the bunched-up blanket. 'But,' she says, 'I don't know you at all. What do you want?' She looks around her. Everything is shimmering blue and gold and green. Invisible birds are calling to each other. 'I just want to be your friend,' he says, and kisses her again. She likes how unfamiliar his lips are. She turns away from him and looks down the bank. The flowers could be a frozen waterfall. There are ragged-winged cream butterflies feeding. He puts his arm around her shoulder and down inside her blouse. His hand covers her breast. She leans against him and feels her nipples harden. She turns, pulls his face toward her and rubs his earlobes between her thumbs and fingers. She sucks his tongue.

They walk through the bluebells until they find a place where the brambles have parted to make a little nest. She watches as he stamps the plants flat and spreads out the blanket. They lie down and gaze up into the mesh of sky and leaves. 'It's hard to take this in, isn't it?' she asks him. He kneels, puts both hands up under her skirt and pulls her panties down. He raises them quickly to his face and breathes in, then puts them in his pocket. She lifts her bare knees and feels the breeze cooling her. He kisses her pubic hair and runs his tongue between her legs. 'Do you like this?' he asks. She doesn't answer him. Instead she pushes his head down with both hands and opens her legs wider. She looks up into the trees with half-closed eyes. She thinks the sky could be water. Everything is mixed up. He tells her to turn around and kneel. She gasps as he forces his penis into her. The smell of the sappy, crushed plants is making her drunk. She pushes herself onto him and he grips her shoulders. She tells him she wants him to come soon. 'Do it as hard as you like,' she says, and lowers her head. She loves the noises he makes, his exuberance. He calls her darling as he comes.

The Business Trip

CECILIA MORREAU

The drive to the airport was as tedious as usual. Anna gazed through the windscreen, admiring the low autumn sun on the trees as she let the clutch out and crawled another five yards forward before braking again. John sat silently next to her biting his fingernails with impatience. Reaching the motorway Anna cruised calmly at fifty-five behind a large and dirty truck. 'Well driven? Call 0720 563 466'. She read the sticker again. She was tempted to get her mobile out and do as the sign suggested, praise the driver and perhaps invite him out for a Chinese. Good job they didn't have a notice like that on the back of John's Mondeo or she would be inundated with complaints every time he took to the road.

'For God's sake! Can't you overtake him?' John's edginess was making his right foot twitch on an imaginary accelerator pedal. Anna was struck by how she reacted similarly when he drove, only it was her left foot that was constantly pushing into the foot well.

'Better five minutes late in this world than fifty years early in the next.' Anna replied smugly. Not that she thought John was likely to last another five decades. A heart attack or some other miscellaneous stress-related fate would get him well before he was eighty. Well, that is if no one murdered him first, mentioning no names.

'Don't bother to see me off. Just pull in. Save you paying

for parking.' John was already reaching in the back for his jacket. *Or save me seeing who is going with you to this 'conference'*, Anna thought. Before she had even put the handbrake on, John leapt out and yanked his suitcase out of the boot. He poked his head through the open driver's window and pecked her on the cheek. 'See you in a week. I'll call.' Anna didn't bother to reply. Doing eighty back down the motorway a smile spread across her face.

'Was that her?' Bryony asked as she pressed her body against John's. A few of his fellow businessmen gave him knowing looks.

'Yes, of course. She always takes me to the airport.'

'They've called our flight, we should go.'

As they passed the departure gate John paused. He remembered other trips, when he first got this job and started flying in and out of this seedy local airport. In those days Anna had followed him through to the departure gate. They had stood just here, not wanting to part. Long lingering kisses made him want to go straight back home and take her to bed. She would wave him off, tears in her eyes. After that the children too would come, wave furiously and try not to cry. Then Mark and Zoe would press their noses up against the glass hoping to get a glimpse of him as he strode across the tarmac and up the steps of the plane. He would always look up at them and do a silly walk to make them smile. Only last week the four of them had stood on this spot, but this time it was Zoe getting on the plane, off for her gap year in Australia. Mark then departed in his own car to university. Time flew faster than the bloody planes.

'Come on sweetie!' Bryony nudged him out of his reverie. *Why the hell am I doing this again?* John asked himself as he followed her sexy swaying bum down the corridor. It was fairly obvious not only to John but to his fellow suited passengers why he was doing it. *Still, what Anna doesn't know won't hurt her.*

Ensconced in the impersonal hotel room Bryony locked the door and draped herself across the bed.

'Come here tiger,' she crooned. John did as he was told, although for some reason he fancied, not Bryony's body, but a nice cup of tea, and maybe a nap. Affairs were supposed to be fun, exciting. When this one first started it had been, but, as with the others, there was always this underlying stress. With a lover you were expected to 'perform', be good at sex, fantastic in bed. Not that he wasn't, he reassured himself, or Bryony wouldn't be here. It was just that, well, it was such a lot of bother. John's mind wandered to the picture of Anna in their marital bed at home. She liked sex, but didn't have these 'expectations'. They had a hug, or they had sex, nice warm sex, or they went to sleep. No one expected hot sex that lasted for hours.

Hot sex accomplished John was just drifting off to sleep when Bryony propped herself up on her elbow and started twisting the hairs on his chest around her finger. John looked down at his curling greying hair that seemed to be increasingly migrating towards his shoulders and stomach over the years. He wished Bryony would stop that, it was hurting.

'Have you talked to her about the divorce?' she asked. John sighed. Why was it the done thing to promise every lover to divorce the wife and marry them? The fact was that he didn't want a divorce, why should he? He suddenly had the frightening realisation that he would rather be at home with his wife drinking cocoa in bed and chatting about the children, than in this bed with his red hot lover. He was either going mad or getting old, neither prospect pleased him very much.

'No,' he replied flatly.

'When are you going to? You've been promising for ages.'

'Never. I'm not going to leave Anna.' Shit, had those words come out of his mouth? This was not part of affair protocol. You were supposed to promise and prevaricate until the next lover came along.

Bryony leapt out of bed yanking out a few of his chest hairs that had caught in her fingernails. John winced.

'You bastard!' she yelled as she gathered her clothes together and put them back in her suitcase. 'To think that I actually believed you! Bloody men, bloody bloody married men!'

John knew he was supposed to cajole her into staying and all that sort of stuff, but somehow he just didn't have the inclination.

Bryony slammed the door behind her. John got up and took a shower, tried to wash the image of Bryony's angry face from his mind. Again he thought of Anna, alone in the house now both the children were gone. He realised that he was looking forward to having her all to himself again. He put his pyjamas on, that was another problem with lovers, they expected you to sleep naked.

Anna arrived home burdened with carrier bags and began to fill the fridge and freezer. She switched the radio on and turned the volume up really high. She was alone now and could do what she bloody well liked. In celebration of this fact she removed all of John's clutter from the kitchen and threw it into his study. Everything that Zoe had left lying around she put in big piles on her bed. Mark's stuff too was deposited unceremoniously in his room. Finding this act supremely satisfying she did the same to the sitting room and the hallway. Coats, spare shoes, wellies, books, magazines, CDs, everything was removed. The whole house took on a new air of tidiness. It looked like *her* house now. She wandered from room to room smiling, no, grinning to herself.

Sitting alone in the centre of the bed she started to write a letter, something to explain to her husband what she was about to do. Page after page she wrote until her hand was sore and there was a pile of crumpled tissues next to her. She looked at the bulk of paper she had covered in her small neat handwriting and realised that she had probably said too much. She started again,

'Dear John,' well, that said it all really didn't it?

Forever

CAROLINE CLARK

I like green, but not that sludgy olive colour. I remember colouring in the squares of my time-table at the beginning of my Lower Sixth year: gold for English, sky blue for History, grey for Games (in the hope of rain stopping play). Latin was divided – light green for old Julius who was OK if a bit tedious, olive for the new unknown, the displacer whom I was bound to hate.

It should have been so different but for the most miserable year of my life the scarlet of love and joy had been absent and now would be so for ever. A lot of things are 'forever' when you are fifteen.

Four years ago I had encountered Latin and love simultaneously in the person of my new form master, Rhodri Jenkins. I had been pretty devoted to the Welsh headmaster of my junior school but he was a fatherly soul rather than a romantic ideal. Mr Jenkins was young, pale and interesting. His profile was perfect as an antique cameo, his hair – a black-bird's wing, and his accent irresistible. Much of the class found it irresistibly hilarious but that only increased my protective affection.

It is quite clear that I required someone to fall in love with. Some of the boys in class were acceptable as acquaintances but certainly not in the frame for adulation. I was not attracted to the prefects and sports captains who caused a flutter among my friends. They offered neither the lure of adult experience nor the actual opportunities for contact of a teacher, especially a form master.

I have no real gift for languages. The decent 'ear' that enabled me to make acceptably French noises was no help in Latin. Nothing but personal devotion would have propelled me to a good grasp of that. However, there is at least one good thing about schoolgirl passion: you know, for the first and perhaps the last time in your life, exactly what your beloved wants – work.

In return there was a kindness. Although he was young, Mr Jenkins was a serious man, rather shy. Looking back, I don't think teaching came easily to him or was very satisfying but he was never impatient, never made fun of me. 'Amo, amas, amat…'

During those two years in his form I accumulated scraps of information about him: his birthday, where he came from in the Valleys, which flat he lived in with his wife. Ovid says 'Every lover is a soldier,' he might have said, 'a spy'. Not a stalker though, perhaps I was more like a pilgrim collecting the tokens of her saint.

His wife… I had at first very ambivalent feelings about her. On the one hand she represented another 'forever', a limit to the imagination of the future, on the other she was his choice, touched by his aura. Perhaps subconsciously I simply chose to like rather than hate her because she was unreachable. It was not that I had no jealousy. There were not many pupils, at least among the girls, whose work was so much better that they constituted a threat. I do remember, I can taste again now, the acid hatred for a gym mistress who flirted with him. Of course I disliked her to start with: someone who made me run around a frozen hockey pitch for no comprehensible reason was not likely to be popular. Maybe her looks and style suggested a sexuality which I had no wish to associate with him on any level.

It is probably hard for a current teenager (especially in a mixed school) to believe how unaware I was; how little I connected this always-present adoration with any kind of sexual desire. There were Biology lessons. There was a lot of literature, including some pretty explicit pieces of Shakespeare which I knew quite well and, on some level comprehended. There were barriers of ignorance but also of imagination. The patterns of romantic (or rather Romantic) love which appealed to me very early on were *The Lady of Shallot* and Andersen's *Little Mermaid* – fatally loving the unreachable or dancing, voiceless, on knives before the kind but uncomprehending beloved. These are not good patterns but they can shape a soul who chooses them.

There was no fall from the pedestal, no scandal or disillusion. He just left. I think they were probably home-sick, especially after they had a baby. Mr Jenkins was not a born teacher. For the one or two enthusiasts who shared his vision of burning Troy – Aeneas flitting from shadow to shadow, stalked by Greeks like starving wolves – there were always a dozen who copied the words, laughed at the Valleys vowels and hardly waited for the bell. He went back to South Wales and into the Civil Service.

For me this left a time of grinding misery. The O Level year is pretty pressured by its nature. It was especially so before the days of coursework and continuous assessment. Everything had to be done at once. Maths was purgatory: class hours of paralysed fear followed by nights struggling first with intractable calculations and then with blinding headaches. I lost my grip on Physics and Chemistry, which seemed to turn into more Maths. Latin, while well grounded, was empty of its meaning. Even in English I became neurotic about my spelling and History held the terror of forgotten dates.

The centre was gone. My mental map had no treasure around which to navigate. I remember hitting myself on the head with the flat side of a large carving knife, in frustrated fury that I lacked the courage to drive in the point and put a stop to it all. Suicide was another 'forever' that seemed more desirable at that time than it ever has since.

Incredibly, the O Level results were really quite good. I permitted myself the tormenting pleasure of writing to Mr Jenkins to tell him this and received a brief, kind reply but with no hope of return. He had been replaced.

So there I was; relieved of the subjects that had become a burden. I was looking forward to the wider horizons of Literature and a much more congenial period in History but Latin could only be an anti-climax.

There were only three of us in the set: Maggie was businesslike, bright and uninvolved; Pat, the real linguist, was talented, of strong opinions and very determined to succeed. I could grind out the work and put it in a decent shape. I was not expecting much more.

What we got was Peter Reynolds.

I was wary, trying not to be hostile, trying not to think of how it might have been. I think this lasted about twenty minutes – as long as it took to get over the formalities. From then on it was a journey up into the sunlight. This was not about Latin, it was not even about falling in love with him instead (although I think we all did that in time). It was about learning to think, question, be challenged in everything, be swept along by a mind like a burning river of light.

His projects went far beyond the requirements of set books. Lucretius' *De Rerum Natura* was on the syllabus so we must read all we could about the pre-Socratics. This meant that we found ourselves wrestling with all available theories on the nature of the universe, the existence of God and the working of human consciousness. We argued passionately, were teased and shocked and turned inside-out. Throughout, we were encouraged by cries of 'Splendid!', Pete's favourite word, said with enormous relish.

That was later. What I remember after our first encounter was coming out into the school garden, the September sun and the scent of roses – feeling the slightly guilty lightness of freedom. There was so much more to think about than I had somehow ever dreamed.

Romantic love is a powerful engine but it makes a lot of noise. I would continue to be carried away by it on many future occasions but from that time came a kernel of determination to live and think for my own sake.

That love's power does not last for ever is a hard lesson; not one, certainly, to be fully learned at once. When, some years later, I had cried myself to a standstill over a departing boy-friend, I walked out into another autumn day and remembered that the world is not just full of other people but much more than that. Infidelity, in many contexts may be regrettable, but it is also a way of surviving – a part of growing up.

'Forever' isn't as long as you think when you are fifteen.

Speaking in Tongues

MARION PREECE

'Yes, that's it,' Larry whispered urgently. He furtively checked the living room door before easing down his zipper and pressing himself into the soft cushions of the sofa.

Manoeuvring the phone against his jaw, his hands gloated over the velvet of his trousers in counter rhythm to the beat of the music from upstairs. As his breathing quickened, he stared unseeing into the round eyes of Little Tony, sitting opposite him. The jester doll seemed to leer in collusion as the man made a soft, agonised noise.

In the ensuing silence, Larry heard the sound of familiar footsteps.

'Linda, I've got to go,' he said quickly and replaced the phone.

He was leaning forward to pick a stray thread from the dummy's jacket, when something hard struck him on the shoulder. Gritting his teeth with irritation, he turned to face his wife.

'What do you think?' Babs pirouetted in front of him in a cloud of blue net and playfully tapped him again with her fairy wand.

He glanced at the roll of fat protruding from her tight bodice and averted his eyes.

'You look fabulous,' he said, and his gaze shifted to catch the glassy, incredulous stare of Little Tony.

She smiled with relief. 'Really?'

No, not really, Babs, he thought. With her faded, brown hair and garish stage make-up, she bore little resemblance to the shy young woman he'd talent spotted all those years ago. She still had the voice of course but everything else had gone south. Although – Larry tried to be honest with himself – the punters still liked her, even if they didn't seem so keen on *him* any more. But all that was going to change when he teamed up with the luscious Linda.

'Yeah, really fabulous,' he drawled and cursed himself as he saw that she'd caught the sarcasm. She was fat, not stupid.

Babs went to the mirror, anxiously scrutinising her reflection and Larry felt a tiny flicker of shame. But then she turned, and her sadness had been replaced with sudden gaiety and graceful, theatrical gestures.

'Tony darling, aren't you the handsome one! Come to Babs, let me look at you!'

The small, wooden figure was swept from the cushions and into the air where it was whirled up and around. The dolls eyebrows jiggled madly and its jaw clacked open into a surprised gape.

'You stupid cow, you're going to damage it!' Larry leapt to his feet and grabbed her by the arm.

Babs stumbled to a halt. 'For God's sake, Larry! It was only a bit of fun.'

'Do you know how much we'd have to shell out to replace him?' Seething with irritation, he lowered the dummy into its case and snapped it shut.

Babs rubbed her arm and glared back. 'And who saves us money by repairing and maintaining him?'

Conceding that she had saved them a packet over the years, and also aware of the fact that they had a show in an hour, he clumsily tried to placate her.

'Aw, come on sweetheart, don't take any notice of me – I'm just in a funny mood that's all.'

He lifted his stick with the bells and shook it in her face. 'I say, I say, I say – my dog has no nose!'

Babs dutifully struck a pose, but her voice was flat. 'Your dog has no nose? How does he smell?'

A muffled voice came from the case. 'Awful!'

'We'd better get a move on,' she said and went to get her coat.

Larry slowly packed his jester's hat and stuck it into his rucksack along with his bottle of scotch. He stared uneasily at the case. He hadn't spoken – he was going to but...

The club was half-empty and the punters were not responding well to Larry's new routine.

Somebody shouted, 'Hey, Little Tony! You look a right state in that outfit – and your dummy looks even worse!'

Larry, perspiring in his velvet suit, tried to laugh, but another voice yelled. 'You'd look much better outside, mate!'

Larry thought uneasily that the hecklers were getting a better response than he was. He glanced over to the corner where Linda sat with her friends. Her blonde hair cascaded over one shoulder of her tight, green sweater as she giggled into her hand. Suddenly conscious of his eyes, she sat up and licked her lips at him.

Babs brought a glass and Larry started the bottle of beer routine – usually a favourite with the punters.

'Gockle a geer! Gockle a geer!'

The familiar taunt had an unusually spiteful sound. A loud raspberry made the crowd roar and perspiration trickled into Larry's eyes as he fought to regain control.

Then a voice yelled: 'Gerroff, you boring old twat!'

Larry's voice was drowned out by catcalls and, in panic, he launched into a Morris dance with little Tony flopping and bouncing about in his arms. The heckling increased in volume, Larry's heel slid in some spilled beer and suddenly, a well-aimed pork pie caught him in the eye.

Babs cut the music and walked forward, admonishing the culprit with her wand.

'Didn't your mother teach you not to play with your food?' she asked teasingly.

The man called out. 'Grant us a wish, Blue Fairy.'

Babs put a finger coquettishly to her cheek. 'Now what can that be?'

The heckler pointed at Larry, who was slinking towards the wings. 'Wave your magic wand, love and make that silly sod disappear!'

'How about a song instead?' Babs laughed, and several of the regulars clapped as her voice began to weave its magic.

Larry tore at his nails as he glared from the wings. Tonight had been all her fault; she hadn't been quick enough with the props or her responses, and now here she was, grabbing the limelight again. He turned as he heard a clatter of high heels.

'Larry darling,' Linda breathed. Her mouth sucked at his while her hand determinedly groped his crotch. Stupid, irritating bitch! He pushed her away and held her at arms' length.

'Look Linda, I've decided to give us a trial run tonight.'

Her eyes widened but he rushed on, 'Do exactly as we rehearsed. Go back to your table and when I give the signal, come up on stage.'

Fifteen minutes later Babs came into the tiny dressing room and stooped down in front of the cracked mirror.

'You okay, Lar?'

She bent over and yards of net puffed up, wafting her heavy odour towards him. Faugh! It was no wonder he couldn't get it up for her any more. After half a bottle of scotch, he didn't even bother to hide a grimace of distaste as his eyes met hers in the mirror.

'Mmm.'

The voice sounded as though it had just licked something delectable.

'What?' Larry jerked around.

Babs looked at him strangely.

'I didn't say anything.'

She spat on her palms and started easing out the wrinkles in her tights.

'Tasty.' The word was sibilant and mocking.

Little Tony, propped upright on the chair, was staring straight at Larry and as he watched, one eyelid clicked down in a lascivious wink.

'The doll…' Larry pointed to Little Tony with a trembling finger.

Babs opened the hatch on the back of the dummy and tutted as she fiddled with the mechanism.

'I thought I'd fixed this. You'll just have to put extra pressure on the control knob for tonight and I'll sort it out tomorrow.'

The hecklers had gone and a new crowd had filtered in to the hall during the break. Seemingly determined to have a good time, they groaned at all the old jokes and laughed at Little Tony's antics. Larry glowed – he was back on form.

'And now, ladies and gentlemen…'

Babs stepped forward.

'We have a change to our programme!' Larry bared his teeth in a feral grin that stopped Babs in her tracks.

'As a professional entertainer, I am always on the lookout for exciting new talent; so this evening,' Larry's smile glittered as he pointed to Linda, 'I want you to give a warm welcome to an up and coming young star – Miss Linda Forster!'

He glanced sideways and caught Babs staring as Linda scrambled to her feet.

Larry clapped loudly and called out. 'Don't be shy Linda, that's the way. Give her a big hand folks!'

There were a few claps as Linda climbed onto the stage, but then somebody wolf whistled and Larry felt slippery with success. His eyes sought Babs' but she had disappeared. He shrugged, easily pushing away a niggling pinch of guilt.

'Ready?' he whispered, pulling Linda around into position in the spotlight. He noted anxiously that her face was set and he could feel her shaking through the thin material of her sweater.

'Say hello to the lady, Tony.'

The dummy's head rotated and its eyebrows waggled. 'Hello lady.' It leaned towards Larry and whispered loudly. 'She's built isn't she?'

This was where Linda should have said: 'You cheeky monkey!' But she seemed mute with fear. In the silence somebody coughed. Larry could smell his own sweat as he brought Little Tony close to Linda and made it roll its eyes.

What happened next he could never explain. His throat clicked as he started to project: 'Have you got a sister at home?' But what came out of Tony's mouth was: 'Hey, lady – are those knockers real?'

Then somehow, the dummy's head was swinging around to stare into Larry's horrified face.

A man in the audience guffawed as Linda's eyes slowly turned to the dummy. 'You cheeky bugger,' she said, 'sod off!'

Larry's fingers fell away from the controls in Little Tony's body, but the doll continued to move. As the laughter of the audience washed over him, Larry's teeth began to chatter as he heard the dummy say: 'I'd like to give you one, Linda. Right now on this table.'

The audience gasped, waiting for her reply.

Linda tossed her hair and examined her nails. 'Sorry Little Tony, I'm not into wooden... legs.'

Larry gaped at her through bulging eyes. That was fast for her – the little bitch was enjoying herself!

The whole audience was laughing now as Linda slipped her sweater off one shoulder and fluffed up her hair.

Moaning, Larry twisted his head towards the darkness of the wings, searching frantically for Babs.

The dummy waggled its head. 'Larry tells me that he's always hard; always ready for it.'

Linda snorted. 'You've got to be joking!'

Little Tony's eyebrows shot up and the crowd roared laughing. Larry glared at Linda, but she was totally immersed in the dummy.

'Bit of a limp rag is he?' Little Tony leaned against Linda's shoulder and batted its eyelids. 'I bet you wish that *he* had a wooden... leg.'

Larry was trapped. The noises of the club faded and he shivered as Little Tony's voice boomed and receded in his head. Spots of light began to obscure his vision and the acrid taste of vomit rose in his throat.

'Shall we let these folks into a little secret, Linda?'

Linda nodded happily.

'Shall we tell them that Larry is always on the prowl for naïve little tarts like you? Especially the ones that give good ... telephone.'

Linda's smile faded as Little Tony peeled back its lips in a hideous grin. 'But I'm afraid he also likes his meat young and fresh, and from the smell of you, love, I'd say you're well past your sell-by date.'

The laughter in the hall petered out as Linda began to cry, but the chirpy voice continued.

'Aw look – it's upset! Well, give it a big round of applause, folks. It's not very bright, but you can see why he'd prefer it to saggy old Babs.'

Several people booed, Linda ran off the stage and the props table crashed sideways as Larry's head hit the floor.

Eight months later, on the advice of his psychiatrist, Larry attempted a reconciliation with his wife. After several fruitless phone calls, Babs agreed to meet him at the theatre where she would be working.

The Alhambra Theatre was busy as Larry walked around to the stage door and was directed to her dressing room.

Smoothing back his hair, he took a deep breath and knocked on the door.

At first he thought he had the wrong room, then his jaw dropped.

'Babs?'

She looked fabulous. Her hair was darker and shone in the light as she moved. Her makeup was flawless and her figure…

'Come in, Larry. I've been expecting you.' Babs turned and he blinked at the way her black, beaded gown clung to her generous curves.

She sat down and began to apply lip-gloss with brisk movements.

'How are you, Larry?'

He swallowed. 'All the better for seeing you.' He tore his eyes away from her and glanced nervously around.

'What do you want?'

He coughed, checked around the room again and said, 'I'm better now.'

'And your point is?'

'I think we could make a go of it again.'

Babs smiled at him through the glass. 'This is a one woman show, Larry.'

She was laughing at him but he forced himself to relax as he'd been taught.

'I thought maybe the position of manager? You owe me, Babs.'

'All right.'

'What?'

She turned to face him. 'I said all right. I need someone who knows the business and it might as well be you.' She rose to her feet and his eyes flickered greedily from her face to her breasts.

'Make yourself comfortable until the show has finished,' she said. 'And then we'll go over details. There's whisky in the cupboard.'

Larry checked every corner and niche in the room before settling down with the bottle.

'So, for one night only, please welcome... our very own ... Barbara Mandrell!'

As the small loudspeaker in the corner relayed the compere's voice, Larry gulped down his drink. Thunderous applause died down as Babs began to sing and he listened intently to her rich voice. Why had he never realized how talented she was?

Three more glasses of whiskey later, he leapt up, punching the air with excitement.

'Larry boy, you've landed on your feet!'

Wrenching open the door, he weaved his way over to the wings.

He was watching the show with a dreamy smile on his face when he heard the voice of his nightmares.

'I've been waiting for you, Larry.'

His bowels turned to water as a grinning face appeared around the curtain.

Bab's voice soared as Larry backed away, babbling. 'No! You're not real! I've had treatment for this and you're not real!'

'Shut up, Larry. You always did talk a load of shit.' Little Tony seemed to float towards him.

A distant, rational part of Larry's mind knew this couldn't be right, and his eyes searched for hidden wires as the dummy closed in, wafting the smell of oil, and something … else.

'Hey, Larry. Wanna see something really scary?'

Larry's eyes bulged with horror as its lips receded, revealing a crooked row of razor-sharp teeth that glinted wickedly in the half-light.

Larry had turned to run, when pain exploded in his leg. Thunderous applause drowned out the sound of his screams as he fled out into the night.

Babs took her final bow and made her way over to the gloom of the wings. Pushing aside the curtain, she saw the small figure slumped forward, in a child's wicker chair. She laughed softly as her fingers moved over the buttons of a slim control box and Little Tony, immaculate in a white tuxedo, snapped upright. The dummy's jaw clacked open and shut as a hidden recorder played: 'So long, sucker!'

Because of the size of Larry's ego, her talent for mimicry and throwing her voice had been kept under wraps. Once however, out of boredom, she had impersonated Linda over the phone. It had been mildly distasteful.

She'd known that Larry wouldn't be able to resist coming down to watch, and it was a pity that she hadn't been there to witness the look on his face, but there, you couldn't have everything.

The audience was calling for an encore, and as she turned, she paused momentarily to frown at some dark red splashes on the floor in front of her. At that moment, the orchestra started to play, so, lifting the hem of her gown, she gingerly stepped over the sticky mess.

She walked back into the spotlight and began to sing.

Safe Haven

SHELAGH MIDDLEHURST

I'd already told her too much. Tongue loosened by the wine, the warmth of the log fire, the soothing comfort of her presence. I'd known Mona since we were eleven and loved her, but there were some things you shouldn't even tell your best friend. Things like slipping out of the house at 3 in the morning to meet a man. Making love on the cold damp earth in a secluded spot at the top of the garden; a space strewn with rotting leaves, rotting apples. My lover. We'd lie on a tartan picnic rug and I'd look up at the sky, the stars above his head, while he moved inside my body.

His name? Jay, or was it Jai? We didn't speak much. He'd arrived at my front door asking if I wanted trees lopped, hedges cut. A young man with a shy look, a slight smile. His hair was dark, longish. His skin sallow. His eyes black. He pushed his hair off his face with strong fingers.

I wondered what his hands would feel like on my body.

He knew.

'Do you do any other gardening, any landscaping?' I asked him. My garden needed a path. And in the wasted area away from the house behind the garage, I wanted an arbour. Seasons had come and gone and Oliver never seemed to have the time. I'd already decided to get it sorted out myself. All it needed was simple paving, a wooden frame and seat, then planting with climbing roses, honeysuckle and jasmine.

My own little haven.

I took Jai up the garden and showed him the space. It was filled with sacks of garden rubbish, old plant pots and bits of wood. But it was a pleasant spot, secluded from neighbours behind a laurel hedge, a suntrap on summer mornings. Jai took a good look around. The sky was blue. The air mild and warm.

'Not take long.'

'That's okay, take as long as you need. I'll supply the materials and a plan of what I want; all you'll have to do is the work. Right?'

I was looking up into his face, speaking in my best 'woman of the house' voice. Who was I trying to kid?

'Is easy, I do good job. What price?'

'Ermm, two, three hundred pounds?'

'I give you my very best work for that price,' his smile widened, showing white teeth. I imagined what they would feel like, biting me.

Walking back to the house I sensed him near me. We drank tea in the kitchen and finalised details. He started work the next day.

'All sounds very Lady Chatterley,' Mona laughed and poured more wine. 'Passion between the mistress and the gamekeeper, or in your case, gardener. Your bit of rough was he? God, I could do with a bit of that myself, Nick's so bloody boring, know what I mean, predictable. Always same place, same time. I tried to seduce him in the kitchen after a dinner party and do you know what he said, 'Hadn't we better load the dishwasher first?' I nearly hit him! Bloody well left him to it and went to bed with my vibrator. Thank God for Anne Summers.'

'Mona, you're the best!'

'Come on then, Becky, don't get sidetracked I know

there's more.'

'I wasn't going to tell you any of this but you always make me spill the beans.'

'Sisters, remember?'

I did.

I remembered how we swore an oath to each other. An oath sworn in blood: menstrual blood. Like true sisters our monthly cycles were synchronised and we walked into the school toilets arm in arm and locked the door.

'What do we do?' I asked.

'Put your fingers inside your knickers.'

I put my hand up my skirt and wiggled my fingers inside the leg of my navy-blue knickers. I manoeuvred past the lumpy sanitary towel and put my finger into the entrance of my vagina.

'What does it feel like?' Mona asked.

'Slippery and wet.' I pushed my finger in further, it was a tight fit. 'God, can a boy really get his *thing* in there, it must kill!'

'At first,' Mona said, 'then when you're "broken in" it gets nice.'

'How do you know?'

'Ellie, the one with the big boobs in form five, she told me.'

'What did she say?'

'Well, you have to touch it...'

'Eeek,' I screamed, 'I hate snakes.' We both fell about laughing.

'Then,' Mona continued, 'it gets really long, kind of grows, and he lies on top of you, you open your legs and he puts it in.'

'God, how yukky.'

'Then,' Mona continued, 'he moves up and down really

fast, till all this white stuff comes out.'

'And that's supposed to be nice? I think I'll become a nun!'

'Oh, and he takes your bra off and feels you, but Ellie's used to that.'

For a moment we both pondered the experiences that were to come.

'Anyway,' Mona said, 'I'm not doing it until I'm married.'

'I'm not doing it *ever.*'

'Oh, you're such a goody two shoes, but I bet you do it with the first boy who asks. Anyway, let's forget about all that, and do the blood-sisters ceremony.'

So we linked our bloodied index fingers chanting, 'Sisters forever, till death!' Mona adding, 'Let no man put asunder!'

Friends forever.

We stayed close even after careers, husbands, children intervened. And despite living hundreds of miles apart Mona visited whenever her busy schedule allowed. My new baby was to be christened on Sunday and she was to be her Godmother. We had the whole weekend to catch up with each other.

Mona had grown to be clever, ambitious and very, very sexy. Men fell over themselves to please her and she let them. Nick was her third husband and was, she assured me, her last. I asked her, 'Why him, why Nick?' When both her other husbands had been richer, sexier, better-looking. 'He loves *me* Becky, you know, really loves me, even when I mess him around he's still there for me.'

Her only pregnancy had ended in stillbirth. She named her son Isaac and held him for hours, not letting anyone, not even Nick, come near. He called me in the early hours, his voice twisted with emotion, 'Talk to her, Becky, please, talk to her, I can't reach her.' So I cried with Mona down the phone while he gently lifted the dead baby from her arms.

'You're not telling me everything, have another glass.'

I sipped the warm red wine and remembered. Early morning, the air cool, a ring at the bell. He stands there.

'Is early enough?'

'Yes, perfect timing.'

Oliver's car backs out of the drive. A smile, a wave, he's gone. My little daughter, Rosie, takes Jai's hand and leads him through the house. She stays close by him all morning, watching him clear the ground.

'Is she bothering you?' I walk up the garden with a tray of tea and biscuits.

'No, children I like very much.' He's taken off his shirt and has his back half turned. The pale supple skin is scarred in three places. I stare then apologize, 'An operation?' Rosie peers up in his face.

'No, in my country we are punished for who we are. I never go back.'

I want to touch the ribbed, puckered marks. To kiss away the past, to kiss away his pain. Instead, I mutter about milk, how much sugar and does he like chocolate biscuits.

He works steadily all day, stopping for a midday break. Refusing my offer of ham salad, crusty bread; accepting coffee and a glass of water.

'He's eating big round floppy bread,' Rosie informs me as I sit in the nursery, breast feeding five-month-old Harry. 'Let's show him our baby,' she insists. So when Harry is full, clean and smiling I show my son to Jai who unexpectedly takes him out of my arms, lifts him in the air, lowers him, lifts him again, making Harry squeal and giggle with pleasure.

'My turn!' Rosie clamours when Jai hands Harry back. So Rosie is swung and thrown, caught and thrown till I decide, enough.

'Leave him, Rosie, he's got work to do.'

Jai's eyes look at the ground. He turns his back and gets on with digging. I take the children into the house. Rosie is difficult all afternoon. 'Why wouldn't you let me play with him?' She glares at me before stomping upstairs to lie on her bed, Paddington tucked under one arm. I look in later and she's fast asleep. I put Harry down for his nap and walk up the garden.

'How's it going?' I speak to Jai's naked back. The scars stand out, livid in the afternoon sunlight. 'Look I didn't mean...'

'Yes,' he replies, 'I understand. I work, you pay. I go.' He averts his face and carries on digging. I feel reduced, petty.

'Jai,' I call softly, moving closer, 'the children sleep for a little while now.'

He stands up and faces me. His gaze is steady.

'You feed baby,' he touches his own nipple, 'is good.'

Damp circles show through the thin cotton of my dress. He holds out his hand and I give him mine. We move into the overhanging shade of next door's apple tree and sit on the partly cleared earth. We can't be seen. His arm is around me, light and strong. Something inside me gives; eases, shifts, moves. He is close to me. He smells of soil and sweat and garlic and bread; of oil and wine and air; of sunlight and darkness and pain and death and love. He holds me and in silence we kiss. In silence he strokes my damp nipples. Milk flows. I undo buttons on my dress, he drinks me deeply. Never has Oliver done this. My womb contracts, opens, and I pull him into me. The sky is blue above his head. The branches of the apple tree rise and fall in the breeze.

Mona pours more wine, exhaling deeply. 'Phew!'

'He was wonderful.'

'In broad daylight! And how did you manage this middle of the night stuff? Didn't Oliver wonder where you where?'

'No. Out like a light. Takes those herbal sleeping things, besides I'd often sleep in the nursery after feeding Harry, especially if he was grizzly.'

'How long did it go on?'

'I met him that night, and the next and then...'

'What? What happened?

'Oliver.'

'Shit! Oh my God. Did he forgive you? I always said that underneath that stuffed shirt beat a heart, if not of gold, then at least a heart!'

'No he didn't find out, something worse. Not for me, for Jai. Oliver came home from work a couple of days later hot and bad tempered; you know the way office politics pisses him off. I met him at the door, all bright and shiny, with two cheerful children in tow.'

'Has he gone?' were Oliver's first words.

'Has who gone? Oh, you mean the gardener, you've just missed him. Come and see what a good job he's doing.'

'Pay him off tomorrow, give him half of what you agreed. I'll finish the job myself.'

'But you won't, you know you won't, and we'll be left with a mess.' My voice was rising. I took a deep breath, sent Rosie to play upstairs and put Harry down in his cot.

'Watch Harry for me, poppet, while daddy and I have grown-up talks.'

I returned. 'Why?'

'Because he's most certainly an illegal alien, and I don't want to get mixed up in all that.'

'In all what?' I was furious. 'Since when did you become Mr Citizen of the Bloody Year. He's doing a better job than you ever could!'

'Look, it's done.' Oliver went to the fridge and poured

himself a glass of wine from a half empty bottle. 'Anyway these people come here with forged papers. If they're genuine why come through the back door?'

'You *know* why,' I screamed.

'Don't take it so personally, if he is genuine they'll let him stay, if not…'

'Do you realise what you've done? And I thought you had principles, what a load of bullshit!'

'They were waiting for them next morning. Immigration. Ten young men were arrested as they got out of a mini-bus before they dispersed to their casual jobs. It was even on the local news. I caught a glimpse of Jai as he turned around to look straight at the camera. Straight at me. I never saw him again.'

Mona gulped her wine and looked stricken. 'But Becky that's awful.'

'Don't worry, Oliver's paying.'

Mona's eyes widened.

There was a wail from upstairs and Rosie came to the door clutching Harry's hand.

'The baby's awake, come on Auntie Mona, let's go up and fetch her.'

Mona opened her mouth to speak.

I put my finger to my lips and nodded.

After Melissa

MARLIS JONES

The coffee is hot and very sweet; so sweet that I can't taste it. Of course it might have been tea. Coffee, tea, cocoa, arsenic, who cares anyway? I'm sure I don't, and I don't suppose the girl in her white starched blouse cares either. I wonder how often she changes her blouse in a day? It was so white, and not a wrinkle in it. Creases, yes. Sharp crisp creases that screamed 'cared for'.

She wasn't abrupt, in fact she was quite calm and business-like. She'd done this before. Many times before. I bet they called for her especially every time. I can hear them now.

Hello, Miss Efficiency. Can you come down here, please? We've got another one for you.

And down she comes. She's done it time and time again. She's not bored; she's not fed up. She'll do it again and again with the same efficiency, the same detachment. Yes! That is it. Detachment! She's not part of it, yet she is involved. That is exactly the situation I am in. I am part of it, yet I am not involved. Well, not really involved. But were it not for my actions, I would not be here now drinking dissolved sugar.

The polystyrene cup is warm, and if I squeezed it, it would crack and the hot drink would pour over my hand...over my dress...over the floor. I don't want to mess up this shiny tiled floor. I didn't want to mess up the hall floor either. I didn't want that to happen. I didn't want to make any mess. I just wanted to avoid a mess... But they can't understand that. Miss Efficiency in her white starched blouse does not understand, nor does her friend in his dark suit.

He will be here again soon.

'Have you finished your drink?' he'll ask, and I shall answer, *'Yes, thank you.'* Then he'll say, *'Now what have you got to tell me, Mrs Finch?'* But what can I tell him? He knows the important bit. But he does not understand. He does not understand why. How can I make them understand? If they had been there with me all the time, perhaps they would understand a little bit. Mr Dark Suit will probably say something about starting at the beginning. But does he really want me to start at the very beginning? The beginning is a very, very long time ago.

I suppose the very beginning was at my cousin Esther's third birthday party. I can remember bits of the party. Johnny Day was sick behind the sofa, and Esther's dog licked it all up. When you're only five, you remember things like that. Charles nearly fell into the fire in *blind man's buff.*

They don't want to hear about the very beginning. They don't want to hear about the skiing trip, although that too was very early on. Nor do they want to hear about the engagement, or the wedding.

Melissa's birth was another beginning, so was her accident. Perhaps the accident was the beginning of the end. That was when Charles started to withdraw into himself. It was to be expected, I suppose. He absolutely adored Melissa. I did, too; but I tried to keep my feet firmly on the ground. Someone had to keep an even head.

'You are too strict,' Charles would say. And I would reply that he was too lenient. We'd argue a bit, but never quarrelled. People who love one-another don't quarrel. They disagree. We did not always see eye to eye, but we never quarrelled.

Not seriously. Oh, I know I got fed up with him at times. He did have some annoying habits. Now and again I would get on his nerves. He would get fed up with my foibles.

Charles resented the time I spent going to see Father. I would sometimes remark that money was tight. We discussed the shortage of money, but did not quarrel. We were careful how we spent the money. Charles never let Melissa want for anything. We disagreed, sometimes on what Charles bought for her, but they were not rows. We never quarrelled over what Charles gave Melissa.

Perhaps. Just *perhaps* it would have been different if Melissa had been Gavin, the son I had hoped for. Or even if Gavin had come later. But that was not to be. After Melissa, there would be no more babies. So that was the end of my dream. No son. No future Mr Finch. The end of the line.

Could I make these people understand that Charles meant everything to me? Their questions sometimes seem to presuppose that I hated him. That is what they think. I know that Miss Efficiency believes that Charles and I were not friends. She can never understand the depth of our feelings for one another. Ours was a pure love that lasted through forty years of marriage.

I'd always known Charles. We grew up together. We attended infants school, junior, and secondary school together. We were friends. Real good friends. He knew all about my family. I knew all about his family. We never had any secrets. Even before we started courting properly we knew all about one another's romances. I knew that he had slept with Ruth. He knew that I smoked secretly. He knew that I had been stupidly blind drunk at Kerian's house that weekend. And I knew that he had stolen a book from Smith's. We had no secrets. Our marriage was special. Not many couples stay together for forty years. I loved him. I understood his problems. I could live with his impotency. It was Melissa's accident that was at the root of it. That, and the fact that I could not have more children. But we never quarrelled about it.

At times, his lack of interest in sex would get me down. I would think that it was my fault, perhaps he did not find me attractive any more. Perhaps he had someone else. After all he worked with some very smart ladies. I knew most of them but I could not imagine his having an affair with any one of them. He was dedicated to his work, and his fellow workers, men and women were a means to an end. I used to tell him to think of them as people, not items at work.

While I knew Charles was faithful to me, I did lapse. Esther's husband started calling when his work brought him to our neck of the woods. At first, I was delighted to see him. It was very pleasant to have company for an hour or so in the afternoons. One day he rang suggesting that we met for lunch, and I suggested that I'd cook lunch for him.

The wine he'd brought with him made me very giggly and light headed. I lost my usual sense of propriety and really let my hair down and had a most wonderful afternoon.

Then I realised what I'd done. I blamed him, he accused me of leading him on. He threatened to tell Charles that I had been unfaithful to him. The silly fool! Charles knew about his every visit. He knew the gist of all our conversations too.

I did not spell out to Charles why the twice-weekly visits had stopped. I merely said that Keith was not welcome any more. But did Charles suspect that I had been unfaithful that once? He never asked me. I never admitted it, although the guilt never left me. From then on I never let anything come before Charles.

The episode proved to me that I was not unattractive. It also showed me how important to me was Charles. In a way, it did me good without harming our marriage. In fact, I think it strengthened Charles's and my relationship. We both knew that we were true to one another. I knew that my one infidelity was because of drink and a mad afternoon of fun. Neither Charles nor I ever mentioned the matter again.

I'm convinced that it was a feeling of guilt that changed Charles after Melissa's accident. She was barely twenty. A normal, happy young girl doing what she enjoyed and succeeding in her job. She was popular and always on the go. Her group of friends did everything that decent young people do. Her great passion was mountain climbing, or rock scaling, as she used to describe it. There was nothing she liked better than to pack her rucksack and leave on Friday night for Snowdonia. No matter what the weather was like, or how bad the forecast would be, off they'd go. A minibus full of friends all eager to challenge the rocky mountains around Llanberis or Capel Curig.

During the holidays, they'd venture further afield, The Lake District, perhaps, or Scotland. They were planning to go climbing to the Pyrenees in the summer. Melissa had all the guidebooks; she prepared well before every trip. She kept herself fit, and practised on the climbing wall in the gym. We had no qualms about her climbing. It was a sport she adored, and at which she was becoming very competent. She was the youngest member of a group that respected the mountains, and the vagaries of their weather. Even so, my favourite sound was the sound of the minibus stopping outside our front door on Sunday evenings.

Melissa was living life to the full. It was a cruel blow to all when the accident happened. She, who often defied death on the mountains, was taken practically on her own doorstep. It was during the October storms in the eighties, when Charles and she went out to see the waves breaking on the promenade. I had a bit of a cold and decided to stay at home.

I shall never forget the look on Charles's face when, eventually he returned home accompanied by a police officer. I had dozed in the chair and had not realised how late it was. It took me some time to understand what Charles was telling me. The policewoman was very understanding and helped me cope with the terrible news. A freak wave had swept Melissa off the promenade and hurled her against the wall. She had no chance. Charles could not do anything. Luckily, other sightseers had witnessed the accident. But for their intervention, Charles would instinctively have jumped in to try and save her.

It is said that time is a great healer. I don't believe it. Not all the time to eternity could heal our sorrow after Melissa's death.

We carried on existing. On the surface, I suppose it appeared that we were coping. Only we knew the emptiness in our lives. The years dragged on, bringing with them greying hair, wrinkles and all the other evidences of time's passing. Charles's eyes had dimmed considerably. No longer did they sparkle like the sea on a summer's day. I noticed that he did not wear his clothes as smartly as he used to. They were his usual clothes, but lately, they did not look right somehow.

Then, about two or three months ago, I realised why. He had lost weight. He had never been overweight, although he was quite well built. Now, he had begun to look really skinny. He no longer went to play golf, nor did he go fishing. When I saw the blood, I realised that something was seriously amiss. With difficulty, I persuaded him to see Dr Weaver. Then the tests began. I knew before the Doctor told me what the trouble was.

I did not want to see Charles suffer. I could not bear to think of him going through weeks of chemotherapy, or undergoing operations. Charles, who had never had a day's illness in his life, would not be able to face months or even weeks of illness. His passions were golf, fishing and football. He, who enjoyed being outdoors would not be able to endure weeks of hospitalisation. His days were numbered.

Maybe I could prevent his suffering. Yes, there was a way I could help him shorten the weeks of agony that were in front of him. The inspiration struck me last night.

Last night was just a little bit different because of that football match. Usually, Charles goes upstairs first, and I stay to tidy the lounge and make sure that the kitchen is tidy for the morning. But last night, I had finished my chores before the last minutes of the match, and was at the top of the stairs as Charles laboured up. I was amazed at how slowly he climbed the stairs, and how heavy his steps were. I had not realised how much of an effort it was for him to move. I had an overwhelming desire to pick him up in my arms and carry him up. There was nothing I could do but watch his painful steps, one after the other until he reached the top.

'That was an enormous effort, Darling.' I said.

'I manage,' he said. His face smiled, but his eyes were dimmed with pain.

'I love you so much,' I whispered and placed both my hands on his shrunken chest. 'I can't bear to see you suffer. Tell Melissa I'll be with you both soon.'

Ticking of a Clock

CAROLYN LEWIS

When Martin suggested we take a trip to the garden centre, I said yes straightaway. I wanted bulbs and terracotta pots to put on the patio.

'Got to make a call first, check over a house, might be worth buying. You don't mind, do you?'

No, I didn't mind. Why should I? That's what Martin does, he buys old houses, usually rundown terraced ones. He does them up, new plumbing, damp course, that sort of thing, then either sub-lets or sells them.

'It won't take long,' that's all he said as we got into the car. My mind was chasing over the number of daffodil bulbs I'd need. Tulips too I thought and then I wondered if I should plant up my own winter baskets or let the garden centre do them for me. That's an expensive way of doing it, but money was hardly a problem.

Martin had retired. Five years ago he left his company, a major construction firm where he'd been Sales and Marketing Director; he'd been with them for years. He left with a hefty golden handshake and he told me that we could travel. 'All over the world,' was how he put it. For two years we did just that. America, Africa, most of Europe. We had a wonderful time.

Then, when Martin's father died, his will came as a bit of a shock: there seemed to be such a whopping great chunk of money. There was too much, it hovered around us, it felt almost indecent and I knew Martin was bothered.

'I'll have to do something with it,' he'd say over and over again.

'Invest it,' that was all I could come up with. If I'm honest, I didn't want anything to do with it. Martin's always handled our money, right from the day we were married. He saw to the bills, the mortgage, everything.

The truth was I forgot about it for a while. I was more than content, our life was fine, running smoothly like the ticking of a clock. I'd given up work when Martin retired; there didn't seem to be any point in me being at work if Martin was at home. I'd only worked a few days a week for a charity for the homeless. I wrote press releases about money raising ventures, got local TV presenters to open charity shops. Keeping my hand in I suppose. Before I'd got married I'd worked as a journalist, quite a high profile job at the time. I gave it up when the boys were born, being home with the kids took over my time and the job didn't seem so important to me then.

Anyway, when Martin told me what he wanted to do with his dad's money, it sounded perfectly ok to me.

That's how it started. Martin went along to various auctions and made his bids. At first, I went with him. I liked the idea, I thought it would be dramatic. In the end I only went to three. Seemed to me that they were all held in large, unheated rooms in grotty hotels. We sat on uncomfortable chairs, the carpets were threadbare and stained and, when I went, I was the only woman there. I just couldn't get excited about a grubby room full of seemingly bored people bidding for rundown properties.

That wasn't the only reason I stopped going, I lack Martin's vision. He can see potential where I see only outside toilets and damp walls. He sees what these houses will eventually look like; he knows what areas will be coming up the ladder of desirability. Martin is usually right, he's only lost money on one deal. He says he's learned a lot.

When Martin said this call we were making was in Riverside, nothing warned me. There was no bell ringing inside my head.

We sat side by side in Martin's car. We sat in the silence that married people have. *Companionable.* Suppose it is, but it's more than that. It's a comfortable silence too, not just the comfort of the car but comfort in the feeling between us. A sort of *well-off* feeling. That's what we were, well-off.

When Martin stopped the car, I had an impression of a tatty mid-terraced house, looking like all the others that Martin buys and converts. Even now I'm not sure what made me open the door of the car. Normally I wouldn't get out and look at any of the houses that Martin buys. But this time I did. I opened the passenger door and it was only then I realised where we were.

The park at the end of the street had an enormous Redwood tree, so tall it dwarfed all the others. As I looked at it, it shook its leaves, like an old dog shaking itself after a bath and then I knew.

No. 39, Backwell Park. Martin had the details in his hand. I hadn't looked at them, why would I? Our home is littered with estate agents' descriptions of houses just like this one.

I stood on the pavement. No. 39 had a dusty privet hedge that had been savagely pruned; someone had slotted empty crisp packets into the gaping holes of the hedge. It was an old privet hedge, it had stood in front of No. 39 for years. I knew that for a fact. I'd seen this house for the first time thirty five years ago.

Martin was at the front door, he'd put a key in the lock and was grumbling something about damp, the door was warped. He turned to look at me.

'Coming in?'

'Yes, I will, in a minute.' My voice was quiet and I don't think he heard me. Martin disappeared into the house. I walked slowly towards the porch and the open door. The porch smelt of cat pee and, oddly enough, of cinnamon.

I was nineteen years old when I saw this house for the first time. Just started my first job. 'First rung on the ladder,' that's what the careers officer and Dad told me. Working in the newsroom of the local paper, a trainee journalist. It was exactly what I'd always wanted.

The newsroom looked like every one I'd ever seen in films. Incessant ringing of telephones, photographers dashing in with black and white photos; a circle of sub-editors, pens shoved behind their ears. They barely glanced up as I was introduced. I remember feeling disappointed that they weren't wearing green eyeshades.

My desk was behind a battery of small switchboards. I had to learn everything, I knew that. My first job was copy-taking. One of the sub-editors flapped a hand at the desk. 'Put the earphones on, listen carefully and type, type as fast as you can. You *can* spell?'

I'd met his bored gaze with indignation. 'My spelling is perfect. I always got the highest marks and my typing is above 120 words per...' I was talking to a space. I was on my own.

I struggled that first week. I spoke to the district reporters daily. They were abrupt, their stories were a mind-numbing round of court details, traffic violations, parking fines. I could remember thinking how flat, how dull everything was.

'Got any change? For the coffee machine?'

I hadn't seen him before and he smiled down at me. Unfashionably long, silky blond hair resting on the collar of a dark brown leather jacket; hand outstretched, silver coins on the palm.

'I'm Neil,' he said, blue eyes twinkling.

'Yes, hi, somewhere I've got...' I had to turn away. I didn't want him to see the blush but it gained ground and, when I handed over the coins, my face was brick red.

I watched for him every day, looking out for the purposeful stride of his long legs passing my desk on his way to the coffee machine, listening for the creak of the leather jacket. He was chief reporter and he also wrote a motoring column. I watched the way he typed, using just two fingers at a furious speed. I learnt disjointed chunks of information about him: he was twenty-nine, he'd trained in London, he drove an old American jeep. He was married.

At nineteen my concept of boyfriends was centred on youth club dances, Saturday night cinema seats and mid-week pubs. Not married men.

Neil began stopping at my desk, resting his arms on the top of the switchboard. I felt that, no matter how hard I tried to avoid his eye, like a butterfly collector, he captured my gaze.

He told me about where he'd been, the films he watched, the books he read. We shared the same favourite Stevie Wonder song, *Uptight*. My childhood stammer re-emerged and I spent hours curbing my curly hair. I swear he knew, he knew how hard I tried not to look up each time his head appeared. He must have heard my heart thumping, he smiled when he heard the hesitancy in my speech.

'Fancy a drink?' It was a quiet Saturday, a late afternoon shift, just Neil and I and two sub-editors working on the other side of the big newsroom. I didn't recognise my voice. It sounded surprised and quiet. 'Yes please, thank you.'

We sat on a mock leather bench, a careful distance apart. 'Cheers.'

The fact that I can't remember what we talked about has nothing to do with the years that have passed. I couldn't remember an hour later.

Neil drove me home, the exhaust on his jeep was throaty, it rattled the peace of my parents' suburban street. I *can* remember fumbling with my handbag and the catch on the door of the jeep. I wanted to be inside my front door, I can remember that urgency. His smile I remember too, he knew what was going on inside my head.

That began the pattern: drink after work, a chat about the paper, the personalities working there. I remember the first time I asked Neil about his wife. I juggled the word around in my mouth, like a child with a searingly hot potato.

'Elizabeth? She works in the Infirmary, as an almoner.'

My smile was weak. I'd no idea what an almoner did. 'Sounds interesting.'

Elizabeth. At home, in the triple mirrors of my dressing table, I said her name out aloud, watching my reflection as my mouth made exaggerated shapes with the syllables of her name. Elizabeth. I saw her as a tall, dark-haired woman. Someone with a name like Elizabeth would be poised, elegant. Someone called Elizabeth would spend her working day wearing shoes with a heel, she'd carry files in her arms, her hair would be sleek, her mind wouldn't search around searching for soft words, words she wouldn't stumble over. Someone like Elizabeth would be in control.

I didn't ask Neil anything else about his wife and I didn't tell anyone about Neil. I can remember the agony of keeping Neil apart from my other life. I couldn't introduce him to my friends and family. In some way I felt that if I ever merged the two, I'd draw attention to his *marriedness*. I made myself believe that, if no-one knew, then I wouldn't be doing anything wrong. I couldn't hurt anyone. If I locked our relationship inside my head, then that would be ok.

One evening we went to a pub just outside the city. We'd been there before and, as Neil came back to the table with our drinks, he told me about a friend's flat.

'Mike Thompson, used to work on the city desk, spends all week in London, comes back at the weekend. He says that I, that we can go there.'

'Where is it, this flat?' I can remember asking, stupid really, what difference would it make *where* the flat was?

'Riverside, No. 39, Backwell Park.'

Didn't mean a thing to me and Neil didn't mention it again until he drove me home.

'What do you think? Do you want to see the flat? It's ok, whatever you decide, that's fine with me.'

'Yes, ok.' My voice often surprised me. My head, my sensible life, said 'no' and then this unexpected voice, the one that was locked inside my head, said 'yes'.

I'd followed Neil up steep, wooden stairs, my shoes making a hollow clicking on the bare treads. Neil had been silent as he unlocked the door and pushed it open. The flat was warmed by the late afternoon sun. Neil tugged and pulled at the thin curtains, trying to make them meet. Posters tacked on the emulsioned walls showed Monet's garden: a curving bridge, a small forest of nasturtiums. A double bed was in the corner, a faded lilac eiderdown, fussy frills touching the floor.

I remembered the silence in that room. In the middle of an old, empty house in the middle of a week. No sound of children, cars, voices, not even the songs of birds making their way to the park at the end of the street. I remember too my blue silk blouse as it tumbled to the floor. My sudden thought about going home: my mother, she'd ironed that blouse, would she notice the creases?

Neil and I stayed in that room, we'd lock the door and we

pulled at the curtains. No-one knew where we were and that made it perfectly all right. If no-one knew then I could quell my doubts, my guilt. I could leave all those feelings there inside that room.

I could hear Martin tapping at something and I walked up the stairs to see him. There was worn carpet on the treads, my shoes made no noise. The door was open and I could see Martin peering up at the ceiling. He muttered something about '... state of the roof.'

I felt a ridiculous wave of disappointment as I stood in that doorway. There was no sign of Neil, no hint that the two of us had spent time there. No sign of anything in this small, stuffy room. The walls were different, pale, cream wallpaper now with a tracery of gold leaves. The posters of Monet's garden had gone; oddly enough Martin and I had visited Giverny two years ago. I hadn't given any thought to the posters, hadn't remembered them at all as we walked around the gardens.

There was no furniture in the room and, on the walls someone had left a collection of simple line sketches: a bird, a sleeping cat. Martin was crouched over, tapping at the floorboards.

I looked at the back of his neck, he'd had a haircut on Saturday, the skin on his neck looked exposed, vulnerable.

When I spoke my voice sounded high-pitched, `So, what do you think? Worth buying or too much work?'

Martin straightened up, wiping his hands along the seam of his trousers. 'Nah, needs too much spending on it. It's not worth it, I'll leave it for someone else.' He gave me a quick lopsided grin. 'All done here, you go down first. I'll make sure everything is locked up.'

Walking downstairs I let Neil's name wander inside my head, like a tongue probing a jagged tooth. He'd be sixty-four years old now. I can't think of him getting old. When I'd told him that it was over and I wouldn't be coming back to this room, he'd smiled, shaking his head, blond hair flying, hiding his eyes.

As I waited for Martin, I stood near our car and I watched as the branches of the big redwood tree swayed in the wind. From where I stood, I could hear the rustle of the leaves.

Mrs Morgan's Boulders

FRANCES-ANNE KING

I stand gazing at the vast stones. My eyes are blank, reflecting only the grey blue sheen of granite before me. Motionless, I am caught on the cusp of the present and Pentre Ifan's past.

The air is still, trapped, suspended between each blade of grass. The ewes and their lambs are silent. The light shifts over Dinas Head rippling across Newport Bay and snaking up the estuary.

In my hand I clasp a jar of primroses. Kneeling on the soft grass before the ancient Burial Chamber, I remove the fragile flowers and scatter them across the ground. Then I raise the jar aloft and slowly trickle the clear mountain water into the earth at my feet as ritualistically as any ancient Celtic priestess. My lips are stiff. I move them awkwardly as if the granite around me is slowly leaching into my body. 'You are free now, Bethan. Fly light with the wind and the tide. I won't tell. I promise I won't tell.'

I was seventeen in 1940 and new-day bright with innocence and hope. North Pembrokeshire seemed far removed from the war, apart from the fact that it pushed us young ones into positions of responsibility we wouldn't normally hold. That's how I came to meet her on 29th April. The day I grew up.

Mrs Bethan Morgan of Bwthyn Bach Farm, Newport.

Well, Sister Jenkins said it was Newport, but it was half way up the mountain, and by the time I'd walked the five miles from the bus stop in Market Street up to Bethan's little farm I was hot and sweaty and longing to throw off my heavy nurses coat. But Sister Jenkins was a tarter where uniform was concerned. 'Full uniform for home visiting, Nurse Thomas. You have to look professional at all times.'

Well, I can tell you I didn't feel professional that day. The stone hedge banks along the road tumbled with pale primroses, dog violets, celandines and those early purple orchids and the sunlight sang notes of pure green and gold.

That's what I remembered afterwards: the colours, the scent of wild garlic and the strange remote stillness of it all.

Bethan's farm was only a stone cottage really. They used to dot the Preseli mountains back then; small holdings consisting of a couple of acres. The whole place seemed asleep, apart from the birds and the sound of a mountain stream by the side of the house. It had a shuttered, neglected look about it so I felt odd calling out as I knocked at the front door. 'Mrs Morgan? It's the nurse from the Cottage Hospital come to visit.' And then, as an afterthought, thinking it added a stamp of authority, 'Sister Jenkins sent me.'

No reply. So I opened the door and wandered down a stone flagged passageway into the kitchen.

What a kitchen. Every visible surface gleamed. The table was scrubbed to a near white. Bunches of herbs lay in serried ranks along its surface, their mirror images reflected in great labelled jars arranged behind them. A dresser, heavy with spotless china, stood against one wall and a wooden settle bright with patchwork cushions was drawn up to an empty hearth. The contrast between the scabby, flaking exterior of the house and this pristine interior was strange. I felt I was stepping back into a different world.

A faint but audible tapping from the ceiling above me

drew me to the narrow wooden staircase in the far corner of the room and so up to Bethan Morgan's bedroom. It was a tiny fragile doll I found lying in the bed, all brown and wrinkled like a walnut shell. There was an aureole of white hair tied in a plait and a faded patchwork quilt over the bed. But these were hazy recollections, as if viewed through a fine muslin; a backdrop for her eyes. Eyes as startlingly blue as Newport Bay on a shining morning, and a smile of such piercing sweetness that my hot sticky body sloughed a skin and was bathing in the mountain cool of spring water.

'My name's Gwen Thomas, Mrs Morgan. Sister Jenkins sent me to see how you were getting on.'

'Come in, cariad, sit yourself down here by me. I'm not so good this morning. It's the boulders, you see.' And she waved a little brown leaf of a hand at her chest. 'They're so heavy today, I can hardly breathe.'

Well, I couldn't see any boulders on her chest. But she was ninety-four and I knew the old sometimes had these fancies so thought it best to play along. 'How long have they been there, Mrs Morgan?'

'How long,' she echoed back; a whisp of a laugh in her tone. 'Eighty years, cariad. Eighty years ago the angels from Carningli gave me the first one.'

'Carningli?' I repeated, puzzled.

'Carningli, the mountain behind the house,' she said softly. 'St Brynach used to walk from Nevern to talk to the angels on Carningli. It's so beautiful up there, you think you're on top of the world. On a fine day you can see Snowdonia and the Wicklow hills in Ireland. But the angels were angry with me, see. They made me carry boulders all these years and I can't do it any more, cariad. They're crushing me.'

She started plucking at the patchwork quilt, her distress so palpable I had to think of something to soothe her.

'Will you let me take them away for you, Mrs. Morgan?'

She shook her head 'You can't, cariad. The angels won't let you. But perhaps, if I told you about them, it might make the burden a bit lighter. I don't think the angels would mind that.'

Have you ever lain in the hot sand dunes and listened to the wind winding through the blades of grass? It's like an opiate, gradually detaching you from reality. Bethan's voice was like that; so soft and murmuring that I had to lean close to catch all the words. I had to listen so carefully that all other senses fell away. But they came back later – the pain, the shock and the horror.

'Do you know Newport, cariad?'

I shook my head. 'I'm from Fishguard, Mrs Morgan.'

She patted my hand gently. 'Never mind cariad, you can't help that. It all started at the white house down near the estuary,' she whispered. 'I loved my house then, when I was little. It was so close to the sea. I'd escape from the garden and run like the wind down the path to the Parrog. There were always little boats ferrying the estuary and the fishermen knew me there and would give me a row over to Newport Bay.

'Hours I'd spend, lying in the warm sand looking for cowrie shells and listening to the sea. Sometimes I'd lie there with the sea just a shimmering lick of silver blue and the spread of sand at eye level. I'd watch the wind dip its fingers into the soft sifting grains and whip them up into tiny whirlwinds that flew across its surface. The sea was before me, the estuary behind. My spit of sand was an island where I just wrapped the sun around my heart and knew heaven could be no better. Time meant nothing then and Mam would come down to the Parrog to look for me; she knew where I'd be, and although she scolded if it was late, I knew she wasn't really cross.

'Then Da died when I was ten. He'd been ill for a while

with the coughing sickness. In the end, he was coughing up his lungs and it was only a husk of a man left, not the Da I remembered. Things were never the same after that. Mam became thin and quiet and worked all day and half the night doing other people's washing. I didn't get down to the Bay much after that, but I was always thinking about it.

'Three years later she married again. Mr Huw Jones. Everyone said wasn't it wonderful for Mam and me, but I didn't like him, even though he brought me sweets and took us on outings. He had a way of looking at me that I hated: like nails dragged across stone. It made my skin crawl. But Mam was happy again so I said nothing.

'When she said I was going to have a little brother or sister I was pleased. But when the baby started coming all the pleasure flew away: fear and pain took its place. They buried Mam with my baby brother in the churchyard of St Mary's. You can see the sea from her grave and the fields above the bay, where a trick of the light makes the cows look like cardboard cut-outs pasted against the sky.

'The night after her funeral Huw Jones came to my bedroom. It was late and he'd been drinking heavily. I could smell it on him as he leaned over my bed and put his hand across my mouth to stop me screaming. I fought him as hard as I could but he was strong. I couldn't stop him. When he'd finished, my body was one long howling scream; jagged and raw. I was defiled and dirty: I'd never be clean again.

'He came to my room the next night, but I was ready for him this time. I had the kitchen knife in my hands and told him if he ever touched me again, I'd stab him. He was frightened then and backed off, but I knew I wasn't safe in the house any more, so next day I went to the Vicar's wife and offered to live in and help with their seven children. I never went back to the white house again.

'The angels gave me the first boulder then and it lay heavy

on my heart. So unclean I was I'd creep away when I could and wash in the mountain stream till my body became numb with cold. I had this idea that if I washed in the mountain water long enough it would purify me; sluice all my filth down the mountain and out to sea. That perhaps the angels would take pity on me and take the boulder off my heart, but they didn't, though sometimes they'd carry it for me for a few hours.

'There's a wood below Pentre Ifan where the Vicar took us to pick bluebells once. He told us it was thousands of years old. The trees were twisted into strange shapes like hump-backed old men, with moss and lichen growing up their bark and through their branches which trailed on the ground like knotted old fingers. I could hear the silence of the place; layered magic it was, lapping round me like the sea. I knew there were spirits living in those trees that had been there forever and nothing would surprise them.

'I remember wrapping my childish arms around one and whispering my secrets into its rough bark. The angels took pity on me then and lifted the boulder off my heart for an hour or two. So I played with the Vicar's children and we collected huge bunches of bluebells which we carried home in the pony and trap, singing *All Things Bright and Beautiful* into the gathering dusk.

'Four years I stayed with the Vicar's family and then I married Evan Morgan. He was a big blonde man, slow in his movements and his words. He started to court me when I was seventeen. Brought me little presents to church on Sundays. A blackbird's nest, a bunch of spring flowers or some freshly laid chicken's eggs with the feathers still on them. I grew to be at peace with his slow, gentle ways.

'It was as if the warm sand of Newport Bay had come to rest all around me and I thought the angels had taken my boulder for good. I stopped bathing in the mountain stream because I didn't feel unclean any more. He never tried to touch me, just held my hand sometimes in a friendly sort of way.

'He didn't talk about his family much. He'd lived alone since his parents had died fifteen years before. No brothers or sisters. He was forty years old and I was eighteen when we wed, and the next five years were the happiest of my life. I loved the rhythm of our days. The farm work was hard, but I didn't mind that, and I cleaned this house till it gleamed like the wet driftwood kissed by sun on the beach. He dug me a little patch at the back of the house so I could grow my herbs. The Vicar had taught me all about herbs and Evan was proud of my knowledge then. He bought me a set of bell jars for my nineteenth birthday to store the dried ones in. Then one day all that happiness just drained through my fingers and drifted away. The angels didn't mean it to last, I suppose.

'It was late afternoon, I'd been working on the herb bed and had become so engrossed in it I hadn't noticed the lengthening shadows. When I saw how late it was I hurried into the house thinking Evan would be back soon from the fields wanting his supper. But I found him already home, sitting at the kitchen table with a strange dark haired man I'd never seen before. Evan turned on me a look of blinding joy. Such a smile on his face as I'd never seen before. "Bethan, look who's here. It's Dai, my cousin Dai. He's come home, see."

'I was bewildered. He'd never mentioned a cousin to me before, and what did he mean, "He's come home?" But I remembered my manners and walked forward to greet him. Dai turned to look at me then and my blood ran cold as I saw the eyes of Huw Jones staring out at me from Dai's face. Horrible probing, stripping eyes and I felt the angels place the boulder back over my heart.

'Everything changed after that. Not so as others would notice, but I knew it. Dai seemed to have some hold over Evan, who became remote and strange. Not that he'd ever been a talkative man, but the old easy ways were gone. He hardly spoke to me and when he did it was polite like, as if he was talking to a stranger.

'And then the drinking started. Evan had drunk very little before Dai came. But now they'd come back from the fields in the evening, eat their dinner and then go off down to Newport to the public house. I'd hear them come back at two or three in the morning, drunk as pigs. I started to take the carving knife to bed with me each night, but I needn't have bothered, they were only interested in each other. I might as well have been invisible. I didn't expect anything to happen during the day, but then things never happen when you expect them, do they?

'It was an afternoon in late summer. I had the farm to myself. Evan and Dai had gone off to the far field to harvest and I was in the barn feeding the chickens and searching for stray eggs. You know how they like to go and lay them in odd places. It was one of those beautiful balmy days, when the whole world seemed drowsy. I'd stopped looking for eggs for a moment. I was just standing gazing at the sunlight on the barn floor. Shifting it was, little circles of opaque golden light, reminding me how it used to shine on the shallow rockpools down at the bay and for a moment I forgot all my sorrow and fear and became that small girl hunting for shells.

'Suddenly it was gone and I was in pitch blackness. The barn door had been shut and by the time I'd adjusted my eyes to the dark he had me by the waist and was dragging me to the ground. I fought him like a wild cat, I did. Biting, scratching, kicking, but he only laughed and hit me so hard across the head I tasted my own blood, before I lost consciousness.

'When I came round he was heavy on top of me saying the most terrible things about Evan, I didn't want to hear and couldn't understand. He kept saying Evan belonged to him and had never been mine and never would be. Cariad, I thought I'd fallen into Hell that afternoon and that Lucifer himself was tearing my heart and body apart. When He'd finished he just got up and walked away whistling under his breath. God help me, I would have killed him then if I'd had the strength but I was so battered and bleeding I could barely move.

'I don't know how long I lay there, my head still dizzy, from his blows, but when I eventually dragged myself out of the barn it was dark. I found my way to the stream and knelt down in it to wash away the blood and filth. I remember looking up at the night sky and seeing the first star glittering and wondering why was it there, how could everything look the same when the world was such a changed, evil place to me?

'I was numb with cold by the time I got back to the house. The men had already gone down to Newport and I knew they wouldn't be back till the early hours. I pushed the chest in front of the bedroom door and then lay on my bed, wide eyed, all night, just thinking what was to be done. It came to me stealthy like, in the backbone of the night. You're too young to know that hour yet, cariad. It's the darkest time, when all the stars have gone out and hope is asleep and only fear prowls huge and silent. The solution just crept in and curled itself up in my mind.

'I got up early next morning and set off up the mountain. I knew where to look for it: the Vicar had shown us on one of those botanical walks he liked to take us on. It was there in the same place, its tiny black berries glistening like snakes' eyes. I knew the men would have left the house by the time

I got home so I had all day to prepare it. When it was done, I mixed it into his ale and poured it into the mug he always used. Always the same mug; Evan had given it to him a few weeks earlier. It was pewter and had belonged to his father. Then I just waited; sat on the settle darning socks and waited.

'They came in together at the usual time, Evan silent as ever and avoiding my eyes, the other, just stared at me, bold like. I said nothing, just went on darning, but my eyes followed his hands as they went to grasp the handle of his mug. He drank deep and noisily and then to my horror he did something he'd never done before. He turned and looking straight at me, handed his half-drained mug to Evan to finish. I could do nothing. I just sat there paralysed and watched my husband drink.

'I've often wondered since why Dai did that. I suppose he thought he was showing me how inseparable they were. Well, he'd made sure of that, hadn't he? They ate the supper I'd prepared and then went out as usual. I never saw them alive again.

'I hadn't wanted Evan dead. Part of me thought if I could only get rid of Dai, things would go back to how they had been before he came. Afterwards I had years to think about it and I realised then that nothing would have been the same. Evil like that scorches deep and leaves wounds weeping forever. Three weeks later, I had to go and identify the bodies; what was left of them. They'd been washed up further down the coast. The Coroner's report said they'd died from drowning whilst under the influence of drink.

'God help me, I felt safe then, cariad. Safe and more alone than ever before in my life. All feeling seemed to have withered up in me. I thought the three boulders I now carried had crushed so hard and deep into my heart that no blood remained in my veins, just a fine grey dust flowing through me. I was sure I could never feel again, but the angels had one more boulder to give me and it was to be the heaviest yet.

'When the sickness started and my belly began to swell, I knew it was Dai's child and every fibre of my body rose up in revolt against it. I stopped eating and took to walking the mountain day and night, whatever the weather. My physical battle with the elements was nothing compared to the mental chaos that raged inside me. I wasn't brave enough to take my own life, but how I wanted to die! To rid myself of this spore of evil growing inside me like a dark fungus. I mixed bitter purges from my herbs, but they only made me sick and weak.

'Four months it clung on to me and then sensing how I was rejecting it, it just gave up hope and came away one morning. Poor, helpless, bloodied little girl. And when I saw it lying there such a flood of pity and horror engulfed me. What had I done? I knew then how I could have loved and cared for her and perhaps she would have loved me in return. Such a loss, cariad, such a bottomless pit of loss that I've lived with for the rest of my life.

'I couldn't bear to be parted from her then: I had to keep her close by. I buried her tiny body in a patch of ground by the stream, where the grass is green velvet and the spring primroses are stars dropped from the sky. I've been there every day since and I talk to her. Tell her all the things I've done and all those things we might have done together.'

Bethan Morgan's voice died away like the susurration of a gentle wind through leaves. Her eyelids closed and she seemed to sleep; her breathing so shallow I had to search for her pulse. The room became thick with silence. I don't know how long I sat there, but the next thing I remembered was the room awash with moonlight and Bethan Morgan lying like a little marble effigy on a tomb: smooth, serene and utterly at peace with death.

When dawn came I went out to the stream and collected the cold mountain water to wash her little body with. I found her best nightdress in a drawer and laid her out with a bunch of primroses between her cold hands. And then I just sat and waited. Perhaps I should have said a prayer for her, but my mind was frozen over. All I could feel was the pressure of those boulders.

It must have been around eight o'clock when I heard a car drive up the track. There was the murmur of voices in the kitchen below and then old Doctor Davies was standing beside me. I was glad it was him. He was a kind wise man whose eyes always spoke more than his mouth. He just put his hand on my shoulder and said 'Well done, child. I'll take you home soon. Mrs Jones is downstairs and she will look after Bethan for you now.' I nodded, wordlessly.

Somehow I found myself out by the stream again. I'd filled a jam jar with primroses and mountain water, some primal instinct telling me what I had to do next. I'd been there once on a school outing. Set up in a fold of the hills it was, above the bay; an ancient Neolithic burial chamber. When I asked Doctor Davies to take me there, to Pentre Ifan, he just nodded and didn't utter another word until we arrived.

'Take your time, Gwen, no rush now, I'll be waiting here for you.' That was all he said as I walked off across the still dew-soaked grass, towards the vast gaunt stones.

Bethan would have her burial at St Mary's Church, near her mam, but this was something private between her and me. The laying to rest of dark knowledge with the spirits of her ancestors.

I scattered the primroses at the foot of the stones and poured the mountain water in a slow trickle onto the damp earth. I looked over to Carningli where tiny white clouds scudded across the sky shifting patterns of light and shade onto the dappled mountain side. Like angels wings, I thought, angels wings in flight.

My lips moved awkwardly as if the power of speech was new to me. The words tumbled out on top of each other, halting, ungainly: a clumsy pile to be sifted and carried away by the wind. I whispered my goodbye to Bethan Morgan and only realised later, years later, that I'd said goodbye to the remains of my childhood at the same time. It's there, on the Presili mountains, in the dappled light of angels wings.

Erik

JENNY SULLIVAN

One day, I became invisible.

High Street, flanked by daughters visiting from college, and this pair of lads coming towards us. I straightened my shoulders – like you do, you know – batted the old eyelashes, pouted a little and then realised that their eyes had skimmed right over the old tart in the middle as if I didn't exist. Beth one side, belly button glinting gold, Mali on the other, her boobs bubbling in the cauldron of her t-shirt, and, well, to all intents and purposes, yours truly was invisible.

At home I looked in the mirror. Wasn't totally past it, was I? I mean, not quite ready for Crumblies Care Cottage yet. OK, maybe I was a wee bit overweight, but not what you could call gross, and some men quite like a bit of flesh to cling on to in times of stress. There's a bit of grey in my hair, but I get it streaked regularly, and I've still got all my own teeth, give or take a porcelain crown or two.

Maybe what I needed was a makeover, like on the telly. You know, Thingy and Whats'ername trash your entire wardrobe, reduce you to tears and then pat your back and give you two thousand quid to buy new stuff. I could do that. I thought about writing to the Beeb, but then decided it was a quick fix I needed, not a telly programme.

Please don't run away with the idea that I'm not married. I am, but not so you'd notice. It's a twin bed sort of marriage.

I've been married to Charlie for twenty-eight years, and it's true what they say, the first forty years are the worst. The first year, if we'd put a jelly bean in a jar every time we had it away, we'd have had enough to keep Ronald Reagan happy for years – or was it Bill Clinton? No, he was cigars, wasn't he? Anyway, just lately, like the last ten years or so, Charlie's sort of lost interest in that sort of thing, and by the time he gets to bed it's sleep he's interested in, not me, so forget the jelly beans. I looked in the mirror again. Maybe it was me. Maybe I needed to spice up our love lives a bit.

So I went to this underwear party my friend Marilyn next door was having, and bought this little red satin job with poppers in appropriate places. When it arrived a week later, I took it out of its poly bag – funny how stuff like that never looks quite like it did when you ordered it... after seven white wines and an egg and mayo sandwich – stripped off, and climbed in.

Well, it did something for me all right. Turned me into an animated polony, that's what. So I put it in the Oxfam bag and had a Baileys for elevenses.

That night, after several more of the same, I decided to go for broke. I pitched up in the bedroom door in my sexiest undies, stretched one arm up and draped the rest of me along the doorframe, thus elongating my shape and getting rid of a couple of chins and a belly or two.

Charlie lifted a bleary eye over his duvet. 'Aw, love, back bad again? I'd go and see an osteopath if I were you. You can't go on like that.'

I whinged to Marilyn over coffee next morning. 'My life's over, Maz,' I said, dunking a chocolate suggestive. 'I've had all the sex I'm ever going to get. Just got to put up with it. Or without it, more to the point.'

'What you need, my girl, is a nice bit of infidelity,' she said, recognising a crisis and getting out the Cointreau.

'Somebody young and gorgeous, with shoulders like tallboys and a nice little arse in a pair of tight jeans.'

'Doesn't everybody,' I said bitterly, 'but they don't stock nice little arses in supermarkets. Besides, I don't approve of adultery.'

'Who mentioned adultery?' she said. 'I said infidelity. Infidelity's fine. It's only adultery when *they're* married. And if they're younger than you, it doesn't count as adultery anyway. Look at it this way. Adultery has calories, infidelity doesn't.' She grinned. 'Leave it to me.'

She rang me that night. 'Marge? You in tomorrow?'

'No,' I said, gloomily. 'I'll be lounging on a beach in the Seychelles.'

'Good. There's a bloke coming round to see to your garden.'

'My garden? What's wrong with my garden?'

'Grass needs cutting, trees need trimming, flower beds need hoeing, and you need some eye candy.'

'What?'

But she'd hung up. I forgot all about it until the knock on the door next morning.

I put down my cornflakes and paddled to answer in my downtrodden slippers. On the doormat was six feet of wildest dreams, marred only by a woolly bobble hat.

'Erik,' he said, removing the hat, allowing a mass of surfer-blonde hair to tumble round cheekbones like chainsaws. 'You Marge? Marilyn sent me. Said you wanted some stuff done in your garden.'

He had the faintest of Australian accents and a wide white smile. And dimples. And stubble, and... 'Oh, I do, I do,' I said, 'I really, really do.' Stuff in the garden, stuff in the laundry room, on the kitchen table, under the apple tree...

I showed him through and did a quick change worthy of Gypsy Rose Lee, although I had to lie on my back on the carpet to get my jeans zipped. Braless seemed a good idea in theory, but the reality was a bit Belgian lop-ear, so the old Gossard push-me-pull-you went back on again.

Erik, shirt off, was mowing the lawn. I gazed from the kitchen window and watched bronzed back, rippling muscles, slim waist disappearing into skin tight levis and a bum that just ached to be patted. No, squeezed. No, bi… Oh, forget it. Oh, God.

Then he turned round, and the narrow line of hair that started at his belly button and travelled south set me off again.

Coffee, I thought, wildly. That's it, give him coffee. 'Erik,' I bleated, in that curiously strangled voice one gets when one's gut is sucked in so hard it's touching one's backbone, 'would you like some coffee?'

He stopped with the mower and drew a tanned forearm over a moist brow. 'Coffee? No thanks. Never touch it. But a glass of water would be great.'

Water? Water? Oh yes, tap, turn it on, water. I tripped out to the garden with a pitcher clinking with ice, and stood mesmerised watching him drink. I'd never appreciated the erotic appeal of the Adam's apple before.

Trouble was, he was a fast worker and I wasn't. I spent so much time fantasising about baby oil and brown skin that I hardly spoke to him, and meantime he finished the lawn, strimmed round the trees, hoed the flower beds, raked the gravel and trimmed the shrubs. By four o'clock I had eyestrain from sneaking peeks at him through every window at the back of the house, and a dry mouth from drooling. I had also discovered that even the top of his head was sexy, the way the crown twirled ever so slightly, and when he bent to free the string of the strimmer, his jeans descended everrrrrr sooooo ssssslightly, exposing the beginnings of his... Oooooh, God how my head was hurting!

He came to the back door, by which time I'd changed the t-shirt for a tighter one, put on another layer of mascara and chugged down four aspirin and a large brandy.

'That's about it, Marge,' he said, re-applying the bobble hat. 'Unless there's something else you'd like me to do?'

He had to be joking. Please, please, please – a fast bit of something else over there by the water feature would be good... No, forget it. Just forget it, Marge. It's not going to happen.

'Trees!' I heard myself croak. 'Trees. Need lopping. Yes, that's it. Trees.'

He was busy the next day, so it was Thursday before he came back and by then I'd stiffened up the sinews and summoned up the blood. As soon as he arrived I shot upstairs, had a quick shower and slithered into the black negligee trimmed with crimson ribbon I'd bought under Marilyn's guidance the day before, that propped up everything that needed propping, revealed what was still worth revealing, and veiled what wasn't. The possibility of al fresco sex made even walking in a straight line difficult, and no, it wasn't the cherry brandy I'd had on my muesli.

I flung open the back door. The garden appeared empty. Had he got down wind of my perfume and scarpered?

'Erik?' I called, 'Erik? You there?'

'Up here,' came a voice from the ash tree. A pair of endless legs emerged from breathtaking shorts. I seemed to be purring.

I washed into the garden on a flood-tide of lust. He looked down. From fifty feet up an ash tree the view of my cleavage must have been awe-inspiring, and I saw a slow smile cross his face as he began the descent.

Unfortunately, he wasn't wearing a safety harness or even a hard hat. The noise he made hitting the ground reminded me of the time I dropped a honeydew in Safeways. I knew he wasn't going to get up. Ever.

Between ringing 999 and the arrival of the ambulance I managed to change into something a bit less revealing and kick the seduction kit under the bed to dispose of later. He didn't have a wife, which was good, so I went to the funeral and mourned him, mourning even more my last decent shot at lust. I wouldn't bother again, but all the same there was a miserable feeling of unfinished business.

A week or so later, I was lying in bed trying to ignore Charlie's snoring, and remembering those lean, long legs in the little shorts, the way the muscles rippled under the taut skin of his back, the way his Levis had hugged his... Oh, sod it. There was just this awful feeling of misery, and missed chances, and life stretching ahead like an endless pile of ironing.

Then, in the dim light from the bathroom, I saw the curtains stir and sway, although the windows were closed, and suddenly the air took on a strange, almost tangible electricity that caught my breath and made the blood hum in my head. The room was soundless: even Charlie had stopped snoring.

The dark room was filled with waiting, with longing, with expectation.

I felt the edge of my duvet slowly, slowly lift. The bed sagged, as if under an extra weight, and a lithe, cool body slithered in beside me. A long leg, rough with hair, crooked companionably across mine. A hand, slightly roughened by outdoor work, crept slowly and sensuously up my thigh.

I shot upright and put on the bedside light. My bed was entirely empty, except for me.

Oh, and the hand gliding up my leg, and the smooth, muscular chest against my hip…

With an about to be satisfied smile, I lay back down. Finest kind, I thought. Infidelity, and no body to worry about.

Biographical Notes

Kay Byrne is a journalist with a long and varied career in newspapers, television and new media. She has also written extensively about food. Fiction writing is a more recent venture, and she is currently working on a novel. Kay was born in West Yorkshire but has lived in Swansea for eighteen years and now considers south Wales her home. She loves the company of family and friends, travel, cooking, real ale, the outdoors and her dog Dudley.

Caroline Clark was born in the Midlands but has lived in Aberystwyth for twenty-seven years, married to Alan, a university librarian. A former member of the Shakespeare Institute, she has contributed to publications on Shakespeare and Ovid. Having always written poetry, with some success over the years in magazines, local and national competitions, she is presently working on a collection of poems inspired by the landscape and history of north Ceredigion. Most of her short story writing has been in fantasy genres. While living in Wales she has been involved with theatre and dance groups; costuming, performing and directing. She has worked in wardrobe for Aberystwyth University's Theatre Department and has been active for many years in the Drama Association of Wales. More recently she has been an advisor on Welsh Arts Council committees. However, family commitments have meant that for the past year she has been a full-time carer at home.

Holly Cross was born in Carmarthen in 1981, but her family moved to Somerset shortly after. Whilst a certain 'Welshness' was ever-present in her identity, the West Country retained its sense of home for her until she returned to Wales to study at Swansea University, where she took an English degree followed by an MA in Creative Writing taught by Welsh writers. Wales' wilder landscape and proud creative tradition appealed to a young woman whose inspiration and drive has always come from a connection with the earth and the struggle to communicate the need to care for it. Although, post university, Holly is often in Pembrokeshire, where her parents have now settled, she is currently now travelling around Britain and mainland Europe in pursuit of her muse, while working for community projects and organic farms.

Christine Davies was brought up in Burry Port in Carmarthenshire. At eighteen she left Wales to study biological sciences at University College London. She subsequently obtained a PhD degree at the University of Bristol and went on to hold posts in biomedical research in England for several years. In the 1990s she returned to Carmarthenshire with her husband and daughter, now a teenager, and currently lives in Pembrey, She teaches and lectures part-time in science and higher and further education and also helps to run her husband's small business. She also tries to find time to indulge in her two favourite pastimes – walking her Labrador dog along the beach and writing fiction.

Deborah Davies has lived nearly all her life in the Gwent Valleys where she was born, but has recently moved to

Cardiff. Her short stories have twice won awards in the Rhys Davies competition, and have been published in Mslexia magazine as well as being broadcast on BBC Radio 4. Her poetry has appeared in many magazines and anthologies including Agenda, New Welsh Review, Planet, Poetry Wales and the Parthian anthology, *Pterodactyl's Wing*. Next year Parthian will bring out her first collection of poems, *Things You Think I Don't Know*. She has performed her work in the USA and throughout the UK, including Cardiff, London and the Hay Festival. She has taught Creative Writing at Cardiff University and the University of Glamorgan.

Maria Donovan was born in West Dorset. She lived in Holland for several years and trained as a nurse. A variety of jobs followed, from gardener to magician's assistant, and she travelled around Europe. A mechanical breakdown left her sitting in a caravan on a mountainside in Asturias with time to face up to her desire to write. Later that year she came to Trefforest to study at the University of Glamorgan with the aim of making a permanent space in her life for this work. After graduation she moved to Llandaff and has been teaching fiction and non-fiction at Glamorgan while also working towards an M.Phil. in Writing. Her short stories have appeared in *Mslexia* and *New Welsh Review* and her ultra-short fiction is published by the-phone-book.com. Her biography of Megan Lloyd is published in *Sideways Glances*, edited by Jeni Williams. She lives with her partner Mike and dog Bertie.

Marlis Jones was born and brought up in Bethesda. She was educated at Ysgol Dyffryn Ogwen and trained as a teacher at Bangor Normal College. After teaching for some years at Llandudno she married a farmer, settling eventually at Llanbrynmair. She started writing in 1991 in her early fifties and attended creative writing courses at the Wales Writing Centre at Tŷ Newydd. She competed in Eisteddfodau with some success, winning the crown for prose at the Powys Eisteddfod in 1998, 2000 and 2002. She writes mostly in Welsh and has had many short stories published including two collections, *Blaenwern a Straeon Eraill* and *Rhyddhad?* (both published by Pantycelin). After many years farming she and her husband enjoy retirement in their country cottage, being very involved with the local primary school and church activities. Her hobbies include gardening and cross stitch.

Ruth Joseph grew up in Cardiff and dreamt of writing fiction while working for IPC magazines as a freelance journalist. After graduating with an M.Phil. in Writing from Glamorgan University she was approached by Accent Press to publish her collection of short stories, *Red Stilettos*. She is a Rhys Davies prize winner, Cadenza prize winner and won the Lichfield Short Story prize. She has also had work accepted by Honno, New Welsh Review, Loki and Cambrensis. One of her scripts forms part of the Cardiff Centenary exhibition in the Old Library. Her second book, *Remembering Judith* – a memoir – relates her situation as a child carer to an anorexic mother traumatised by the after-effects of the Holocaust. It was published in September 2005. Her husband Mervyn, children, grandchildren and rescue-Labrador Bobbi, are a source of inspiration, encouragement and comfort.

Frances-Anne King was born in Glasgow in 1951. She was brought up in Glamorganshire and south Pembrokeshire, from where her great love of the sea originated. She started writing poetry as a child and had intended to read English at university. A quirk of fate led her into nursing. She trained at St Bartholomew's Hospital in London and has worked in both primary and secondary care, specialising in hypertension and asthma. In 2002 she decided to concentrate on her writing and is currently studying at Bath Spa University for a BA in Creative Writing. She has a small cottage in north Pembrokeshire and feels her writing is influenced by the wild, mystic beauty of the area, the poetry of R S Thomas and Gillian Clarke and the paintings of John Knapp-Fisher. She is married with three sons and lives in Bath.

Carolyn Lewis was born in Cardiff in 1947. Married twice with three daughters and four grandchildren, she now lives in Bristol. Writing since she was eight years old, her work has been published by Honno, Accent Press, Redcliffe Press, Mslexia and QWF and her stories have won a number of competitions. Earlier this year she came second in the Mathew Prichard Award and is currently working on a novel and a collection of short stories. In 2003 she graduated from the University of Glamorgan with an M.Phil in Writing.

Melanie Mauthner is a social science lecturer at the Open University. In the 1990s she was involved in setting up and teaching Women's Studies at Swansea University. She has a background in journalism and social research. She has written *Sistering: Power and Change In Female Relationships* (Palgrave 2002) and co-edited two collections about feminist research (*Ethics In Qualitative Research*, Sage 2002 and *The Politics of Gender and Education; Critical Perspectives*, Palgrave 2004). Her short story *The Lido*, won first prize in Lambeth's *Impressions of Brixton* competition 2003. She lives in South London.

Barbara Michaels was born in Birmingham and moved to Wales ten years ago. The mother of three children and a grandmother of six, she is writing her first novel as part of a BA degree in English Literature at Cardiff University, where she is in her final year as a mature student. Previously published by Honno in the award-winning anthology *Laughing, Not Laughing*, she was the winner of a Writers' Forum competition and has had several short stories published. She is on the editorial board of Bimah, the quarterly magazine for the Jewish community in mid and south Wales. After leaving school she worked on local newspapers, then married and moved to London. She subsequently returned to journalism as a freelance writer. Her interviews with celebrities and articles on homes, gardens and antique collecting have been published in magazines and newspapers worldwide.

Shelagh Middlehurst was born in Liverpool in 1950. She made a speedy arrival onto the kitchen floor after her mother had taken a dose of castor oil. She married in 1970 and has two grown-up daughters and two grandsons. She lived in Lancaster for a while and spent a number of years in the Middle East. She has lived in Cardiff since 1987 and shares a house in Rhiwbina with her husband, three retired greyhounds and one cat.

Candice Morgan was born in 1973 in Pontypridd. In 1999 she graduated with a First Class Honours degree in Creative Arts from the University of Glamorgan. She has worked as a researcher and currently teaches creative writing and calligraphy. She has had poems published in a collection of new writing from the South Wales Valleys, *Out of the Coalhouse* (Underground Press, 1994) and *World About Us* (Poetry Now, 1995). In May 2002 one of her short stories, *Shrine*, was translated into Spanish and published in a popular South American culture magazine, *Tierra Adentro*. Another of her short stories, *Metamorphosis* was published in Cambrensis magazine (December 2002). Her most recent project has involved editing a collection of writing produced by learners who attend her creative writing workshops at Coleg Morgannwg Writers' Forum.

Elizabeth Morgan was born in Llanelli and has worked in the entertainment business as an actor/writer, both in England and in Wales. She has appeared in numerous television productions which include 'The Old Devils', 'The Two of Us', 'We Are Seven', 'The Dick Emery Shows' and 'Dad's Army'. She has also performed at the National Theatre and provincial venues, notably the Sherman Theatre Cardiff and Theatre Clwyd, plus several tours in the USA with her own one-woman plays. She provided the voices of Destiny and Rhapsody Angels in the 'Captain Scarlet' series, and continues to voice animated cartoons.

She has worked extensively in radio particularly with the BBC Radio Drama Company, and recorded Under Milk Wood with Sir Anthony Hopkins. Recently she played Caitlin in a new play about Dylan Thomas at the Dylan Thomas Festival in Swansea.

She has written 26 performed plays for Radio 4, several short stories and four television plays. A regular contributor to magazines and newspapers, she is now working on a sequel to her book, *Can We Afford The Bidet* (Queen Anne Press). Her first novel *The Girl On The Promenade* is published this year.

A devoted Francophile, she spends half the year at her home in the South of France, easily recognisable by the Welsh flag 'Y Ddraig Goch', which flutters from the balcony.

Cecilia Morreau is a lost American who has been living happily in Wales for twenty-five years. She is the mother of two teenage girls and the owner of a large, unruly garden. She has just gained a First Class Honours degree in Creative

Writing from the University of Glamorgan. She used to own a restaurant in Cardiff, perform in a circus, work as a gardener and make quilts (not all at the same time). She is also a qualified yoga teacher. She writes poetry, short stories and has completed two novels. As well as writing, taxiing children and wondering why the house is so dirty and the garden such a mess, she is director of a new publishing venture, Leaf Books, which aims to promote short story writing and reading.

Marion Preece was born and educated in Swansea but now lives with her partner in a two hundred year old cottage in Garnant in the foothills of the Black Mountains. She has a son and daughter and four grandchildren. She has studied under the guidance of several prominent Welsh poets and writers, notably Penny Anne Windsor and Peter Thabit Jones. Currently in her third year of a BA in Creative writing at Swansea University, she still finds time to work on her first novel. She is co-founder of the local writers' group, Hooker's Pen, andis a founder member of the Peacock Vein Scrip Shop. She was a prize winner in the Kilvey Writers short story competition and has had a short story, *All The Woods May Answer*, published in Cadenza magazine. Marion loves anything to do with Hollywood but is terrified of snakes and ventriloquists' dummies.

Kitty Sewell was born in Sweden and has lived variously in Spain, Canada, England and Wales. After running an estate agency in the frozen north of Canada she trained as a psychotherapist and then as a sculptor. Since 1991 she has written a popular agony column which is published in various newspapers around Britain. Her first book, *What Took You So Long?,* a biography, was published by Penguin in 1995. Her first novel, *Ice Trap*, was published by Honno in October 2005. She lives in Cardiff with her husband.

Jenny Sullivan was born in Cardiff, the fourth daughter of six children. She left school at fifteen without qualifications but at the age of fifty she bit the bullet and did an MA at Cardiff University, where she later gained a PhD. Her mother, now aged 99, is still wondering why. Jenny is a prolific children's author – her many published books include *Gwydion and the Flying* Wand, *The Magic Apostrophe* and *The Caterpillar That Couldn't*. She has also had several short stories published and her work has featured in five previous Honno anthologies. She is currently living in Brittany following her husband's retirement, but is still writing. She tries to return to Wales every few months to get a fix of Welshness, and also to spend some time working with children in schools as well as visiting bookshops to launch whatever is latest. Jenny has three grown-up daughters, two married, one determinedly single, based in Ealing, Northern Ireland and Epping.

Joy Tucker is a Scottish writer who has lived in Wales for many years. A former columnist with The Glasgow Herald, she has had several short stories published in newspapers and magazines throughout Britain, as well as having her work broadcast on BBC Radio 4. Her radio credits include children's stories and poems, some of which she wrote for her own son and daughter. Now she writes them for her grandchildren. She has recently turned to play-writing, with two one-act dramas produced at the Landmark Theatre, Ilfracombe. Joy lives on the Gower Peninsula with her Welsh husband and finds that the countryside and beaches of south-west Wales have many similarities with her native Ayrshire. Searching for the similarities and differences around the countries and regions of the UK – in the people and their traditions, dialects, even their food – is a major interest.

Jo Verity was the winner of the 2003 Richard & Judy Short Story Competition, which attracted 17,000 entries. She also won the Western Mail's short story competition in 2004. Her first novel, *Everything In The Garden*, was published by Honno in May 2005. She has also had numerous short stories published and broadcast on BBC Radio 4. Jo is the mother of two daughters and lives in Cardiff with her husband.

Vashti Zarach was born in Bangor, North Wales and currently lives in Llanberis. She studied Archaeology and Anthropology at Cambridge and also lived for a while in Brighton, where she achieved her childhood dream of dancing in a carnival parade. She is currently studying part-time for a Heritage Management MA at the University of Wales Bangor, working part-time for the university and writing a children's book about dragons and magic. She has been writing stories and poems since she was a child and this is her first published story.

It has unfortunately proved impossible to contact one of the authors, **Karen Buckley**. We regret this very much and hope that she will be able to get in touch with us.

AFTERWORD

These stories have been gathering since Honno first put out the call for submissions in the year 2000. There has been a steady trickle of brown envelopes, but the project suffered a serious set-back when a package containing twenty submissions, was lost in the postal labyrinth somewhere between Honno's office in Aberystwyth and my home address in Cardiff. Honno have tried their best to trace the authors, but in some cases this was not possible as the covering letters were stapled to the submissions.

I apologise profusely to anyone who, having submitted their stories in good faith, never heard back from Honno. Such a thing can and does cause a budding writer to lose an already fragile confidence in her writing, though, having said this, anyone who is trying to become a writer will be well acquainted with the feelings of indifference, dismissal and rejection. As all published writers know, the only road to success is to grit your teeth and, like a dog with a bone, *keep writing*. So please submit your stories to any and all forthcoming anthologies.

Kitty Sewell

Dip into another superb Honno collection

Mirror Mirror

This rich and diverse anthology contains realist, fantasy, historical and experimental stories on the theme of the Other Woman.

* A first wife haunts her garden while the second wife tries to make it her own
* A teenage girl gets drawn into the tensions between a husband and wife at her first grown-up party
* A desperate woman steals her counsellor's handbag – but isn't ready for the secrets inside.

Are you ready to meet your Other Woman?

ISBN: 1 870206 576 £7.99